Books by Valerie Burns

Baker Street Mysteries
TWO PARTS SUGAR, ONE PART MURDER
MURDER IS A PIECE OF CAKE

Books by Valerie Burns writing as V. M. Burns

Mystery Bookshop Mysteries
THE PLOT IS MURDER
READ HERRING HUNT
THE NOVEL ART OF MURDER
WED, READ & DEAD
BOOKMARKED FOR MURDER
A TOURIST'S GUIDE TO MURDER
KILLER WORDS
BOOKCLUBBED TO DEATH

Dog Club Mysteries
IN THE DOG HOUSE
THE PUPPY WHO KNEW TOO MUCH
BARK IF IT'S MURDER
PAW AND ORDER
SIT, STAY, SLAY

Published by Kensington Publishing Corp.

Murder is A Piece of Cake

A Baker Street Mystery

VALERIE BURNS

Kensington Publishing Corp.
www.kensingtonbooks.com

KENSINGTON BOOKS are published by

Kensington Publishing Corp.
119 West 40th Street
New York, NY 10018

Special book excerpts or customized printings can also be created to fit specific needs. For details, write or phone the office of the Kensington Sales Manager: Kensington Publishing Corp., 119 West 40th Street, New York, NY 10018. Attn. Sales Department. Phone: 1-800-221-2647.

The K and Teapot logo is a trademark of Kensington Publishing Corp.

ISBN: 978-1-4967-3826-4 (ebook)

ISBN: 978-1-4967-3823-3

First Kensington Trade Paperback Printing: July 2023

10 9 8 7 6 5 4 3 2 1

Printed in the United States of America

Acknowledgments

Special thanks to Jessica Faust at BookEnds Literary Agency. John Scognamiglio, Michelle Addo, Larissa Ackerman, Carly Sommerstein, and all of the other wonderful people at Kensington Publishing.

When you write crime fiction there are a lot of unusual questions that most people will think are bizarre. I have been fortunate to have met many experts who have been generous enough to share their expertise with me without judgment, no matter how crazy the questions. Thanks to Alex Savage for the military advice, Dr. Alexia Gordon for medical advice, and Carson and Christopher Rucker for their fashion expertise. Thanks to Michael Dell for editing assistance, Debra H. Goldstein for legal advice and always providing honest, critical advice and suggestions; also thanks for listening. And thanks to Kellye Garrett for the sprints and for all of the unicorns who lent a critical ear, a kind word of encouragement, and a laugh when needed.

In addition to professionals, I have been blessed with good friends and family who have supported me in so many ways. Thanks to Ben Burns, Jackie, Christopher, Crosby, Cameron, and Carson Rucker, Jillian, Drew, and Marcella Merkel. As always, I have to thank my close friends Shelitha McKee and Sophia Muckerson, who provide both emotional support and tough love.

Murder is A Piece of Cake

CHAPTER 1

For a moment—one moment—I forgot who I was. In the heat, nay the thrill of filming, baking, and acting, something switched. In an instant, I was no longer the inexperienced, non-baking owner of Baby Cakes Bakery in New Bison, Michigan. No, I was Shonda Rhimes and Julia Child all wrapped up in one. In my commercial-style kitchen, with my ring light casting a soft pink glow while it held my iPhone perfectly angled over a bowl of frothy egg whites, I knew that I not only looked like a chef, but I felt chef-ish. Despite Southwest Michigan's humidity, my natural hair was perfectly curled with zero frizz. I'd spent extra time on my makeup, and my newly arched brows were inverted Vs of perfection. And even though New Bison was far from McMullen boutique, thanks to the marvels of modern technology, my stylist had hooked me up with the latest in high fashion. Wide-legged Khaite jeans, simple white T-shirt, and my crisp chef's apron, branded with our new logo featuring the face of my English mastiff, Baby. Add in the latest in athletic footwear—black and blue Pyer Moss Sculpt sneakers—and I was set. I knew I looked fantastic. I was a fashion maven. An Iron Chef of cakes and pies! I smiled into the camera.

"Pride comes before the fall," Hannah Portman said. Hannah was a sixty-something-year-old Black woman who had been best friends with my great-aunt, Octavia, for more than fifty years. She'd worked side by side with Aunt Octavia in the bakery for most of those years. She was spirited, sassy, and an excellent baker. Now in the early stages of dementia, Hannah continued baking and working whenever she was able. She also happened to be my new boyfriend Michael's grandmother, so I couldn't blow her off, no matter how much I wanted to.

"You need to focus when you're baking or you're going to have a mess on your hands," Hannah said. She made the best sweet potato pies I'd ever eaten, but when it came to videos and social media, that was my wheelhouse. Videos of me learning to bake were trending on TikTok, Instagram, and Twitter, not to mention a host of other less well-known social media platforms. I was even doing well on Facebook, which was popular with New Bison residents. I was a social media influencer long before I inherited my great aunt's bakery and moved across the country to Southwest Michigan. Now, I'd found my niche and was putting Baby Cakes on the map.

I turned away from Hannah and rolled my eyes at the camera. Even at twenty-eight, I knew better than to let an older Black woman catch me rolling my eyes. Confident that beating egg whites would be a breeze, I smiled and turned on the stand mixer.

My first mistake was failing to secure the bowl. The moment the power was turned on, the bowl rocked and thumped against the counter. My second mistake was failing to turn the mixing speed down after the last time I'd used the beast. My third mistake was screaming when the mixer started flinging the slimy liquids in my face, hair, and around the kitchen. Note to self, *Never open your mouth while egg whites are flying through the air.*

With one eye closed and eggshell innards dripping all over my previously sparkling clean kitchen, I managed to get close enough to turn off the mixer.

Hearing my screams, Leroy Danielson, my head baker, rushed into the kitchen in time to see me with egg whites dripping from my hair and Hannah Portman laughing like a hyena. Leroy was five feet ten, thin, with shoulder-length dark wavy hair. His brown eyes were hidden behind a pair of thick, black-rimmed glasses, but even buried behind the frames, his eyes sparkled with laughter.

My fourth mistake was taking time to remove the egg whites from my hair before reaching for my iPhone. Leroy beat me to it. With a wicked grin and a few quick swipes, I knew that video was on its way into the cosmos.

"Your followers love these outtakes." He chuckled as he handed me my phone.

I glared, but it didn't do any good. He'd pulled out his phone and was watching the video from the beginning. Even without the sound, I knew when he got to the egg-white debacle because he guffawed.

Baby, the two-hundred-fifty-pound English mastiff I'd inherited from my great-aunt Octavia, along with her house, bakery, and a bit of cash, had followed Leroy into the house. Baby glanced in my direction and then loped over to the corner and hoisted himself up onto the custom-made corner dog bed that I'd ordered for his lounging pleasure. It was the size of a twin-sized bed and upholstered with a soft gray velvet that looked great in the adjacent white custom kitchen.

I stared at the massive canine that I'd grown to love in the short time that I'd been in New Bison.

He put his massive head down on his paws and sighed.

That sigh made my eyes water. "Something's wrong with him." I rushed over and climbed into the dog bed and put my arm around him. "What's the matter, boy?"

He gazed at me, lifted his massive head, rested it in my lap, and sighed again.

I gave Leroy an accusing look. "I thought you were going to take him to the vet?"

"I did, but the place was chaos. Michael had to do an emergency C-section on a goat, and the staff were rescheduling everybody else." Leroy saw the concern in my eyes. "I sent him a text, and he promised he'd come by as soon as he could."

"A goat?" I wiped the tears that had welled up in my eyes and leaned down and rubbed my chin on Baby's head and kissed his nose. "It's late. How long does a C-section take? Where is he?"

"Right here." Michael Portman, Hannah's grandson and my boyfriend, hurried in. "I got here as fast as I could." Michael placed a backpack that I knew contained his most-needed medical equipment on the counter. He looked tired but still smiled as he walked over to me.

He stood in front of me and stared down. "Hey, Squid."

I took the towel that I kept near the dog bed to take care of Baby's drool and swatted him. "Oh, shut up. I'm not in the mood for Navy slurs . . . any slurs."

In addition to being my boyfriend, Michael was a veteran of the Army, and Baby's veterinarian. As the daughter of a Navy admiral, I often bickered with him and tossed around military slurs without hatred or ill will. There's a frenemy kind of relationship between all branches of the military. He called me "squid" or "swabbie." I called him a "grunt" or "a dumb Joe." No bad feelings, but I wasn't in the mood.

"Don't pay her no mind," Hannah said, chuckling from the seat in the dining room. "She's just upset 'cause she's got egg whites all over her expensive new shoes."

I looked down at my Sculpts. Before moving to New Bison, I never would have thought twice about spending six hundred dollars for a pair of shoes. In the circles I hung around with in

L.A., I would have not only bought the latest Pyre Moss Sculpt sneakers with bright blue bottoms, but I would also have bought a pair in every primary color. My dad wasn't Elon Musk or Jeff Bezos rich. But U.S. Navy Admiral Jefferson Augustus Montgomery had served in the military for more years than I'd been alive. He earned a good living but didn't spend it on anything except me. He didn't need to spend a lot of money. The military provided his clothes, housing, and travel, and the Admiral had few vices. An occasional cigar and a taste for good cognac didn't break the piggy bank. My life as the only daughter of a too-busy-to-raise-a-kid-alone Navy admiral who could command thousands of men without breaking a sweat was one of financial indulgence and emotional neglect. I was determined to prove that I was a responsible adult, capable of taking care of myself and making important decisions when necessary, and that meant paying my own credit card bills. At least, that's what my new friends told me responsible adults did.

"I'm not upset about my shoes. I'm upset because I have egg whites dripping from my ceiling." As if on cue, a wad of the slimy whites fell from a pendant light, just missing my shoe.

I stared at the glop and used Baby's towel to wipe it off.

Michael squinted at me. "What's wrong with your eye?"

I pulled a compact from the pocket of my jeans and looked at myself. One glance was all it took to see that I was missing one of the false eyelashes that I'd carefully applied earlier. I glanced at Baby, who was using a paw to swipe at what appeared to be a spider on his nose.

I reached down and plucked the now limp and badly mangled lash off his nose.

Baby gave me a brief glance and then sighed and put his head back down.

With one quick tug, I removed the remaining lash. "Can't you see Baby's sick. He's been moping around here for two days. He doesn't play with his toys, and earlier today I opened a bag of potato chips, and he didn't even bother to lift his head."

Michael's lips twitched, and he worked to keep from smiling. "That does sound serious."

I glared at him. "I'm serious. He barely eats and he's lost his . . . his . . . zing." I turned to Leroy. "Hand me that T-R-E-A-T we put away for him."

Leroy was an excellent cook and was teaching me to prepare basic meals. Of course, the fact that he had a massive crush on my tenant April Johnson was probably another motivator for him to spend as much time here as possible. He went to the fridge and pulled out a large bone that we'd saved from dinner last night. He handed the bone to Baby, who sniffed it but didn't bother to look at it.

I gave Michael an *I told you so* look, but I didn't have to say a word. I could see that his demeanor had changed. In a few seconds, he switched from boyfriend to veterinarian, and he was now staring at Baby with concern.

He grabbed his backpack from the counter, walked over to the dog bed, and sat next to Baby. He stroked his head and his body, but I could tell that his petting had a purpose as he gently poked the gentle giant. Eventually, he pulled out a stethoscope and listened to Baby's heart and lungs.

The mastiff barely moved.

Despite my best efforts to contain myself, a few tears overflowed and ran down my cheek. My makeup was ruined, but I didn't care.

Michael asked about his input and output and a host of other questions, which I answered to the best of my ability. Input was something I could speak to, but I had to admit that I hadn't been watching his output. Yuck!

Baby lay listlessly by his side until Michael put on a pair of rubber gloves and pulled a large thermometer out of his backpack and inserted it where the sun don't shine. Baby wasn't pleased, but Michael spoke softly to him. When the indignity was over, Baby put his head back down.

Michael took alcohol wipes and cleaned the thermometer before returning it to his bag along with the stethoscope. "Temperature is normal. Heart and lungs sound clear. I can run some blood work tomorrow, but . . . he looks healthy."

"Healthy? How can you say he's healthy? Look at him." I spread my arms toward the mastiff.

Baby took that moment to sigh loudly.

A thought ran through my mind that made my heart skip a beat. I swallowed the lump in my throat. "Could it be an infection from getting shot?"

Michael looked at the scar that was the only sign of Baby's heroic attempts to save me from a deranged killer. "I doubt it. Everything appears to have healed well. He doesn't seem to have any tenderness."

While Michael probed the area, I couldn't help but stare at his arm, which bore a similar scar where he too had been shot saving my life.

"Maddy." Michael stopped poking Baby's scar, reached over and gently lifted my chin. "You didn't shoot Baby or me. And we've both healed just fine."

I nodded and wiped away the tears that were flowing faster now.

"Now focus, Squid. When did you first notice the change in his eating habits?"

I took a deep breath and thought. "He's been this way for about two days."

"Two days ago, he was at the clinic, and he seemed fine. In fact, he was frolicking around like a puppy."

"Frolicking? My two-hundred-fifty-pound English mastiff doesn't frolic. You must have been busy and gotten Baby confused with some other large dog or pony at the clinic."

"Not likely. I could never confuse Baby with any other dogs."

"I've never seen him . . . frolic." I stared down at the mastiff.

Michael grinned. "He was definitely frolicking."

Something in his smile made me curious. "What happened?"

He stole a glance at his grandmother, who was sitting at the counter.

Hannah intercepted the look. "Don't mind me. I care about Baby too." She sipped a cup of tea.

Michael rubbed his neck. "Baby was there to fulfill his . . . contractual obligations with a young beauty named Champion Xena Warrior Princess." He gave me a pointed look. "He took care of business, but he also met a little cutie named Daisy." He winked. "That's when our boy here got a twinkle in his eye. Some bounce in his step. And the frolicking commenced."

Baby was a champion show dog with good health and many fine characteristics of the breed. Before she died, my great-aunt Octavia set him up as a stud dog. A few days ago, Michael had given him a physical and introduced him to a dam named Daisy. Daisy wasn't under contract to mate with Baby, but her owner had heard good things about him and had reached out to me. Before inheriting Baby, what I knew about dogs was less than what I knew about baking. And that isn't saying much. I couldn't look at a dog and tell if she met the breed's standards and would produce champion-worthy pups, so I'd asked Michael to do the introductions. Besides, I found Daisy's owner to be pushy and arrogant, and I'd initially declined her request. But my friend and tenant, April Johnson, suggested that I cut the dog some slack. She reminded me that few people get to pick their families, and Daisy couldn't pick her owner.

"I thought you said he liked Daisy," I said.

"He did like Daisy. He *really* liked Daisy." He raised his eyebrows.

It took a few seconds for his meaning to sink in. "Are you trying to tell me that Baby's in love?"

He shrugged. "I don't know that I'd go as far as *love*, but he was strutting around like he was the king of the world. Now you're telling me that he barely eats. He has no interest in playing or treats. It sure sounds like he's at the very least infatuated."

I stared at Baby. "This isn't the first time he's . . . mated. Did he act this way the other times?"

Michael shook his head. "Not that I recall. If he did, Miss Octavia never mentioned it."

I glanced over at Leroy and Miss Hannah. "Well?"

They exchanged a glance and then shook their heads.

I looked into Baby's eyes. "Are you trying to tell me you miss Daisy?"

I don't know if he understood me, but he raised his head for a second, snorted, and then put his drooly jowls back down on my leg and sighed, again.

"What did you think about Daisy?" I asked.

"She seems to be in good physical health," Michael said. "Her heart and lungs sounded good." He hesitated.

"What?"

He paused and shook his head. "Nothing. Everything sounded okay, but I can't say for sure without an ultrasound. Sometimes a heart condition can't be detected without really looking at it. But that would just be a precaution. She's got paperwork from her veterinarian that states she's OFA certified."

"What's that?"

"Responsible breeders have their dogs checked out and certified with the Orthopedic Foundation for Animals to confirm there's no signs of congenital heart problems."

"Was Baby checked?"

"Miss Octavia took care of that, and all of Baby's certifications are current and up to date. Of course, the certifications only last for one year, but I just automatically complete his paperwork."

"Thank you." I leaned over and kissed him. "If Baby is pin-ing after Daisy, then I want to make sure that she's healthy before I let him . . . well, you know . . . mate with her. Great Aunt Octavia entrusted Baby to me and I have to make sure that I'm doing the right thing for him. What about Daisy's certification? Is she healthy?"

"Daisy was registered, but her OFA certification is out of date. It may not mean anything. Her owner just may not have gotten the paperwork done yet. Anyway, her eyes were clear. She's one-hundred-sixty pounds, which is a little small, but otherwise, she looked healthy. I'm a veterinarian. I can tell you if she's healthy, but I'm not an expert when it comes to winning dog shows. I'd suggest you talk to a breeder like—"

I was already shaking my head before the words left his mouth. The only English mastiff breeder I knew was Jackson Abernathy. Heck, the only dog breeder that I knew, period, was Jackson Abernathy. When I first arrived in New Bison, he made an offer to buy Baby, which I rejected. Even if I wanted to sell him, Aunt Octavia's will stipulated that in order to inherit, I had to live in New Bison and run her bakery, stay in her house, and keep Baby for one year. It hadn't taken more than a day before I realized that selling Baby was the last thing I wanted.

"Look, I'm not suggesting you sell Baby to him," Michael said. "All I said was talk to him and see if he knows anything about the owner and the quality of her dogs. The dog show world is fairly small, especially in Southwest Michigan. You could just see if he knows the breeder and find out what his opinion is of her dogs."

"That's not a bad idea," Miss Hannah said. "Octavia knew all the mastiff breeders in the country. Her issues with Jackson Abernathy were personal."

I glanced at Leroy.

Leroy cleared his throat. "It couldn't hurt to talk to him. There's the town meeting tonight. It'll be his first since he took over as mayor."

"He'll be strutting around like a turkey on the day after Thanksgiving," Hannah said and then sipped her tea.

"That should put him in a good mood," Leroy said.

I wasn't good at making decisions. As an admiral in the Navy, my dad said I needed to assess the situation thoroughly before making a decision. He should know; he made important decisions that impacted thousands of people every day. I, on the other hand, had a long history of bad decisions that I'd made hastily or based on emotion rather than facts. But I didn't have time to research and assess all of the facts objectively. Doing nothing could jeopardize Baby's health and well-being. "Okay, I'll talk to him."

"Besides, now that he's taken over as mayor, he's bound to be less of a jerk," Michael said.

I hoped he was right, but in my opinion, once a jerk, always a jerk. Nevertheless, I pulled out my phone, snapped a picture of Baby, and posted it. **#MyBabyHasTheBlues #IveGotA-CrushOnYou #EnglishMastiffisinLove**

CHAPTER 2

"What do you think the mayor's big surprise is going to be?" Leroy whispered as we sat in the hard folding chairs that were arranged in the public room of the New Bison City Hall building. The front of the room had a raised platform and seats where the mayor and city council members sat. Each of the board members had a microphone. There was a standing microphone on the floor facing the council where the public were allowed five minutes to speak their piece. Behind the microphone were about fifty folding chairs for the public.

"I have no idea." I looked around the room. Every chair was filled except the one Michael, Leroy, and I were saving for our friend Tyler Lawrence.

As if on cue, Tyler made his way through the crowd. He strained his neck as he looked around the room. We made eye contact, and he wove through the standing-room-only throng to our row. Then he sidled past several people to take his seat.

I leaned across Leroy and whispered, "What took you so long?"

"Business has been booming. Thanks to you." He nodded toward me. "Since you've been posting pictures online, I've been crazy busy. Not that I'm complaining. I'm grateful, but it's exhausting."

Tyler was a small-framed man with dark hair and vivid blue eyes. He was a wizard with yarn and owned a custom knitwear shop.

"I wish I could take credit, but your bespoke knitwear sells itself. I just helped folks find you."

"Bespoke." Leroy chuckled. "It sounds so much more expensive than homemade."

The council members entered and went to their seats at the front of the room. The conversation level had reduced to a low rumble as the crowd prepared for the main event.

Jackson Abernathy was a red-faced man with wisps of blond hair on either side of his head. Abernathy was new to the role of mayor, having fallen into the position after Paul Rivers, the previous mayor, was murdered.

New Bison was a small town with a population of less than two thousand, so the mayor wasn't a paid position. Abernathy supported himself by breeding English mastiffs and managing his father's insurance agency, New Bison Casualty and Life. He liked being the center of attention, so the role of mayor was perfect for him.

I glanced around at the crowded room. I was struck by the amount of flannel and denim. It was spring, but still a little cool beside Lake Michigan, so most of the women had a denim jacket or a sweater to combat the wind. Sadly, one glance told me the sweaters were not from Tyler's knit shop. The quality of the yarn and boring machine designs screamed blue-light special. In my past life, I would have chosen death before I'd have allowed myself to be seen in those outfits. However, my past life hadn't worked out so well. In fact, six months ago my life was night-and-day different from what it was today. Six months ago, my highest aspiration was to marry a doctor and be a good trophy wife. I never dreamed I would be living in a town that wasn't a metropolitan hub, like New York City, Los Angeles, Paris, or London. I saw myself at the center of a bustling, exciting life, dressed to the nines in the latest in haute couture. I'd have a huge diamond on my left ring finger. The stone would be so large that when the sun hit it, I could use it like a laser to blind my enemies. I smiled. I'd had that life. Most of that life. I'd lived in Los Angeles, built a career as a social media influencer, snagged a doctor, and was on my way to the altar, when everything came to a screeching halt. My former fiancé, Elliott, dumped me at the altar in the middle of our live-streamed wedding, and I thought my life was over. #HumiliatedBeyondBelief

I planned to find a big rock to hide under for a few years until things died down, but my great-aunt Octavia died. Now, instead of hiding out, I was running a bakery, dating a vet, and sitting at town hall meetings in New Bison, Michigan.

A nudge in the ribs brought me back to the here and now. I glanced at my friend, head baker, and assistant, Leroy. "What?"

"What's wrong with April? She looks like she's seen a ghost." He nodded toward a door near the front of the room.

I followed his gaze and had to agree. Just a few minutes earlier, my rosy-cheeked, bright-eyed friend looked like a tough-as-nails cop, which she was. In just a few minutes, the blood had drained from her face. Her eyes were wide and a bit wild, as though she was ready to run. "You're right. She looks . . . frightened." I followed her gaze, which was focused on an older man who had just walked up to the front of the room.

The man looked to be in his forties, but I was willing to bet my new Telfar bag that he was in his midfifties and well preserved. He wasn't as tall as Michael, so I'd put his stats at five foot ten and two hundred pounds, give or take a pound. His thick dark hair was cut to perfection. In fact, I doubt that your layperson would have guessed that his hair color came from a tube. However, I had spent too many years in high-end salons not to recognize the signs. His hair was perfect; too perfect. There were highlights and lowlights in the exact right places, which was my first clue that it wasn't natural. Nature isn't perfect. He was tanned, and I knew with every fiber of my being that he wouldn't have tan lines. However, the most dazzling thing about him was his teeth. When he smiled, those on the front row would need to shield their eyes or suffer from retina damage. He wore a dark blue English-cut, bespoke suit that fit like a glove, and money oozed from every pore.

April wasn't the only woman in the room whose gaze was fixed on the stranger, but she was the only one whose gaze he returned. His stare reminded me of the leopards I'd seen on a safari in Botswana. Our guides warned us never to stare at the leopards. These large cats will lie perfectly still, relying on their camouflage to hide them. It's possible to walk right by a leopard without seeing it. However, if you stare into a leopard's eyes, he knows his cover is blown and will attack. Leopard-like, this well-groomed stranger looked ready to pounce, and his target was my friend.

I squeezed Michael's arm.

"Ouch."

"Sorry."

At the front of the room, Mayor Abernathy whispered something to the man and laughed.

The man turned away from April. He gazed at the mayor and forced a smile, which looked more like a grimace. The spell was broken.

April fumbled with the doorknob of the door behind her, but finally wrenched it open, stumbling through the door and out of the room.

For a split second, I was torn between staying to find out who the man was and helping my friend. My normal indecisiveness didn't have time to kick in. I got up and started sidling my way out of the aisle. "Excuse me."

Outside in the hall, I saw the back of April's head as she turned a corner that I knew led to the ladies' room.

I hurried after her and arrived just in time to hear her retching in a stall. I waited at the sink until she finished, flushed, and came out.

She bent down and used the sink like a water faucet and cleaned her mouth and then splashed water on her face. When she finally stood, I handed her a mass of paper towels and waited.

April took several deep breaths. "I look horrible."

I tried not to notice her hand shaking or her ragged breath. "You want to tell me who that man was?"

"Not really."

I waited.

"You're not going to let sleeping dogs lie, are you?"

"Nope."

"Then, I suppose I'll have to." She took a deep breath and closed her eyes.

"Yep."

"His name is Clayton Jefferson Davenport. CJ to his friends, but I don't know if he has any of those." She paused for a few moments.

"Okaaay, but *who* is he?"

She chuckled. "Never heard of him?"

I thought for a moment. "It kind of sounds vaguely familiar, but . . . no. I don't know him."

Her laugh increased and sounded a bit strange.

"April, are you hysterical? Do I need to slap you?"

She shook her head, held up a hand, and forced herself to calm down. "You don't need to slap me. I'm not hysterical. It just struck me as funny. You not knowing who he is would really irritate him."

I raised an eyebrow. "Oh? So, he's someone who I *should* know?"

She stared. "Clayton Jefferson Davenport is one of the wealthiest men in the Midwest. He's not as wealthy or as well-known as Bill Gates, and I'm sure that's eating a hole in his gut. But he's wealthy."

"Okay, he's got money. Great, but who is he to you?"

She paused so long I was about to repeat my question when she said, "Clayton Jefferson Davenport is my husband."

I stared at her. I knew April had been married, but she didn't talk about it. If asked, her response was always, *It's complicated.* I hadn't thought much about her ex-husband, but given that April wasn't wealthy and the little bits of information she'd shared about her life before I moved to New Bison, I had made assumptions about his wealth that were obviously not true.

"He's not exactly what I envisioned your ex-husband would look like, but—"

"No. Not my *ex-husband.* We never got divorced. CJ is my husband."

CHAPTER 3

I stared in silence.

"Say something," April said.

"Wait. What do you mean, your husband?"

"I told you, it's complicated."

"Complicated? You're either married or you're not. How is that complicated?"

April opened her mouth to respond but stopped when the bathroom door opened. A woman came in clutching the hand of a young boy, who looked to be three years old. The boy was screaming. "I don't wanna go in there. That's for girls."

The young mother picked up the screaming boy and carried him into the stall, mumbling, "Just get in there."

"Maybe we should go someplace where we can talk in private," April said.

I nodded, and we left the bathroom.

"Baby Cakes? I want to see how the renovations are going, and we won't be disturbed there, but you'll need to drive. I came with Michael."

April agreed.

I sent Michael a text letting him know to pick me up at Baby Cakes, and we headed out.

The drive from the town hall to Baby Cakes Bakery was short. We could have walked, but the breeze from Lake Michigan was brisk, and I'd opted for style over practicality and changed from my sneakers into the cutest-ever pair of tangerine-colored pumps. The four-inch heels weren't a problem. I could run through the airport in four-inch heels without breaking a sweat. The problem was that the weather in Southwest Michigan was unpredictable, and while a Bottega Veneta pump could hold up to a lot of wear and tear, unlike the postal service they were not intended to endure rain, sleet, snow, and hail. All of which could make an appearance any given moment in Southwest Michigan.

April drove the short distance. Retail stores lined both sides of the two blocks of the area New Bison residents called *downtown*. Baby Cakes Bakery was on the corner of Main and Church Streets and was somewhat larger than the other businesses that occupied the block-long brick building filled with retail shops. The previous mayor used to own a hardware store next door. Now, his wife, Candace Hurston Rivers, was in the process of converting the hardware store into a high-end coffee shop. She'd converted the upstairs into a small apartment that she hoped to rent out. I was as excited for Higher Grounds Coffee and Tea as Candy was. While I was adapting to living in a small town, not having a high-end coffee house was one area where I hadn't adapted. I longed for a truly good cortado or a red eye for those exceptionally difficult mornings. Michael said I was a coffee snob, and I'll own it. I love a good cup of java. I was surprised to learn that Candy was so knowledgeable about coffee. When we met, she'd been a waitress at the New Bison Casino. However, the casino had a first-class coffee bar, which is apparently where she perfected her craft. Besides, a coffee shop next to a bakery would be good for business, so I was excited.

Next door to the soon-to-be coffee shop was Tyler's Knitwear, followed by a small café and a store that sold used furniture, which the owner generously referred to as "antiques." Across the street was a shop that sold soap, candles, and essential oils; Garrett Kelley's bookshop; a small boutique women's clothing store; and a custom jewelry store. Change in small towns is slow, but after the deaths of both Mayor Rivers and Garrett Kelley, things started changing quickly. There would be the new coffee shop, and a lot of activity had been happening at Garrett's bookshop. Although, no one knew exactly what was planned for the space. The new owners were keeping their plans on the down-low, but I was making connections in New Bison, and I planned to unleash them to find out who had purchased the building and what their intentions were.

April and I went in through the back door. A few months ago, Baby Cakes had suffered damage when a fire was deliberately set to hide a murder. In the vein of converting lemons to lemonade, I'd used the insurance money to update the space. The kitchen had undergone a remodel previously, so that space had simply needed the replacement of anything damaged by smoke or water from the fire department. One side of the bakery had been where the baked goods were displayed and sold, and it had a few bistro tables. There was a wall that separated it from another space where Aunt Octavia had sold bakeware. I'd had the wall removed and opened the customer area up so that the bakery was light, bright, and airy. I'd gotten the idea of removing the bakeware and installing a kitchen where we could demonstrate baking techniques and offer cooking classes. The space wasn't large. Leroy and I had argued over the configuration. However, after I saw the price tag for my dream—albeit pared down—version of Le Cordon Bleu, I nearly passed out. My design was beautiful, but April showed me that affording it with my budget would have meant giving up cable, internet, food, and shopping for two years. I probably could have managed without most of those things, but no shopping for two years was a deal breaker. Instead of a true cooking school with twelve moveable islands complete with ovens, cooktops, and prep areas, a space that would have made angels sing—and the Barefoot Contessa, Ina Garten, weep—we had a galley-style design with one massive island. There was an oversized double oven, two sinks, and a built-in refrigerator, but mostly the space was ideal for sitting around the island watching Leroy demonstrate various techniques.

April and I pulled up stools to the large white marble-topped island and sat. It took a few moments for her to gather herself enough to speak. I waited.

"I grew up not very far from here in a town a lot smaller than New Bison, if you can believe that."

I couldn't. Before moving to New Bison, I didn't realize there were towns with only one zip code, one high school, one post office, and no shopping malls.

"Growing up, the only thing I had going for me were my looks. My mom entered me in one beauty pageant after another. By the time I was sixteen, I had a room full of trophies and ribbons and a closet full of expensive pageant dresses. I wanted to get away, do something with my life, but I wasn't smart enough to do anything but walk in heels while wearing a bathing suit with a smile plastered on my face like the Joker from a Batman movie."

Take away the bathing suit and Joker-esque smile and I saw a lot of myself in April. True, I'd attended a prestigious college, but deep down, we both lacked self-confidence. "April, you're smart, brave, kind, and intelligent. You're the freakin' sheriff, for Gawd's sake."

She shrugged. "Maybe now, but back then I was just a scared kid who believed I was only good for one thing." She gave me a pointed look.

I reached over and squeezed her hand.

"Clayton was one of the investors in the beauty pageant. I had just turned eighteen, and he was twenty years older, but he was handsome and rich. He showed me a world I didn't know existed. Private planes, penthouse suites, and access to anything I wanted."

She paused and I prodded. "But . . ."

"But there was another side to him. When it came to business or money, he was vicious. He had to win. There was nothing he wouldn't do to win. If he thought someone had gotten the upper hand, he was relentless in seeking vengeance." She stared into space as though gazing into a crystal ball of the past. "Clayton's family had been poor, and he vowed he would *never* go through that again. He fought his way to the top of the financial dung pile. Only the best would do. He had to have the fastest cars. The biggest, most lavish houses . . . he had several. The most expensive custom-made suits."

She grew quiet, and I added, "The prettiest wife?"

She nodded.

I gave her hand another squeeze. "What happened?"

"I couldn't take it anymore. He didn't love me. I don't even know if he cared two cents about me. All he wanted was perfection. I had to be the best. The prettiest. The most perfect wife at all times." She took a deep breath. "He got into a battle over a business he wanted to acquire. But the guy he was fighting was just as rich and ruthless as he was. It was like some vicious chess match. Whenever one of them made a move, the other countered. CJ was furious. Whenever he thought he was making progress, he met a brick wall." April frowned and tilted her head to the side. "The weird thing is that Clayton never met the guy. I mean, no one knew who he was or what he looked like."

"How is that possible?"

She shook her head. "I have no idea, but I know Clayton tried everything to find out who he was. Apparently, he had dummy corporations set up in several countries and . . . well, I don't understand it, but somehow, the guy sent Clayton a message offering to settle, on one condition."

"What?"

"Clayton was to trade me for the business."

I blinked several times and shook my head as I'd seen Baby do to clear the cobwebs. I couldn't have heard that right. "Excuse me?"

I saw a tear drop onto the counter. I got off my barstool, went to the bathroom and got a box of tissues, and came back. I placed the box in between us and slid several tissues into her hand.

She wiped her eyes and blew her nose. "I promised myself I wouldn't cry anymore."

When the waterworks slowed to a trickle, I said, "Please tell me Clayton told the guy exactly what building he could take a flying leap from?" Her silence hit me in the gut, and for a split second, I thought I would puke. "Are you kidding?"

She shook her head.

I reached across and pulled her into an embrace. I could feel her body shaking and felt her tears on the back of my neck. In that moment I was so angry, I could have happily strangled Clayton Jefferson Davenport with my bare hands. No human being deserved to be treated like a baseball card. We hugged until the tears slowed.

She pulled away, grabbed several tissues, and handed them to me before grabbing more for herself. We wiped away the residue of the conversation, but I couldn't imagine what could erase the wounds left by her revelation. Whoever said *Sticks and stones may break your bones, but words will never hurt you* was wrong. I couldn't imagine any physical violence that cut deeper than words.

I dreaded asking, but I had to know. "What did you do?"

"I walked out. I left the money, credit cards, clothes, everything."

I was grateful that she valued herself enough to leave, but

something bothered me. "He doesn't sound like the type of man to just let you walk out. Did he try to find you?"

April avoided looking me in the eyes, and I knew she was holding something back, but now wasn't the time to press her.

"Did you ever find out who the other man was?" I asked. "The one who wanted to . . . trade you?"

She shook her head. "At first, I didn't want to know. I just wanted to avoid anything that would connect me to Clayton. Later, when I became sheriff, I tried. I hoped I could arrest him, but technically he hadn't done anything wrong or illegal."

"Nothing wrong? He's a—"

April held up a hand to stop my tirade. "Nothing happened. So, propositioning a man to hand over his wife in exchange for business considerations isn't illegal."

"But . . . surely Clayton . . ."

"Still not illegal. Now, if he tried to *force* me to comply, then that would have been illegal." She shrugged. "I was just so disgusted. If he thought he could have gotten away with it, he would have. The way he said it . . ." She shuddered. "I knew . . . I could see it in his eyes. When he saw my reaction, he flipped a switch. Suddenly, he was outraged by the audacity. But it was too late. I'd seen inside his soul, and I knew it was dark and evil. That was eight years ago. I haven't seen or heard from him since."

"Why is he here now?"

"I have no idea." She gave me a hard stare. "But I'm scared."

CHAPTER 4

"Scared of what?"

We were so engrossed in our conversation that neither of us noticed we weren't alone and that Leroy and Michael had come in through the back until Leroy spoke.

April quickly turned away to hide her face. We had all grown close over the past few months, normally sharing everything. However, it was clear from April's body language that she wasn't ready to share this aspect of her life. Not yet anyway.

I wasn't a good liar. When I was nervous, I tended to over-share. I racked my brain to think of something that would ring true. "April's worried about all of the new people and businesses moving to New Bison. She thinks the criminal element is going to move in and cause a massive crime wave and her small team won't be able to handle things." All of which was true. She'd talked about it extensively a few nights ago.

Leroy frowned, and I was sure he didn't believe that was why April was upset now, but he had the common sense to keep his mouth shut.

Michael and I exchanged a glance that told me that he didn't believe me either. True to his nature, he came to my aid by changing the subject.

"This place looks great. Are they going to be finished by the start of the Spring Festival?" Michael glanced around. "It's only a few days away, and it looks like there's a lot of work left."

"It better be done. I've already planned a grand reopening to coincide with the start of the Spring Festival. I've been building up a social media frenzy for Leroy's carrot pecan cookies and Hannah's sweet potato tarts." I held up my phone to prove my statement.

Michael held up a hand. "I know. I follow you. **#Baby-CakesGrandReopening #CookingClasses #SweetsAndTreats.**"

Leroy grinned. "Don't forget **#MastiffApprovedBaked-Goods**."

"All true." I smiled. "Leroy's first class is already sold out."

"Sold out is misleading," he said. "There are only twelve students."

"Twelve students who have signed up to learn how to make croissants, but I've also sold observation space."

"What's observation space?" Michael asked.

I turned my back to the counter and spread my arms wide. "That is observation space. I'm going to put folding chairs here. I have another twelve people who are willing to pay half price to sit and watch. Next time, we should offer two classes. One in the morning and one in the evening."

Leroy shook his head. "Who knew Ted Turner was running Baby Cakes?"

April pulled herself together. "Maddy's a genius when it comes to promotion and social media. Who else would have been able to keep Baby Cakes Bakery going by selling baked goods from a detached garage turned roadside food stand at her house for three months while the bakery went through renovations after the fire? Every morning, the line of cars outside the house gets longer and longer. I had to threaten to arrest three people if they didn't move their cars so I could back out of the driveway."

An unfamiliar voice said, "Sounds like a good problem to have."

We turned in surprise, and there stood the man who had caused April so much grief and cost us both a lot of tears just a few moments earlier.

"How'd you get in here?" I asked.

Clayton Davenport flashed a toothy grin and motioned to the back door. "The door was unlocked."

I glared. "Well, we're closed. So, you can just turn around and walk out the same way you walked in here."

Michael stiffened. I could tell he was surprised by my reaction, but he immediately took a step forward, so he became a barrier between me and Davenport. As angry as I was, I could have happily delivered a knee to a sensitive location.

Clayton Davenport wasn't nearly as tall as Michael, and while he might have considered himself in good shape, he wasn't as young, muscular, or tough. There was something in the way Michael carried himself that even though he wasn't wearing a uniform, you knew he was former military. He wouldn't start a conflict, but once engaged, he wouldn't quit as long as there was breath left in his body. Proceed at your own risk.

Clayton Davenport may have been a big guy on Wall Street, but in a physical battle in New Bison, my money was on the military. Davenport clenched his jaw. A vein on the side of his head pulsed as though an alien could leap from his skull at any moment. His eyes were cold, but he must have recognized there was no way he could win this. Instead of engaging in a battle that would surely ruin his expensive suit, he made a tactical retreat. He held up his hands in surrender and flashed his toothy grin even wider than before. "I didn't come here for a fight. I just wanted to talk to my wife and check out the competition."

"Wife!?" Leroy said, and he stared from Clayton to April.

April's face turned beet red.

"Competition?" I asked. "What competition?"

Davenport had pulled a surprise attack and caught us unprepared. He grinned. "I've seen all of the promotion you've been doing on social media and decided to enter the fray. So, I bought the bookstore across the street, and I'm opening a bakery."

"Across the street? You bought Garrett's bookstore?" My mind raged. There was only one bookstore in town. It had to be Garrett Kelley's bookstore. Still, I couldn't believe this was happening.

He folded his arms across his chest. "Don't tell me you're afraid of a little *friendly* competition."

My stomach sank to my knees, and it took everything inside me not to wilt like a leaf of lettuce. Instead, I folded my arms across my chest and glared. "We'll wipe the floor with you. Baby Cakes has a reputation, and *local* residents believe in supporting *local* businesses, not some franchise with frozen pastries shipped from Chicago or New York."

"That's why I've hired a master chocolatier and pâtissier from Belgium. He should be here in a week." He chuckled. "Your reign in New Bison is over. You might as well throw in the towel and quit now. You can save yourself the humiliation of being beat by a *real* chef."

My knees wobbled, and I felt the blood rush from my face. But, in that one moment, I heard my great-aunt Octavia's voice in my head: *Oh no he didn't.* And I remembered who I am. A picture of Admiral Jefferson Augustus Montgomery in full military uniform and spitting commands at the speed of light flashed across my eyes. The Admiral never backed down from a challenge. I hadn't spent most of my life surrounded by dedicated sailors who didn't know the meaning of the word *failure* for nothing. My spine transformed into a steel rod. I stood tall with my head high and shoulders back. Suddenly, all of the clichés I'd heard drilled into soldiers for the past twenty-plus years made sense. "I will never quit. I persevere and thrive on adversity."

Davenport looked confused. He must not have spent much time with sailors. He tilted his head to the side and frowned. "What?"

"Bring it on!"

"You seem awfully confident for someone who can't even beat eggs." He grinned. "Although, you've got great taste in clothes. Maybe I should clarify. We're talking about a *baking* competition, not a fashion show."

I didn't like conflict and avoided it like the plague. However, when there was no other alternative, I was all in. I barely blinked at his jab. He'd done his homework and was obviously following me on social media. I would figure out a way to use that to my advantage. "Mr. Davenport, I don't like you, and you don't like me. So, let's make this brief. I accept your challenge."

"You talk a good game, but can you back it up?" He paused, and I continued to glare at him. "We both know New Bison isn't big enough for two bakeries. So, let's make things easy. Winner takes all. If you win, I close down the bakery and move out of town. And, if I win, you sell out. You close Baby Cakes, and leave."

I heard April gasp behind me. "No. That's not fair. Nor is it reasonable. You're just taking your anger at me out on my friend."

The blood was rushing in my head. Leave New Bison? I didn't want to leave. I needed to stop and think, but I was too angry to stop. "Deal."

Everyone started to object.

"But only on one condition," I said over the dissent.

He waited.

I walked around Michael and whispered in Davenport's ear.

If I hadn't been so close, I wouldn't have noticed the rage that rose up his neck and caused the tips of his ears to turn red. Eventually, he pulled himself together, turned, and glared. "Deal."

If looks could kill, I would have dropped dead after the evil look Davenport gave me. But, with Michael standing immediately behind me, I knew he wouldn't be foolish enough to take his anger out on me physically. Nevertheless, I felt Michael take a step closer. "Now, get out."

"You're real brave with your boyfriend behind you," Davenport sneered.

I smiled. "I don't need anyone to take care of a weasel like you. I can swing a pretty mean skillet."

Davenport frowned, unfamiliar with my previous skillet-wielding encounter. For a brief moment, it looked like he wanted to say more, but before he could, Michael intervened.

"You heard her," Michael said with steel in his voice. "Out."

Leroy held open the door.

Davenport marched out.

CHAPTER 5

For several seconds after Davenport's departure, we stood in a tense silence. Then, the avalanche hit and the silence was gone.

"Are you out of your mind?"

"You can't do that."

"What were you thinking?"

My head was spinning as I was hit with the barrage of comments questioning my sanity. In one moment of anger, I went from cripplingly indecisive to bold impulsivity, and the swing made me light-headed. I held up my hand and sifted through a bazillion thoughts to give a response that could explain what I'd just done. Nothing came to mind.

"Wow! Who peed in his Cheerios?"

I turned to see who had just spoken and caught sight of Candace Hurston Rivers.

Candy was small, not more than five feet tall, but she knew how to use her assets to her best advantage. She wore heels that appeared to add at least a foot to her small frame. The heels made her already short skirts seem shorter, and her shapely legs looked as though they went on forever. She teased her hair so that it gave the illusion of another couple of inches. Her eyes were prominent, probably due to her preference for the overly dramatic drag queen lashes she wore. Michael was fascinated that she was capable of opening her eyelids with the excessively thick, overly dramatic lashes, but she had skills.

"How'd you get in?" I asked.

Candy pointed toward the back of the building. "I came through the tunnel."

"Tunnel? What tunnel?"

"The tunnel that connects your store to mine." She stared. "You didn't know?"

I glanced at Leroy, who shrugged and shook his head.

"The construction folks found it while they were renovating the coffee shop. It's old and dusty, but it works, and it looks like someone has been through there recently. I assumed you knew. I guess it's true what they say about assuming. Come on, I'll show you."

Candy led us toward a door to a closet off the kitchen. She pushed aside the mops and cleaning supplies, and at the back of the closet was another door. She twisted the knob and opened the door.

A dank, earthy scent wafted through along with a breeze that sent a shiver up my spine.

That's when I noticed that Candy had a cobweb hanging off the back of her skirt.

"Come on." She picked up a flashlight that she'd left on the kitchen counter and stepped through the door.

I shook my head. No way was I going through that tunnel. "Classic slasher horror movie mistake. Never take the tunnel down into the dark abyss of doom."

Michael smiled at the running joke we had shared since our first adventure. He hesitated for a moment until Candy yelled, "Hey, are you guys coming or what?" Then, he shrugged and followed Candy.

"I can't believe this has been here the entire time and Miss Octavia didn't know," Leroy mumbled and then headed through the closet.

April and I exchanged looks. She patted the gun holstered to her leg. "I suppose I should go too, in case the boys need cover. I am the only one packing heat." She headed toward the closet, but before she descended, she turned. "You coming?"

"Absolutely not. I'm staying here with my finger on my phone, ready to call nine-one-one if you don't come back in ten minutes."

She nodded and headed through the closet.

"Or if someone screams," I mumbled to myself. "And to think, I used to dream of visiting Narnia."

I waited for fifteen minutes and was just about to call for reinforcements when I heard voices from the closet.

Leroy came out first with his hair full of cobwebs and brushing dirt from his shirt. Once he was out, he turned and held out a hand to help April and then Candy. It didn't surprise me to see that Michael was the last one to emerge.

"I guess now we know how Mayor Rivers got into Baby Cakes the night he was murdered," Leroy said.

April swiped his arm and glanced in Candy's direction.

"Oh, I'm sorry," he apologized.

Candy shrugged. "It's okay."

"So, where does it lead?" I asked.

"Next door," April said.

"I gathered that much." It took a great deal of effort for me to swallow the *Thanks, Captain Obvious* retort, but I did. "I mean, is that it? Why build a secret passage that leads next door? I mean, was one of these buildings ever a bank?"

April shook her head. "Not that I know. Why do you ask?"

"It just seems odd, sort of like a Sherlock Holmes story I read."

"Not another Sherlock Holmes book," Michael said. "Between you and your great-aunt Octavia, everything boils down to a mystery by a *fictional* detective."

I made a point of ignoring him. "It was 'The Red-Headed League.' There's this redheaded guy . . . I can't remember his name." I swiped my phone and asked Siri, "What are the names of the characters in the 'Red-Headed League' by Sir Arthur Conan Doyle?"

Siri rattled off the names, and I stopped her after I heard the name I was looking for. "Mr. Wilson. Wilson was this redheaded man who owned a shop. He had hired an assistant named Clay who encouraged him to respond to a newspaper ad offering a job by the Red-Headed League. The League supposedly had an endowment that provided money to a redheaded man to copy the encyclopedia."

"The encyclopedia?" Michael asked. "Whatever for?"

"Actually, it turned out to be busy work. They just wanted him out of his shop because his shop was across the street from a bank. So, while Mr. Wilson was out copying the encyclopedia, his assistant was digging a tunnel so they could break into the bank. Once their tunnel was done, they ended Wilson's assignment. Wilson hired Sherlock Holmes to find out why."

April narrowed her eyes. "I can check at the clerk's office, but I don't think there was ever a bank here. At least not since I've lived here." She glanced at Leroy, who shook his head.

Michael had only lived here a year longer than me. He'd had a successful veterinarian practice in Chicago but moved to New Bison when his grandmother was diagnosed with dementia. I was the new kid on the block.

"What happened to Mr. Wilson?" Candy asked.

"Nothing. Sherlock Holmes figured out what the assistant was up to and set a trap. When the gang tried to break into the bank vault, Holmes was waiting for him with the police."

Candy stared. "That's fascinating. I'll bet that's what happened here. Maybe Paul wanted to break into Baby Cakes and steal . . ." She glanced around at the bakery kitchen.

Leroy chuckled. "What? Cookies? What's here worth stealing? Miss Octavia's secret recipe for Chocolate Soul Cake?"

Candy snapped her fingers and smiled. "Yes. I'll bet that's it."

April and I exchanged glances, but neither of us spoke. Candy wasn't the sharpest knife in the drawer, but she was nice.

"Since he's passed, I've learned that Paul was into some shady things. I wouldn't put it past him to try and steal Miss Octavia's recipe. I mean, he'd have done anything to get her house and this building. The louse." She stared at April. "Anyway, it sounds like your husband is pretty shady too."

April's cheeks flushed, and she glanced around the room. Candy had apparently been listening to our conversation a lot longer than we realized. She must have heard April mention that Clayton Davenport was her husband, but Leroy and Michael weren't aware of the details. They still thought Davenport was April's ex. April must have realized it was just a matter of time before everyone in town knew the secret she'd been hiding. Eventually, she sighed. "Look, now that he's here, I'm sure everything is going to come out anyway, so I might as well tell you. Clayton Davenport is my husband. We're separated, and I intend to get divorced just as soon as I can. However, I don't want to talk about it." April folded her arms across her chest and stared at the floor.

An awkward silence followed April's statement. After a few moments, Candy walked over and enveloped April in an embrace.

"I completely understand," Candy said. "Some men can be such pigs."

I glanced at Leroy, who was fuming. He had the world's biggest crush on April, so I assumed he was upset at learning that April wasn't divorced and that her husband was actually here in town. I walked over to him. "It's going to be okay."

"Is it?" He slammed his fist on the counter, causing me to jump.

"Of course, it is."

"How? How is it going to be okay? He's rich. He's flying in a master chef from Belgium. You can barely boil water, and you just accepted a challenge from him to a *winner take all* bake-off like some kind of old-fashioned *Gunfight at the O.K. Corral*. What were you thinking?"

Everyone stared at me.

"I wasn't thinking."

"Obviously," Leroy mumbled.

"I was impulsive and irresponsible. Not the first time. I thought I was making progress, but obviously, I just had a relapse. I know on the surface I have about as much chance of winning a baking contest against a professionally trained master chef as a snowball in . . . well, you know, but—"

Michael stopped my verbal bombardment by walking over and giving me a hug. "Never mind, Squid. I'll do everything I can to support you."

I glanced across at Leroy, my head baker and friend. We'd only known each other for a short time, but we'd bonded. He was what I'd imagined it would be like if I had a brother. So, it hurt not to have his support. My heart ached, and I snuggled my head into Michael's chest.

After a few moments, April stepped forward. "I'm no master baker, but I'll do what I can to help. There's no way I'm going to let CJ take your bakery, no matter what I have to do."

I hugged her.

"Well, I probably know even less about baking than anyone here, but I'll help if I can," Candy said.

I hugged her too. Their words of comfort and reassurance helped keep me from having a meltdown. These were my friends. Actually, more like family. I had to take several deep breaths and choke back the tears. "I appreciate the support." I turned to Leroy, who had been surprisingly quiet.

Leroy took a deep breath. "My dad was a gambler. My mom said he would have bet with the devil himself if the spread was

MURDER IS A PIECE OF CAKE / 37

good enough. I don't really remember much about him."
Leroy stared for several seconds. "He walked out on us when I
was a kid."

He never talked about his dad, so I wasn't sure where this
was going. My heart sank when he turned and headed toward
the door.

He opened the door and turned back to face me. "I do remember one thing he always said. *Scared money never wins.*"
He grinned. "You may not be able to cook, but you're brave,
and you're definitely a fighter. My money is on you one hundred percent. Now, if we're going to take on a master chef, we
need to get busy. We can't stand around wasting time."

I smiled up at Michael. "Hooyah!"

CHAPTER 6

It wasn't until I was home that I realized that in all the confusion, I'd forgotten to ask Jackson Abernathy about English mastiffs in general, and specifically about Baby. I remembered when, for the first time since moving to New Bison, I entered the house and wasn't greeted by Baby. Instead of having a two-hundred-fifty-pound dog standing on his hind legs and licking my face as I walked in, I found him lying on his dog bed. He barely lifted his head to acknowledge my presence and confirm that I was not an intruder intent on stealing all of his valuable treats. That experience was horrible. Today wasn't much different and I made a mental promise to swallow my pride and talk to Mayor Abernathy first thing tomorrow.

Once we entered the house, Leroy went into cooking instructor overdrive. "First, we need to figure out what you plan to enter into the contest, and then we will tweak and practice it until you're perfect." He was a natural teacher and I knew once the renovations were completed and Baby Cakes Bakery was open for business, he'd make a great cooking instructor. For now, his culinary abilities were still limited to my kitchen.

We spent several hours talking about various recipes, eating pizza, researching, and debating what I should enter for the contest until the last thing I wanted to do was bake. It wasn't until everyone left and I was alone in bed with Baby hogging more than his share of the bed that the panic hit me full force.

"What was I thinking?"

Baby opened his eyes and gave me his *I have no idea what you're talking about* look.

I hopped out of bed and paced back and forth from one end of the bedroom to the other. "Leroy was right. I can't cook. I can't even use the mixer without making a mess. There's no way I can hope to defeat a master chef."

Baby yawned.

"Hey, wake up." I shook him awake. "If I lose this bet, it impacts more than just me. It'll impact you too." I hugged him. "I should never have made that bet. If I lose, I'll have to move. I don't think I can keep you. It's in Aunt Octavia's will."

Baby put his head on my lap and gazed up at me with his big soulful eyes.

"Don't look at me like that. I didn't do it on purpose. I was angry, and I wasn't thinking straight. If I'd been thinking, I never would have agreed to anything that meant I couldn't keep you." I snuggled him close. "You believe me, don't you?"

Baby stood up and gave himself a shake, flinging drool around the room like spaghetti. Then he hopped off the bed and headed for the door. When I didn't follow, he looked over his shoulder, as though to say, *Well, are you coming?*

I got up, wiped up the drool, and followed Baby. He headed straight for the door. I let him outside, where he answered the call of nature. However, rather than immediately coming in when he was done, he stopped and gazed at me.

"What? I have no idea what you're trying to tell me."

Baby turned and went back to the same tree outside where he had just relieved himself. He hiked his leg, again.

"You're right. Sitting around stressing about things doesn't solve anything. It's time to pee or get off the pot. Is that what you're trying to tell me?"

This must have been what he wanted me to get because this time he came inside.

I was just about to close the door when I noticed a car that I didn't recognize parked at the end of the driveway.

I reached for my cell phone and prepared to dial 9-1-1 when the passenger door opened and April hurried toward the house.

"I thought you were downstairs, asleep," I said. "When did you leave?"

April avoided eye contact, and I knew without being told who had been in that car.

Inside, I folded my arms and stood against the counter and waited.

She sat down at the counter. Eventually, the silence grew too loud for her, and she took a deep breath and broke it. "Look, I know you only accepted that challenge because of me. You were angry, and you were defending me, but I can't let you give up everything for me."

"What did you do?"

"Nothing. We just talked."

"Why don't I believe you?"

Baby walked over and placed his head in her lap.

She scratched the place behind his ear that made his leg jiggle until he couldn't take it anymore and fell over on his side in ecstasy. It brought a smile to her face. "I can't let you lose your bakery, or your house, and I absolutely can't let you lose Baby."

"April, you can't go back to him."

"It wouldn't be forever. You've been here three months. There's only nine months left, and then everything is all yours. Less than one year. It'll just be nine short months. Then, I can leave, and he can't hurt you."

I walked over to her and hugged her. "That's the sweetest

and yet dumbest thing I've ever heard. I love that you're willing to do that, but I can't let you."

She tried to object, but I stopped her. "I couldn't stay here knowing the sacrifice you'd be making. I appreciate it, but *no*. I'll figure out another way."

"How?"

I smiled. "Well, I could always just do things the easy way."

"What's that?"

"I could just win the competition."

CHAPTER 7

April smiled. "Okay, what's the plan? Maybe I can have the Belgian chef arrested before the competition?"

I chuckled. "That'll be our backup plan."

April got up and went to the drawer and pulled out a notepad and a pen. "What's the thing your dad always says about making decisions?"

"You need to assess the situation, weigh the pros and the cons, and then act." I recited the mantra I'd heard the Admiral repeat a million times throughout my life.

"Okay, so the situation is we need to win." April wrote.

"The pros and cons are pretty obvious too. If I lose, then I'll have to walk away from Baby Cakes, Baby, Michael, all of my friends, and tuck my tail between my legs and go back to L.A."

"That's certainly all of the cons, but what are the pros?"

"If I win, then your husband has to leave and . . ."

"And what?"

"And he has to agree to a divorce with no repercussions." I studied April's face. The last part was me getting overly involved in my friend's relationship, but I couldn't stop myself.

"I wondered what you whispered to him." She kept her head down so I couldn't tell if she was pleased or upset until she hopped up from the table and hugged me.

"You're not upset?"

She sniffed and wiped away a tear. "Of course not. It was the act of a true friend, and, I suspect, the main reason why you accepted his challenge in the first place." She gazed in my eyes for a few moments to find the answer. "So, we both have a good motive for wanting you to win this challenge. We're in this together."

"Right, so now I just need to figure out what to make."

We sat down and stared at her notepad. April tapped her pen on the pad while she thought. Eventually, she stopped. "I think you should enter Miss Octavia's Soul Cake. It's delicious. Everyone around here loves it, and it's a proven winner."

"I thought about that, but it just feels like that was Aunt Octavia's recipe . . . I mean, maybe I need to add something to make it my own? You know, like add my own twist."

She looked skeptical. "It's won multiple times. I mean, if it ain't broke, why fix it?"

"Maybe you're right."

We discussed various recipes until April could barely keep her eyes open. It took a bit of persuading, but I eventually convinced her that she would be sharper after a good night's sleep. Reluctantly, she went downstairs to the basement, now her apartment, and Baby and I went back to our room. Even after spending the majority of my early years with a father who rose by four thirty every morning, I was *not* a morning person, except for days like today, when I never went to sleep in the first place. Now, I was wide-awake.

The sun was rising by the time I finally dozed off. I awoke to the most amazing smell of sugar, cinnamon, bacon, and coffee. It was five o'clock, which meant I'd been asleep for about an hour and a half.

After the fire at the bakery, we had reverted to the original plan for Baby Cakes, baking and selling from home. When Aunt Octavia first started the bakery, she baked everything right here at home and sold the goods from a detached garage that she renovated into an adorable roadside stand, which was located close to the street. Hannah mostly baked at home and brought things over each morning. Leroy had a tiny apartment over thirty miles away, which meant that our already early mornings were even earlier for him. Tyler Lawrence offered him a spare bedroom, which he used until Baby Cakes was deemed safe and the construction dust and noxious paint fumes were over. Then, he'd moved upstairs to the tiny apartment above the bakery. It had a small living room that opened up to a kitchen that consisted of a hot plate, dorm-size fridge, and a sink. The space had a tiny bedroom and an even tinier bathroom, but it worked. At least, it worked for a young, single man who didn't have a lot of clothes or shoes or . . . stuff. I liked that Leroy was there during the renovation. Our early starts meant he was often home in the afternoons to answer any of the contractor's questions. Initially, he was reluctant to make renovation decisions, but he was more knowledgeable about baking and better equipped to answer their questions than I was. Questions about the aesthetics, he left to me.

Baby opened one eye when I moved but closed it quickly and was snoring again in seconds. That dog snored like a freight train and could sleep through anything. At first, I was shocked. He was so loud, I had asked Michael to check him out. After a lot of veterinarian mumbo jumbo, he reassured me that Baby was fine and didn't need to have his tonsils removed. I didn't even know dogs had tonsils.

I slid off the tiny sliver of space Baby left for me in the king-size bed and hurried to shower and get dressed.

Hannah and Leroy already had things under control in the garage-makeshift-bakery by the time Baby and I joined them.

Our regular customers knew to come early if they wanted their early morning pastry fix. Without easy access to a kitchen like we had in the bakery, our hours were limited. When we sold out, we closed down. In the bakery, when inventory got low, we could always just go into the kitchen and bake more. Today, selling out was a good thing. The New Bison Spring Festival was only a few days away, and the merchants were having a sidewalk sale to drive more people to downtown New Bison, such as it was. Plus, it would help get the public excited about the festival. At least, that's the way Mayor Abernathy had explained things to us. The vendors on Main Street were planning an early "tasting." So, while Hannah and Leroy managed the sales at home, I drove downtown to the bakery to get set up for the prefestival sidewalk tasting. The others would join me shortly.

The local high school quartet was providing the music in the town square. At that moment, the violin screeches reminded me of cats in heat, but parents would line the block, take pictures and send them to relatives near and far. It wasn't a bad marketing ploy for a small-town event.

Retail stores set up tables and racks outside on the sidewalk proclaiming TAKE AN ADDITIONAL . . . to lure buyers toward off-season specials. It was spring, and Tyler wasn't expecting a large crowd at his knitwear shop, but I'd recommended he go for visual appeal and put out some of his lightweight, brightly colored items front and center. He even had some adorable beach bags and cover-ups that were sure to be a hit with summer just around the corner.

Restaurants included food samples to entice visitors. My baking repertoire was limited to my Great-Aunt Octavia's award-winning chocolate cake and a Baby Cakes signature dish, thumbprint cookies. Leroy had trained me to bake the cookies. The beauty of these thumbprint cookies was that the dough could be used to make three basic cookies. The hardest part was the dough, which really wasn't hard at all. Once you had that down, you could roll it into a ball and cover it with powdered sugar. Or, press your thumb (or a spoon if you just got a manicure that you didn't want to ruin) and fill with either jelly or a simple icing. No heavy-duty equipment needed. Decorating the cookies wasn't my forte, but I managed, and they were *almost* as pretty as Leroy's.

It was a beautiful day. Sunny and warm. I brought Baby's dog bed out and put it in a sunny spot near the door. He climbed in and lay with his large head on his paws. I ordered him a baseball cap with BABY CAKES on it and a pair of *Blues Brothers* sunglasses, which he didn't like but tolerated. I took out my phone and snapped a few quick pictures. **#English-MastiffsLoveSun #NewBisonSpringFestival #BringOnThe-Treats**

Baby was still moping around, so after I posted the pictures, I called Mayor Abernathy and asked if I could talk to him. He promised to swing by when he finished making his opening remarks at the town square.

I was just about finished setting everything up and was ready for business when I was surprised to see April pull up to the curb in her patrol car. I was even more surprised when Clayton Jefferson Davenport climbed out of the back seat. I didn't like Clayton, but I had to admit he had great taste in clothes. Today he was sporting an Italian wool tweed CKC cornflower-blue-and-rust overplaid jacket, skinny-legged rust corduroy pants that hit him right above the ankle and showed that he wasn't wearing socks with his Berluti shoes, and a dark blue turtleneck. I had to commend his stylist. Even at a distance, I got a whiff of his expensive Baccarat Rouge 540 cologne. He might be evil, but he looked and smelled great.

Despite my hopes, he wasn't handcuffed. It was too much to hope that April had arrested him, but I couldn't figure out any other reason why she would be in such close proximity to him.

Lastly, a slim Black woman with short curly hair and large gray-green eyes climbed out. I didn't recognize her, which in a large city wasn't unusual. The Black population in a town the size of New Bison meant that the few Black people who lived here had at least a nodding acquaintance with each other. Most people knew each other or could find a connection with less than five degrees of separation. As a newcomer to the area, I was often greeted in public with, *You must be Octavia's niece?* I had no frame of reference for the newcomer, but I'd grill April later. The look on her face told me this was not a social call.

April stomped past me and entered Higher Grounds Coffee and Tea, followed by Clayton Davenport and the newcomer, who looked as though she'd rather be anywhere else at the moment.

They were barely in the building for more than a few moments when I heard Candy's high-pitched voice. Candy squawked like a parrot and threw out words that would have gotten any sailor under my father's command duty swabbing the latrine.

The screeching increased as April led Candy out of the building and onto the street.

"You can't do this," Candy screamed. "This is my shop."

"Candy, I'm sorry, but I'm only doing my job."

Candy took a few moments to share what she thought about April and her job.

The woman who accompanied April looked as though she wished the ground would open up and swallow her whole. Clayton Davenport grinned like a man who'd just won the lottery, which was a big mistake.

Candy grabbed a knife from the table that I had brought outside to help slice the cookies into smaller pieces and lunged at Davenport, but April was swift. In one motion, she grabbed the knife and wrenched it out of Candy's hand. But if anyone thought that was the end of it, they were sorely mistaken. Candy had just begun to fight. She extended her arms and leapt like a cat. Fingernails like claws, she lunged for Davenport. I was so absorbed by the spectacle playing out on the sidewalk, I didn't realize Leroy had arrived until he came from behind me, grabbed Candy around the waist, and pulled her away. If it weren't for Leroy's quick reflexes, Candy might have clawed Davenport's eyes out.

"What's going on?" Leroy asked.

"She assaulted me, and I'm going to press charges," Davenport said. He pulled out a handkerchief and dabbed at a scratch down the side of his face.

"Clayton, is that really necessary?" April said. "She's obviously emotional. She's had a terrible shock. Her husband's dead and now . . . this. Don't you think you've done enough to this poor woman?"

After the initial burst of emotion, Candy Hurston collapsed into a puddle like a deflated balloon.

April squeezed Candy's shoulder. "I'm sorry."

"Sorry?" Davenport snorted. "What kind of sheriff apologizes to a common criminal who assaults a law-abiding citizen who is taking possession of his own property?"

A crowd developed on the street.

April glanced around. "This isn't the time or the place to go into this. Let's go back to the station and sort this whole thing out." She took a step toward the patrol car but stopped to stare into the crowd. "Okay, there's nothing to see here. Keep it moving."

The crowd grumbled and took a few steps backward, but no one left. This drama was too good to pass up.

"It's not his property," Candy said. "It's mine. I was Paul's wife. I don't care what she says."

The woman who had arrived with April and Davenport avoided eye contact and hung her head.

"April, what's going on?" I asked.

Clayton Davenport held the handkerchief to his cheek. "What's going on is this woman is trespassing on private property." He grinned at April. "As a public servant, it's your job to—"

"I don't need you to explain my job," April said.

"But I don't understand," I said, glancing from Candy to Davenport and then to April. "How does Clayton Davenport own this building?"

"He's trying to take my building," Candy blubbered. "He says he or that woman own my building." She looked to the crowd and went for the sympathy vote by repeating herself. "He's trying to steal my building."

"I didn't steal anything from her," Davenport said. "It was never hers to begin with. That building belongs to the wife of Paul Rivers."

"That's me," Candy sobbed. "I'm his wife . . . well, I was his wife, before he died. Now, I'm his widow. That means it's my building."

Clayton Davenport smirked. "No, this building belongs to the *legal* wife of Paul Rivers." He turned to the woman who looked as though she wanted to melt into the brick exterior. "Mrs. Marjorie Rivers."

"Marjorie?" Candy yelled. "That's his first wife."

"First. Last. Only wife. Paul Rivers never got divorced."

That's the last thing Candy Hurston Rivers heard before she collapsed into a deep faint.

CHAPTER 8

Leroy carried Candy into Baby Cakes. The bakery wasn't designed for lounging, so we propped her in a seat.

I'm not the best help in emergency situations, but I needed to do something. I looked around and then grabbed a platter from behind the counter and fanned Candy, careful not to hit Leroy in the head.

April finished locking up the coffee shop and dispersed the crowd that had gathered to gawk. The scene that had just unfolded was about as exciting as things got in sleepy little New Bison. When she was finished outside, April came in and assessed the situation. Her first move was to take away my platter. "Give me that thing before you hurt someone." She set the platter aside and shoved Candy's head between her legs.

Within a few moments, Candy gasped and then sat up. "What happened?"

"You fainted," I said.

"I've never fainted in my life."

"Well, there's a first time for everything. Today, you fainted."

"Get her some water," April ordered.

Leroy hurried to the kitchen and was back in seconds with a glass of water and a wet compress.

April smiled, and a flush went up Leroy's neck. He quickly turned away and became exceptionally attentive to Candy, but it was too late. I wasn't the only one who had noticed. Clayton Davenport's brow furled, and his eyes narrowed. For one moment, a look flashed across his face that sent a shiver up my spine.

"Mr. Fancy Pants looks like he's 'bout ready to spit nails," Hannah said.

I had forgotten she was there until she spoke.

Everyone turned to see who Hannah was talking about, but I knew. By the time everyone turned back to Davenport, he had control of his face.

"Interesting bunch of people you have here in New Bison." Davenport chuckled, but I saw a vein throbbing against the side of his head. He wasn't as nonchalant as he wanted people to believe.

"These are my friends, so don't even go there," April warned.

Davenport raised one eyebrow and feigned surprise. "I wouldn't dream of mocking your new friends. Like always follows like. You were always rather ... common. I should have known that your true nature would come out sooner or later."

April scowled. "Clayton, don't."

"I offered you the world, and yet ..." He turned and scrunched his nose up as he glanced around. "You prefer this ... hovel. Your father was nothing. Your mother was nothing. And you ... well, they say the apple doesn't fall far from the tree."

Leroy looked like a teakettle ready to boil over. He clenched his fist and seethed. He was seconds away from punching Clayton Davenport, and probably would have if Baby hadn't taken that moment to snap out of his lovesick funk.

A low rumble was the only warning we had that trouble was brewing. By the time I turned, Baby was galloping like a pony toward Clayton Davenport. The scene felt like a nightmare in slow motion, but the drool and the laser-focused look in Baby's eyes were real. Teeth bared and two threads of drool dripping from his jowls, he charged toward Davenport like a bull.

"Baby, *no!*" April and I yelled together.

Thankfully, Leroy did more than yell. He hurled himself in front of Baby and caught him as he prepared to rip out Clayton Davenport's throat.

It took all of us working together to gain control of Baby and convince him that he didn't really want to take a bite out of April's obnoxious husband. Leroy tugged from the front, and April and I shoved from behind. Fortunately, convincing large, stubborn animals to move was a skill I'd mastered in recent months. In addition to pushing, I also used my voice to coax my stubborn mastiff. He was normally well behaved and listened, but he was also two-hundred-fifty pounds, muscular, and as stubborn as any camel I'd ever met in my travels. It felt like it took hours to get Baby under control, but it was mere moments. Hannah opened the door leading upstairs, and as soon as Leroy and Baby crossed the threshold, we slammed the door closed.

CHAPTER 9

By the time we finished, I was sweating, tired, and angry. I turned toward Clayton Davenport. "If you're completely incapable of controlling your mouth, then you can turn around and leave."

Based on the purple color that rose up his neck and the vein that pulsed on the side of his head, Clayton Jefferson Davenport wasn't accustomed to being yelled at.

"Me? You're blaming me for that . . . that beast nearly ripping my throat out? You're crazy. You're all crazy. This whole town is full of crazy people. I should have known. When I heard you were selling baked goods from a garage on the side of the road and that people were actually buying them, I should have known. Where's the health department in this town? That has to violate a dozen health codes. Why don't you post that online, **#HealthCodeViolations.**"

I was so busy trying not to strangle Clayton Davenport I didn't realize the danger until it was almost too late. Just as I was about to provide a scathing response, I was knocked aside.

Hannah lifted her hand, which was clutching a marble rolling pin. "Now, you listen here. Don't you go spreading no lies about Baby Cakes being a problem with the health department."

Leroy came back from settling Baby, just in time to tackle Hannah from behind while April moved in front to block any blows she might land.

"You call yourself a sheriff?" Davenport said. "What kind of town is this? She tried to assault me. I want her arrested. I want both of them arrested."

April whirled around so she was mere inches from him. "This was a great town until you arrived. You provoked her. You provoked both of them. It's what you do. I almost wish I'd let her hit you."

"Crazy. Everyone in this town is batty."

"You're welcome to leave at any time," I said. "And for the record, in this state, the Cottage Law allows people to make and sell specific foods in their home without being subject to inspections or purchasing a food license. However, my great-aunt Octavia made sure that her home, which has a commercial kitchen, meets all the same stringent requirements as our bakery."

"And the detached structure at the front of the property was renovated and is *très* chic," Candy said.

He gave Candy the *You poor, pitiful thing* look.

"Candy's right," I said. "Plus, Southwest Michigan is well-known for our roadside stands with fruits, vegetables . . . oh, and baked goods, but like I said, you're welcome to leave at any time." I stopped short of snapping my fingers and adding a neck roll, but I was so tempted.

"You'd like that, wouldn't you?" Clayton Davenport's nostrils flared. "Well, no one tells me what to do. No one. I'm not going anywhere. In fact, thanks to you and Cujo up there, I've had a change of plans. I'm going to own not only that coffee shop and the bookstore, but I'm going to own this two-bit bakery and this entire town before this week is over. I was going to wait for this, but . . . you brought it on yourself." Like the big, bad wolf in "The Three Little Pigs," he huffed, and he puffed. He pulled out his cell phone, turned, and marched out of the store.

He took most of the oxygen with him when he left, and I felt light-headed. Down from my adrenaline high, I stumbled into a chair and collapsed. The blood was rushing in my ears, and I couldn't hear anything except the pulsing of my heart pumping.

"Maddy! Are you okay?" April shook my shoulders.

"Here, let me." Candy tossed what was left of her water in my face.

"What the—" I sputtered.

"I'm sorry," Candy said. "I couldn't think of anything else to do."

Leroy handed me a dishcloth from behind the counter, and I patted my face dry.

April turned and noticed that some of the gawkers from earlier had slipped inside with the rest of us and were lingering.

"Okay, the show's over." April shooed nonessentials from the building. Before closing the door, she glanced up and saw Chris Russell, one of New Bison's city council members and my attorney, outside standing near the table with the thumbprint cookies I'd been cutting earlier. "Mr. Russell, would you mind stepping in here for a moment?"

The attorney entered, and April closed the door behind him.

Chris Russell was as ordinary as ordinary could be. He was medium height, average weight, balding with glasses. Yet, there was an occasional look that flashed across his face that indicated that he was deeper than he appeared at first glance. Like Transformers, there was *more to him than meets the eye.*

He glanced around. "What's all this about?"

We filled him in.

Chris Russell turned to face the woman who was plastered up against the back wall of the bakery. "You're claiming to have been married to Paul Rivers? May I ask what's your name?"

She had been so still and quiet, I forgot she was there.

"She claims to be Marjorie Rivers," Hannah said. "Marjorie was the slimeball's first wife who ran off and left him, but I can't swear to it."

Marjorie Rivers stepped forward. "It's been a long time. I've changed some over the years. I guess, we all have. I—"

The door to the bakery flew open, and Clayton Davenport stood in the doorway. "Marjorie, come!"

Marjorie Rivers hung her head like a puppy and hurried out the door.

Davenport pivoted and let the door slam closed behind him.

I went to the door and twisted the lock. If Davenport entered Baby Cakes Bakery again, he'd have to break in, and I'd gladly let Baby take his pound of flesh.

"What about the sidewalk sale?" Leroy asked.

"Whatever cookies are outside, people are welcome to them. I—"

Suddenly, there was a loud crash. An amplifier squealed, causing my teeth to rattle. Then, a voice boomed over a loudspeaker.

"HI, NEW BISON! THIS IS CHLOE, AND I WANT TO WELCOME YOU TO NEW BISON'S NEWEST PASTRY SHOP. LET'S ROCK OUT!"

Throngs of people ran down Main Street.

Everyone came to the front door and looked out.

"OMG!" Candy said. "That's Chloe!"

"Who's Chloe?" Hannah asked.

"*Chloe.* The number-one pop singer in the *world*. She's won every award possible this year. Best Artist. Best Album. Best Contemporary Album. Pretty much everything."

"Hmm. Never heard of her."

"OMG! You haven't heard 'Love Is a Four-Letter Word'? Or 'Let Your Fingers Do the Talking'? Or, my personal favorite, 'I'm Your Boo, But He's Mine.'" Candy started to sing the lyrics, and Hannah stared at her as though she'd suddenly lost her mind.

The music was so loud it shook the glass in the front of the store, and while I liked Chloe's music and several of her songs were on my playlist, I wasn't a fan when it was blasting at a deafening pitch through my building so loudly that the items on the shelves vibrated.

"This is violating the noise ordinance," April said. She unlocked the door and marched toward the noise.

Candy was jumping up and down. "OMG! I love Chloe!"

Leroy looked out. "Are those jugglers?"

I followed his gaze. Sure enough, Clayton Davenport had not only hired the top singing sensation in the country, he'd hired clowns, stilt-walkers, jugglers, and . . . "Are those fire-eaters?"

Leroy nodded. "Looks like it."

"There's no way he could have arranged all of this that quickly. He must have been planning this all along. He's been planning this—"

"Long before you made that bet."

"But how could he have known? How could he know that if he pushed me, I'd get impulsive and make some crazy, irrational bet without thinking it through like . . ." I stared at Leroy.

"Like chucking everything, picking up and moving to New Bison after your fiancé left you at the altar in the middle of your live-streamed wedding?" He held up his phone and gave it a shake.

"Ugh." I smacked my hand against my head.

"I don't know anything about Clayton Davenport, but he

strikes me as a man who would definitely do his homework."
Leroy folded his arms across his chest. "He certainly didn't get
as rich as he is by flying by the seat of his pants."

Suddenly there was silence. April must have pulled the plug
on the street concert. However, the crowd wasn't having it and
immediately started booing and heckling her. After what appeared to be a heated discussion, the music continued but at a
much less eardrum-rupturing level.

The crowd roared, and I swallowed hard to keep from
puking.

"We might as well pack up and go home," I said, and opened
the door. Leroy and I pulled all of the items I'd set up back inside. I turned the sign to CLOSED.

I opened the door to the upstairs, and Baby came bounding
down. He trotted around the store as though he was looking
for Clayton Davenport, and then he came and sat by my side.

"It's okay," I said. "The bad man is gone."

Baby sighed.

I jiggled his jowls. "Don't you worry about that bad man.
I'll take care of him, one way or another."

Baby stood up on his hind legs and gave my face a lick.

"Now, let's go home and get some ice cream."

Baby barked and headed to the back door.

"I'm exhausted. Baby and I are going home."

Chris Russell gave a discreet cough. "I'll look into the claims
that Paul Rivers never divorced his first wife. If they're true,
then . . . well, we'll deal with that bridge when we get to it." He
patted Candy on the back. "Don't you worry."

"Would you like a ride to your mom's place?" I asked.
Candy's parents lived near me, and now that April had boarded
up the building, I assumed she'd move back with her parents.

"No. I think I need something to cheer me up. I'm going to
listen to Chloe." She hurried outside and headed toward the
spectacle.

Leroy looked at Hannah. "Would you like me to drive you home?"

But Hannah wasn't there. She'd checked out. Physically, her body was there, but her eyes were blank.

She smiled. "That would be nice, but who are you?"

"My name's Leroy. Come with me, Miss Hannah, and I'll drive you home."

"Such a nice young man." Hannah smiled again and followed him out to his car.

Chris Russell dropped his portfolio, and papers flew across the floor. I turned to help him pick them up, but he stopped me. "Please, I know you're tired. I'll just grab the rest of these papers and let myself out. It'll just take a couple of minutes. You go on."

I hesitated a half second but decided he didn't need me, and I needed to go home and regroup. "Okay, well, the door is locked, just pull it closed on your way out."

Baby and I went home. Normally, the peace and quiet were soothing. There was something about knowing this was my home that made me feel like I was wrapped in love. The bedroom that great-aunt Octavia converted into a library with stunning views of Lake Michigan usually made me feel warm and safe, but tonight it merely made me sad. I couldn't stop thinking that I might lose everything if Clayton Davenport got his way. And, something told me that Clayton Davenport always got his way. After a few hours of fidgeting and pacing, I knew I needed to get away. I packed up Baby, got back in the car, and drove back downtown. I parked in my usual spot behind Baby Cakes Bakery and got out and walked.

One of the things I'd learned to appreciate about living in New Bison was its smallness. At night, you could walk the entire downtown area in minutes and never see anyone. L.A. was sprawled out and required a ride in the car. New York City was very walkable, but the "City That Never Sleeps" was densely populated, and finding a place of solitude was a challenge. Once you found it, the lack of people brought on a feeling of anxiety. At least it did for me. New Bison was different. I didn't feel afraid walking the streets alone any time of the day or night. Of course, that might have something to do with the guard dog that accompanied me on my midnight strolls. Baby was large and intimidating when he wasn't rolling on his back being a goofball.

I was antsy, so I walked the streets in an effort to clear my head. Thankfully, the concert was over and the streets were quiet. The downtown had old-fashioned streetlights that gave the area the look of London in the late nineteenth century. New Bison was a resort town, but there weren't a large number of hotels. The few that existed were closer to the casino or Lake Michigan and the marina. However, there was one large older home that resembled a castle, located near the town square. The Carson Law Inn was built by New Bison's oil tycoon, Beauregard Law. After Law's death, his only daughter, Carson Law, lived in the mansion and raised her family. Carson Law was known for her philanthropy with causes affecting children and animals. She was also known for her passion for haute couture. Her love for women's hats led her to turn her home into an inn so that she could move to Paris to pursue her millinery aspirations. In honor of Ms. Law, the inn sponsored an annual tea to raise money for the humane society each summer. I was looking forward to attending my first tea in just a few short months. The best part was that well-behaved dogs were welcome, so Baby and I had already reserved our table.

My circuit around New Bison took me near the Carson Law Inn, and I wasn't surprised to see a limo parked outside. It was the nicest hotel in town. Where else would a man like Clayton Davenport, who was accustomed to the best, choose to stay while in town? I rejected the urge to pick up a brick and smash the limo's window. It was a petty thought. Besides, the Carson Law Inn probably had security cameras, and the last thing April needed was to have to arrest her friend and landlord.

I walked quickly past the inn, but my thoughts lingered on Clayton Davenport. He was a pain in the butt, and he was probably going to end up owning not only Baby Cakes Bakery but my house and . . . I turned and glanced at Baby. Of course, I'd try to buy Baby from him, but Clayton Davenport would probably have him put down out of spite. I wiped away a tear.

I pulled out my phone and snapped a picture of Baby. **#CuddleBugByDay #GuardDogByNight #LoveMyMastiff**

I posted the picture and almost instantly felt my phone vibrate. Michael's picture popped on the screen. I took a deep breath and braced myself for the lecture I knew was coming.

"Please tell me you aren't walking *alone* in the middle of the night," Michael said.

"I'm not alone. I've got a two-hundred-and-fifty-pound protector."

"Maddy, I know you think New Bison is a sleepy little town where nothing bad ever happens, but you're wrong. Crime happens everywhere. Just because . . ."

I zoned out the rest of the lecture. I'd heard it before. It didn't help that he was right. Crime wasn't the domain of big cities. Small towns had it too.

He took a breath, and I interjected. "I know, and I'm sorry. I just needed a walk to clear my head. I'm only walking downtown where there are streetlights. I have Baby, and I have the taser April gave me." I pulled the small object from my pocket. I always keep it in my pocket.

"I'm sorry. I don't mean to lecture you, but I worry about you. I wouldn't want anything to happen to you," There was a softness in his voice that brought a smile to my face.

"Really, now why is that?"

"I don't want to be the one to have to tell the Admiral what happened to his only daughter." He chuckled.

I disconnected the call.

He was still laughing when he called back. He spent a few moments telling me the real reason he wouldn't want anything to happen to me. Despite the cool breeze coming off Lake Michigan, I felt heat rising inside that made me unwrap the scarf I'd draped around my neck.

"Maybe I need to come downtown and relieve Baby from his guard duty."

"That sounds nice, but I know you have a busy day tomorrow. Don't you have two surgeries? You better get your rest. Besides, we're on for dinner tomorrow."

We spent the next few minutes talking about how much we were both looking forward to tomorrow night. It was just a short distance from the Carson Law Inn to Baby Cakes. Actually, downtown was small, so it was a short distance from practically anywhere in New Bison. By the time we were winding down, I was back at Baby Cakes and getting in my car.

CHAPTER 10

Three months ago, I was awakened in the middle of the night by two police officers who came to my house and asked me to come to the New Bison Police Station because someone had been murdered in my bakery. When the doorbell rang at midnight and the same two policemen came to the door, I thought I was dreaming. It was déjà vu. The last time, I'd only been in town less than twenty-four hours, and I didn't know their names. One of the officers was round and pudgy. He reminded me of the Pillsbury Doughboy. This time, I knew that his name was Officer Al Norris. The other one had a bad case of acne, red hair, and looked about twelve. In an attempt to look older, he'd started growing a beard that made him look like a wire-haired terrier. His name was Officer Jerrod Thomas.

"Good evening, Miss Montgomery," Officer Norris said. "We're sorry to bother you, but the boss asked us to swing by and *kindly* ask if you'd come downtown with us."

Normally, the sheriff and the police were two separate entities, with the sheriff covering an entire county, rather than a small village the size of New Bison. But April's predecessor,

Sheriff Harper, had wielded a great deal of power in his day, and combined the two. When April defeated him and became sheriff, she now held the reins of power, which amounted to an elected title and head of a police force with less than ten people.

"April? Is everything okay? Of course, I'll come. She's not hurt is she?" My mind immediately went there, and even though I knew the likelihood of April getting shot was slim, it was still an occupational hazard. We'd talked about it, but given the size of New Bison, it seemed remote. However, we never dreamed that Michael and Baby would get shot either, but that had happened.

"Sheriff Johnson's fine. She's waiting for us downtown."

In the three months that I'd known Officer Norris, he hadn't changed much. He still wasn't volunteering any information.

"Fine, I'll come, but I need to put on some clothes."

They declined to wait inside. I suspected their reluctance was due to Baby, but everyone at the NBPD knew he was just a big cuddly teddy bear who drooled a lot. Well, mostly, when he wasn't trying to protect me and take out deranged murderers. Regardless, they chose to wait in their patrol car instead.

I hurried upstairs and threw on a pair of black Khaite leggings and a wool asymmetrical sweater that I'd commissioned from Tyler. It was spring, but the wind coming across Lake Michigan could be chilly at night.

Baby looked on from his perch on my bed.

I slipped on a pair of black mules and turned to Baby. "What do you think?"

Baby yawned and rolled over on his side.

"Everybody's a critic." I slipped off the mules and put on a pair of caramel suede loafers with a gold-toned metal kitten heel. "How are these?"

Baby sat up.

"Males," I mumbled. I debated bringing Baby with me. "Baby, come."

He jumped down and followed me outside.

I stopped at the back door long enough for Baby to answer the call of nature and then opened the passenger door, and he climbed into the front seat of my Range Rover. When I moved to New Bison, I rented the SUV at the airport with every intention of returning the car in a week or two. But when Aunt Octavia's will made it clear that I'd be staying here for at least a year, combined with the wear, tear, and drool of a large mastiff, I arranged to buy the car from the rental agency. Baby was a lot of dog for the two-seat, Lexus LC convertible I drove in L.A. And my convertible would never hold up to New Bison winters.

I tooted my horn as I backed out of the two-car garage that was attached to the house to let the patrolmen know I was ready and then followed them toward downtown.

My first surprise came when they missed the turn that would have led directly to the police station and instead turned toward Main Street.

New Bison is a small town that closes at eleven. The few stoplights in town actually stop operating and flash yellow in all directions. When I asked about this, I learned there was no point waiting at a stoplight when there's no traffic. The patrol car pulled up behind Baby Cakes Bakery. April's patrol car and two other cars belonging to the state police lined the back of the building and blocked the alley.

I got out of the car. Out of the corner of my eye, I saw the expensive McLaren Spider that belonged to my lawyer, Chris Russell, parked next door, behind what used to be Candy Rivers's coffee shop. I didn't have time to ponder how or why he was there.

April came outside just as I got out. Based on the look on her face, I knew something awful had happened.

"What is it?"

"Murder."

My stomach contracted into a knot. My throat was suddenly so dry, I had to swallow several times to work up enough saliva to talk. "Leroy?"

"No. Leroy's fine. He's with Tyler."

I exhaled. "Thank God." I glanced at April. "Who?"

She took a deep breath. "Clayton. He's been stabbed."

CHAPTER 11

My relief at hearing that Leroy was okay was short-lived. Clayton Davenport was an evil man, and his death certainly solved a lot of problems. The look on my friend's face reminded me that it also opened up a lot more problems.

"Are you okay?"

She nodded.

I pulled her into a hug. After a few moments, she pushed away.

"He was a horrible husband with few redeeming characteristics, but he was my husband. We may not have lived together, but we made vows, and I honored those vows." She took a deep breath. "We haven't seen each other in more than eight years. Two days after he arrives in town, he's dead."

"Any chance it was an accident?"

She shook her head. "There's no way he could have accidentally stabbed himself in the back."

I cringed. "Is that how? But . . . what was he doing here?"

"I was hoping you could answer that."

"Me? I have no idea."

A stocky man wearing a state trooper uniform came outside. "This the owner?"

"Trooper Bob Roberts, this is Madison Montgomery, owner of Baby Cakes Bakery. Maddy, this is Michigan State Trooper Roberts. He'll be leading the investigation."

He extended a bear-sized hand and crushed mine as we shook. "Trooper Bob."

I flexed my hand a few times to regain circulation. As a military brat, I was accustomed to men who liked to show their dominance in various ways. The Admiral had shown me several tactics to deal with bone-crushers. However, I wasn't sure I wanted to engage the state trooper yet. I glanced at April. "Did you say he'll be leading the investigation? Why?"

"Separated doesn't matter," Trooper Bob said. "Victim was her husband." He grinned and rolled back and forward from his heels to the balls of his feet. "Besides, murder requires an *experienced* investigator who isn't biased."

"What do you mean *biased*?"

April was tugging on my sleeve to get me to back off, but it was too early in the morning, and I didn't appreciate the implication.

He grinned and took off his brown Smokey the Bear hat and rubbed his hand over his bald head. "Well, now no offense to this little lady, but we all know she isn't a *trained* investigator."

It was dark outside, but I could still see the heat go up April's neck, and it lit a pilot inside me. How dare he insult my friend to her face and in front of me. "Really?" I said innocently. "I know she went through the twelve-week police academy training, and she's solved a number of cases, including the murder of Mayor Paul Rivers just a few months ago."

Trooper Bob's grin wasn't quite as broad, and the creases in his forehead would likely be permanent if he didn't stop frowning. "Well, you know what they say. Even a broke clock's right twice a day." He chuckled.

I think he expected that we would join in on the laughter. When we didn't, he looked confused. I was afraid he was about to mansplain his completely inappropriate joke, but I folded my arms across my chest and patted my foot, and I think he finally realized that he was treading in dangerous waters.

"Just a joke. No offense meant. Hope you little ladies know how to take a joke." He reached in his pocket and pulled out a small pouch. He took a pinch of tobacco, shoved it in his mouth, and returned the pouch to his pocket.

I narrowed my eyes and prepared to launch into him, but April stepped in front of me. "It's late, and I'm sure Maddy's tired, so maybe we should get down to business. I'm sure Trooper Bob has some questions for you."

I didn't care what questions Trooper Bob had, but it was late, and there was a dead man inside my bakery, again. I was anxious to find out the specifics. "April's right. Maybe we should go inside where it's warm so we can talk."

Baby had been sitting by my side, but when I made a move toward the door, he stood next to me, prepared to accompany us into the building.

Trooper Bob stopped chewing and pointed. "That . . . that . . ."

"English mastiff," I said.

"Whatever." Trooper Bob pointed at Baby with one hand and edged his other hand toward the gun strapped to his leg. "He can't come in. This is a crime scene. Any decent investigator knows you can't bring a dog, especially a horse like that, on a crime scene."

"Look, Trooper Bob. This is my bakery, and Baby is my dog. And *no one* is going to tell me who can and cannot go into my building. So, if Baby can't come in, then I'm not going in either."

"Baby is a trained service dog," April said. "Legally, he's allowed to go anywhere his owner goes."

I had to work to keep my face straight and not stare at April in the same *You must be joking* stare that Trooper Bob was using.

He frowned and pointed at Baby. "That's a service dog?"

I stood up straight and hoped Baby wouldn't do something silly like rolling over on his back to have his belly rubbed. "Yes."

Trooper Bob was stubborn and wasn't giving up easily. "Where's his vest and harness?"

"The ADA doesn't require a vest, but Baby has one," April said. She turned to me. "Did you remember to bring his vest?"

"Sorry, no. When the patrolmen showed up at my door in the middle of the night, I just focused on getting myself dressed. I'm afraid I forgot Baby's vest and harness." I hoped my nose wouldn't start to grow after all the lies I'd just told.

"The ADA?" Trooper Bob asked.

"Americans with Disabilities Act," April said.

"I know what it is." Trooper Bob stared at Baby a few moments, but then he gave up. "Fine, but you watch him." He glared at me and then turned to April. "If he contaminates my crime scene, I'm holding you personally responsible." He spit a large wad of tobacco on the ground.

April smiled. "I'm sure he won't contaminate the crime scene any more than you . . . or any of your men."

We walked into the back of the bakery. There was a host of men and women snapping pictures, putting little cones on the floor, and scattering black powder over every available surface for fingerprints.

I swallowed the knot in my throat at the mess the platoon had made in my newly renovated building. I comforted myself with the knowledge that at least this time, the killer hadn't tried to conceal the murder by torching my building. The insurance company would find two murders and two fires in three months hard to believe.

I didn't see a dead body, so the murder must have taken place in the demonstration area.

Trooper Bob took two of the folding chairs I'd bought for cooking class overflow and set them down in the kitchen. I sat in one, and April was about to sit in the other when he stopped her. "Sheriff, I plan to do my investigation by the book. So, you can wait outside."

"Wait, I prefer to have April stay," I said.

"Suspects should be interviewed separately."

"Suspects?" I glanced from April to Trooper Bob. "You think April or I killed Clayton Davenport?"

He sucked his teeth and rocked back and forth from his heels to the balls of his feet, again. "Miss Montgomery, I just want to ask you some questions."

"You didn't answer my question."

He glared. "Miss Montgomery, I would appreciate your co-operation."

"If I'm a suspect, then I should have my attorney present." I pulled out my phone and swiped until I found Chris Russell's contact.

He frowned. "If you're innocent, why do you need an attorney?"

"Prisons are full of innocent people. I don't want to be one of them." I pressed Send.

"Maddy, this better be important," Chris Russell said. "Do you know what time it is?" He sounded out of breath, and I didn't want to think why since I knew he wasn't at home.

"Clayton Davenport's dead in my shop, and a state trooper named Trooper Bob says I'm a suspect. He wants to question me, and I remembered what you said before when Mayor Rivers—"

"I'll be right over. I happen to be close by. Don't say anything until I get there."

I could hear him moving around. I also thought I heard Candy Rivers in the background.

"Great. We're in the bakery." I hung up and sat down. "He'll be right over. He said for us to wait until he gets here."

I could almost see the steam coming out of Trooper Bob's ears. He looked like he wanted to bite the heads off nails. "If you need to spit, please do it outside. This is a tobacco-free establishment."

Trooper Bob scowled and then turned and stomped outside.

April stared for a few minutes and then leaned close. "Maddy, please don't make him angry. Trooper Bob may act like an old-fashioned, sexist, country hick who wouldn't know a clue if he stepped on it, but don't be fooled. That's just an act."

"Well, then he must be one helluva good actor."

"Maddy, I'm serious. Don't antagonize him. He's solved a number of difficult murder cases. He's tough, and he definitely won't give up."

"I didn't kill Clayton Davenport—"

April opened her mouth to speak, but I held up a hand to stop her.

"And before you say anything, I know you didn't kill him either. But I'm also not going to sit back and do nothing while Trooper Bob accuses one of us of a crime we didn't do."

I wasn't finished, but a commotion at the back door stopped me.

"You have no right to question my client without her lawyer present."

I turned to April. "Looks like Chris Russell's here."

After a few more words, Trooper Bob escorted the lawyer into the kitchen.

"Madison, are you okay?" Chris Russell rushed into the kitchen. He was wearing the same clothes I'd seen him in earlier, although they were wrinkled, and his hair was a mite disheveled.

"I am. Thanks for coming over so quickly."

Chris Russell blushed a bit and stammered. "Glad to help. I promised to help Candy . . . ah, I mean, Mrs. Rivers with her legal problem and . . ." He coughed. "Anyway, what's this I hear about Clayton Davenport getting stabbed?"

He didn't need to be bashful on my account. Both he and Candy were adults. And both were single, as far as I knew. Well, Candy was a widow, and I had no idea if Chris Russell was married. I don't recall seeing a ring, but regardless, they were adults. What they did was none of my business.

"That's confidential," Trooper Bob said. "I'm conducting a murder investigation, and I'm the one who'll be asking all of the questions."

We stared and waited.

Trooper Bob turned to April. "Now, if you'll just wait outside."

April gave me a look that pleaded with me to be careful.

I smiled.

Baby yawned, walked around in a small circle, and then stretched out on the floor near my chair.

"When was the last time you saw Clayton Davenport?" Trooper Bob asked.

"It was early this afternoon before the concert started." I turned to Chris Russell. "What time would you say that was?"

He thought for a moment. "Four?"

"Were you there, too?" Trooper Bob asked.

Chris Russell nodded. "Yes. I came down to sample the treats and support the local merchants."

"Did you get into an argument with Clayton Davenport?"

Before I could answer, Chris Russell interrupted. "Don't answer that."

"Why not?" Trooper Bob said.

"Maddy doesn't have to answer any questions that might incriminate herself."

"I didn't kill him. So, I don't have to worry about incriminating myself. Yes, I got into an argument with him. He was an odious man who argued with everyone he came into contact with. I argued with him. Candy Rivers argued with him. April—"

Trooper Bob smiled. "Go on. I already know that April argued with him too."

I hadn't intended to share that. Darn it. April was right. He was a wily one. "Great, then you must know that none of us killed him. So, you can stop wasting time questioning us and go out and find the person who really murdered him. Clayton Davenport was very much alive when he left my shop. And I haven't seen him since he stomped out at four this afternoon."

"Is there anyone who can corroborate your story?"

Trooper Bob said *corroborate* as though it were a dirty word. "If you're asking if I saw other people after I saw Clayton Davenport, then the answer is yes. If you're asking if they were with me every second since and can prove that I never came back here and met Clayton Davenport and then killed him, then no."

"Then what is he doing here? How'd he get in if he wasn't here to meet you?"

That had me stumped. My mind raced, and my habit of oversharing when I was nervous kicked in. "I don't know. I mean, it's not like we got along. We didn't. I barely knew him. I can't imagine what April ever saw in him. He knew I couldn't stand him, especially after the way he treated April. Then, when he came here in his expensive suits and tried to run me out of business by flying in a Belgian master chocolatier and pâtissier, well that just made me angry, which is why I made that stupid bet with him that if I lost the baking contest, he'd win the bakery. There's no way I would have made a stupid bet like that, especially since I can't bake very well ... probably not well enough to beat a professional. But he just made me so angry. I kicked him out. But, when I was walking around downtown last night, I saw his limo was still parked at the Carson Law Inn. But I never saw him. Besides, after the fight we had, he had to know he wasn't welcome here, especially after what April told me he—"

Chris Russell placed a hand on my shoulder. "Maddy, I think you've said enough."

Trooper Bob smiled. "What did April tell you?"

Chris Russell squeezed my shoulder to prevent me from answering. He turned to the state trooper. "Are you charging my client?"

He waited nearly a minute before responding. "No, but—"

"Then we're going." Chris Russell took my elbow and pulled me to my feet. "If you have further questions, please call my office, and I'll make an appointment."

Baby followed us outside to my car. I tried to explain, but Russell shushed me until I was in the car and fully out of earshot of the police.

"Maddy, I want you to go home and stay there. If Trooper Bob or anyone else wants to ask questions, promise me you won't say a word unless I'm there." He gave me a hard stare. "Promise?"

"I promise."

He walked around the car and opened the passenger door so Baby could climb in.

I glanced around looking for April, but I couldn't find her anywhere. However, I recognized her patrol car and knew she was still here somewhere. I backed out of the alley and headed home. I prayed that I hadn't just given Trooper Bob a reason to lock up me or my best friend.

CHAPTER 12

The Baker Street Irregulars, the name my great-aunt Octavia gave her group of friends who got together once a week over brunch to help solve the crimes that had stumped the New Bison Police, usually met on Sundays. However, as soon as I got home, I sent out an emergency text requesting everyone who could to meet at my house at nine. I knew April and Leroy would come. April lived here, and Leroy would be here baking or selling, but he'd do anything within his power to help April. Since he had been living upstairs at Baby Cakes, there was no way he couldn't know that Clayton Davenport had been murdered. I'm just grateful he had been with Tyler and wasn't there when it happened.

I posted early this morning that Baby Cakes was closed, so we had plenty of baked goods to eat and wouldn't be interrupted by customers. Still, my cell phone started blowing up early. Michael was first.

U ok?

Y

U want me 2 come over?

You have surgery.
I can reschedule
I'm fine. C U @ Dinner
Sure?
Y
Wanna talk?
Later. I need 2 think
K
Love U
Ditto

I had similar texts from Leroy, but instead of messages of love, he offered food. Leroy's love language was definitely cooking.

Coffee?
Y
Bacon?
Yess!!!

Tyler offered alcohol in lieu of food, but his message was equally heartfelt and filled with concern.

Michael and Hannah were the first to arrive. Michael had a large casserole dish, which Hannah directed him to take into the dining room.

She hugged me. "You okay?"

I nodded. Hannah gave great hugs, and I wanted nothing more than to lay my head on her shoulder and sob, but I knew if I let the waterworks start, there would be no stopping them.

She pulled away, held me at arm's distance, and gave me a hard stare as though she were looking into my soul. "You're good with makeup, but you ain't had no sleep, and you're not getting enough to eat. You're nothing but skin and bones."

Hannah was sweet. She was right about my not sleeping. However, that was probably due to the fact that I had only been home for three hours. It hardly seemed worth it to waste time sleeping when I needed to figure out how to solve this mess. She was dead wrong about the skin and bones part. I wasn't skinny. Five-feet-five and one hundred thirty pounds, I was at the high end of what the outdated BMI chart called healthy. However, I'd long since tossed that chart out the window. As long as I felt good, then I stopped obsessing about losing weight. Thankfully, none of my dates seemed to mind, including Michael.

He returned, and Hannah left to give us a few moments of privacy.

Michael pulled me close, wrapped his arms tightly around me, and held me.

I snuggled close and took a deep breath. He was dressed in medical scrubs and smelled fresh, with a citrusy scent of orange, lemons, and freshly cut grass. I inhaled and allowed his strength to soak into me.

"You okay?"

I didn't trust my voice, so I nodded.

"I can still reschedule. I can see if Dr. Hanover can cover for me. He owes me, and—"

I shook my head and reached up and kissed him.

When he came up for air, he smiled. "If that's what's waiting for me after work, I can definitely reschedule."

I giggled. "You don't need to reschedule. I'll be here when you get done." I took a deep breath. "But I need to work through who killed Clayton Davenport."

I briefly filled him in on what I knew. When I finished talking, the concern on his face confirmed what I already knew. This was bad.

"Geez. I wonder how he got into the bakery. You don't think April—"

"April what?"

We were so engrossed in our conversation and togetherness, we didn't notice April's entry until she spoke.

"When did you get home?" I asked. I hoped to divert attention away from Michael's comment, but I should have known better.

"I didn't kill Clayton, if that's what you're wondering."

Baby must have sensed her distress because he got up on his hind legs and put his paws around her neck.

"I didn't think you had," Michael said.

April let Baby lick her face and then ordered him off. "I don't know why not. That seems to be the popular theory right now. That I lured CJ to the bakery and then stabbed him in the back." She folded her arms across her chest. "Well, I didn't. I would never."

"Anyone who knows you knows you would never kill anyone . . . not like that, anyway."

Now it was my turn to question him. "What do you mean?"

"It's out of character. April's honest and straightforward, but she's also the sheriff. *If* she had to kill in the line of duty, she'd probably have shot him. And she wouldn't have left him on the floor like that. She would have admitted she'd done it and filed a police report." He stared at April. "I don't believe she killed him any more than you do."

A tear fell down her cheek, and she quickly wiped it away. "Thank you."

I pulled her into a hug.

"What's all this hugging?" Hannah said. "The food's getting cold. Where's Tyler and Leroy?"

"Right here," Tyler said. He and Leroy entered the kitchen, which felt small with everyone huddled together near the back door.

Both Tyler and Leroy looked hungover. Their eyes were bloodshot, and their faces had a tinge that didn't look healthy.

Tyler held up a bag that contained several bottles of alcohol, and when the bottles clinked, he winced.

Leroy looked slightly better, which wasn't saying much. He held a platter with fruit and pastries.

Michael said he needed to get to work and offered to take Baby so he could run blood work.

I thanked him and gave him a quick kiss before he and Baby left.

Hannah glanced around at the group. "Well, we better get this meeting started so we can figure out who killed April's slimeball late husband."

CHAPTER 13

We sat at the dining room table, which was laden with food. Usually, our meetings were lively with witty banter back and forth, especially between Tyler, April, and me. Today's mood was much more somber.

"All right, I can't take this funeral service anymore," Hannah said. "How long are y'all gonna avoid the two-ton elephant in the room?"

April sighed. "Hannah's right. I owe you an explanation about—"

"You don't owe us anything," Leroy said. "We know you didn't kill him, but even if you did, we'd understand. He was a lousy human being and deserved everything he got." His face turned red, and his bloodshot eyes flashed.

April gave Leroy a dreamy look and reached across the table to squeeze his hand. "Thank you. I appreciate the vote of confidence, but I do owe you—all of you—an explanation." She glanced at each of us before continuing.

"Contrary to what Trooper Bob believes, I wasn't meeting Clayton last night. I, and most of my team, worked to clear up the mess Clayton started by hiring a bunch of circus performers and one of the hottest pop singers to show up in downtown New Bison without prior warning."

"Did he have a permit?" Tyler asked.

"Apparently, he'd been working on this for months. He told the mayor he had a plan that would make New Bison's Spring Festival even more popular than Woodstock. He was going to put our sleepy little town at the center of the public's eye."

Tyler rolled his eyes. "Oh, brother."

"Let me guess," Hannah said. "That darned fool Abernathy probably just saw dollar signs and didn't ask any questions."

"Exactly," April said. "So, then I looked like the bad guy who wants to shut down everyone's fun."

"Do we know how Clayton got into Baby Cakes?" I asked.

April shook her head. "Trooper Bob's theory is that I agreed to meet him there, after closing, for some kind of romantic interlude."

"In the bakery?"

"He thinks things got rough and I grabbed a knife to defend myself, but rather than reporting it, I panicked and ran away to cover my tracks."

"Because you're just a poor defenseless woman. Lord a mercy, you couldn't possibly handle anything messy like a murder without a big, strong man to come and save you." I fanned myself and batted my eyelashes.

Tyler glanced at me incredulously. "But she's the sheriff."

"He thinks she's too pretty to get her hands dirty with a murder." I huffed. "That idiot is still living in the Ice Age."

"Don't put down women in the Ice Age," Hannah said. "My grandmother told me women have been the same ever since the Good Lord put them on this earth. They had to hunt, gather, cook, clean, and give birth, just like today. Those Ice Age women wasn't no different than you and me."

"He honestly told me that if I confessed, then he would ask

the judge for leniency," April said. "He was pretty sure I'd get it too since the judge is his third cousin."

"You have got to be kidding," I said. "Did he want you to go into court and clutch your pearls and dab at your eyes with a handkerchief while begging the court for mercy?"

April folded her arms across her chest and scowled. "Over my dead body."

"Does he have any suspects?" Tyler asked. "Other than you, of course."

"He's leaning toward me as his number one suspect, but there's a chance that I'm covering for Maddy because of the bet. Or . . ." April flushed. "Leroy."

Leroy turned bright red. "I wasn't there. I have an alibi."

"We were together all night drowning our sorrows," Tyler said. "I have the hangover to prove it."

"You don't count," April said. "You're friends."

"Just because we're friends doesn't mean I'd lie," Tyler said.

Hannah chuckled. "I'm feeling left out. Trooper Bob is willing to believe that everyone at this table murdered Clayton Davenport, except me. I couldn't stand that little Davenport weasel any more than the rest of you. He's only excluding me because he thinks I'm too old to have done it. Well, that's just age discrimination, and it's illegal."

Leroy nearly choked and broke out in a coughing fit.

"Don't be too quick to get on Trooper Bob's suspect list," I said. "We're going to need somebody to post bail for the rest of us."

Hannah frowned and sipped her coffee.

Leroy and Tyler laughed, but April was dead serious.

"We're only joking," I said. "You know that, right?"

April took a deep breath. "I know. It's just . . . I've been suspended from any real police work until this thing is cleared up."

"Can they do that?"

She nodded. "Trooper Bob was right last night when he said

it would be a conflict of interest for me to investigate my husband's murder, but I can't afford to be off work."

"You know you don't have to worry about the rent. I can—"

She was shaking her head before the words were out of my mouth. "No. I can't. And you can't. My moving in here was business, not friendship. I believe in paying my debts, and I can't . . . I won't take charity."

"I can give you a loan until—"

She waved away that suggestion too. "I know you mean well, and that's really sweet, but I'm okay, for now. But we need to get this case wrapped up quickly. Not just for financial reasons, but my reputation is on the line. I'm on desk duty, part-time. I can't investigate anything major. The longer I'm suspended from duty, the longer it'll be ingrained in people's heads that I've done something wrong. Trooper Bob and all his friends who believe I'm only good for one thing will muster their resources, and by the time the next election rolls around, I'll be out on my butt."

"Then we better get down to business figuring out who killed Clayton Davenport." I turned to Tyler. "Would you mind taking notes?"

He reached inside his bag and pulled out a notepad and pen. "Now, let's get down to business."

CHAPTER 14

"Who had a motive for killing Clayton Davenport?" I asked.

There was a long pause before Leroy said, "You mean other than April, you, and me?"

"Yes."

There was another long pause.

Hannah broke the silence. "I can think of three folks off the top of my head."

We all stared, but Hannah's eyes looked sharp and clear.

"Who?" April asked.

"Candy was madder than a wet hen when April closed down her shop," Hannah said.

"That's right," I said. "I'd almost forgotten."

"According to the papers Clayton showed me, she and Paul Rivers weren't legally married," April said.

"Yeah, but this is the twenty-first century, not the Dark Ages," Tyler said. "Nobody cares about that stuff anymore."

"Maybe," Hannah said, "but it doesn't look good for the daughter of a minister."

Tyler tapped his pen. "Yeah, but her dad's a pacifist."

April stole a glance at Tyler before continuing. "I think she had an alibi last night."

Tyler caught the look and held up a hand. "Okay, let's get everything out on the table. Candy and I went out a few times. I thought things were going well, but . . . apparently, she didn't." He shrugged. "I'll admit I was disappointed, which is why I spent last night using rum, tequila, and I think drain cleaner to purge her from my system." He shook his head and winced. "Well, if she wants to hang out with another supposedly wealthy old geezer and miss out on all of this." He motioned from his head to his feet. "Then, that's her loss."

Despite his jokes, it was clear that Tyler was hurt. "I'm sorry, Tyler," I said.

"I don't think she killed the guy, but she's the best we've got right now, so I'll put her on the list."

"I think Candy had an alibi last night." I shared how I'd seen Chris Russell's car parked outside her shop. A thought popped into my head and I turned to April. "Wait. You blocked off the building. How did she get upstairs?"

"Chris Russell filed a restraining order to keep Clayton from moving forward until there was a court case, so I had to let her go back in."

I looked to Tyler. "Do you think she'd talk to you?"

"I can give it a try. We're supposed to be friends. I can give her a call. She wanted help setting up her computer system for the coffee shop, and I still have some papers I need to return."

"I'll try talking to Alma." I turned to Leroy. "We still have some of those croissants left, right?" Alma Hurston, my next-door neighbor, was Candy's mom. She was also addicted to Leroy's croissants.

"No, but I can whip up another batch real quick. Don't worry."

"She loves those. I'll take a plate over and see what I can find out." I turned to Hannah. "Who else?"

"That woman claiming to be Marjorie Rivers. She didn't look none too happy about any of what Clayton Davenport was forcing her to do."

"Claiming to be?" April asked.

"Do you really not remember her?" I asked.

"There's something different." Hannah shook her head. "Of course, it's been years since I last saw her. And my memory isn't what it used to be."

I reached over and gave her hand a squeeze. "None of our memories are what they once were."

Tyler snapped a finger. "I almost forgot. I saw her and Clayton Davenport in a heated argument last night." Tyler held up a hand to halt the barrage of questions and then massaged his temples. "They were in the town square. Abernathy was making his speech opening the Spring Festival. Davenport was standing behind the mayor. That's when Marjorie stormed up and started really letting him have it."

"What did she say?" I asked.

"I couldn't actually hear what they were saying, but based on their body language, she was furious. She was pointing and waving her hands." He shook his head slowly. "Sorry."

"I'll bet Clayton didn't like that," April said.

"His face turned purple, and I thought his head was going to pop off like a Pez dispenser. But again, I couldn't hear what he said." Tyler looked sheepish. "I'm sorry."

"We can talk to Marjorie and try to figure out what the argument was about," I said. "Okay, well, that's two." I turned to Hannah. "Who's the third person who might have killed Clayton?"

Hannah glanced at me, but I could tell it was too late. Her eyes were glazed, and she'd already zoned out. "Do I know you?"

CHAPTER 15

I guided Hannah to the guest bedroom and helped her lie down for a nap. She would sleep for a few hours, and with any luck, she would be back to her normal self by the time Michael came to pick her up.

The moments when Hannah zoned out and didn't remember names or faces were becoming more frequent and lasting longer. Michael and I had discussed her condition. He was concerned, but since there was no cure, he kept her as comfortable as possible.

When I returned, April was sharing her whereabouts the night her husband was murdered.

"It was chaos. Word about Chloe's appearance had spread like wildfire, and people were swarming downtown. Cars were backed up from Main Street all the way to Interstate 94. In both directions. And Red Arrow Highway was a parking lot. People literally abandoned their vehicles and ran downtown." She shook her head. "It was a nightmare. If I had shut down the concert, the crowds would have been furious and caused a riot. You'll never convince me Clayton didn't know exactly what he was doing. And springing that on us at the last minute was irresponsible. If he had told us . . . anyway, I was furious. I could have strangled him." She pounded the table with her fist, rattling the dishes and sloshing coffee.

I grabbed a towel and wiped up the mess.

"I'm sorry," April said.

"How did you get it under control?"

"I called the state police and asked for backup, which is one reason Trooper Bob was on the scene so quickly." She paused. "Then, I told them that the city ordinance required that the music stop at ten. People were upset, but Chloe helped a lot. She said she had a concert the next day in Spain and had a flight to catch, but she would perform a few more songs before heading out. And that's what she did. She performed until ten and then waved goodbye, hopped on her tour bus, and left."

Something tugged at the back of my mind. "Are you sure she left?"

April frowned. "She said she was leaving, but I didn't follow her to the airport. Why?"

I told April about my late-night walk downtown near the Carson Law Inn and how I saw the limo parked in the parking lot. "At the time, I assumed that it belonged to Clayton Davenport, but what if it didn't? What if it belonged to Chloe? I mean, Davenport was in town for at least two whole days, and we never saw a limousine until Chloe arrived."

April stifled a yawn. "I can check at the inn. They'll have a record of the license plate. Which is interesting because later that night, we were called to the inn because of a break-in."

"Really? What was taken?"

"I had my hands full with getting traffic moving. I sent a patrol car. One of the guest rooms was broken into. Someone trashed the room, probably looking for something small they could hock. The hotel didn't want any publicity and refused to file a police report. So, he left and came back to help with traffic control."

"If they weren't going to file a report, why'd they bother calling the police?" Leroy asked.

"Good question," I said.

"One of the housekeepers was picking up trays from the hallway and noticed the door was open," April said. "She looked in and saw the room was trashed and told the night manager. They called the police and then called the general manager. That's who told me neither the guest nor the inn wanted to file a report with the police."

"Interesting. Do you know whose room it was?"

She shook her head. "The inn refused to disclose that information but assured me that they had spoken to the guest and were acting under their direction."

"Don't they have to give that information to you? You're the sheriff."

April yawned. "Not without a court order they don't."

"I might be able to help," Leroy said. "My mom is a housekeeper at the Carson Law Inn. I could ask her. She should be able to find out whose room was broken into."

Leroy rarely talked about his family. I knew his mom lived in New Bison, but I didn't know she worked at the inn. Whenever I asked about her, like April's relationship with Clayton Davenport, he merely said *It's complicated*. My mom died when I was a baby, but having been raised by the Admiral, I understood *complicated*.

I glanced at my watch. "I have to meet Mayor Abernathy to ask about Daisy's owner and to pick his brain on ideas of why Baby is moping around. How about we meet for lunch at the Carson Law Inn?"

April nodded.

Tyler was texting. He finished his message and put down his phone. "Sorry, I can't meet for lunch. I'm meeting Candy. I'll let you know what I find out."

We agreed and spent the rest of the meeting talking about

the bakery and the Spring Festival. Leroy was going to bake and make sure we were well stocked for opening up tomorrow.

Tyler left to open his store before his lunchtime meeting with Candy.

April yawned again.

"You've been up all night, and you're exhausted," I said. "Go downstairs and get some sleep." She revved up to object, but I cut her off. "You're not going to be any good to us if you fall over from exhaustion. Plus, your little gray cells need to be well rested if you're going to help figure out whodunit."

She smiled at my reference to Hercule Poirot, one of my favorite fictional detectives, but the smile didn't make it up to her eyes. "All right, I'll try, but I don't intend to sit back and do nothing while you're all out following clues and tracking down a killer. I need to work . . . investigate. I've got too much at stake."

CHAPTER 16

I stuck my head into the guest room to check on Hannah before leaving. I found her sitting on the side of the bed. "I didn't mean to wake you."

"You didn't wake me." Hannah shook her head. "I don't remember coming in here." She paused. "I seem to be taking a lot of naps lately."

"You were tired. Maybe you should try to go back to sleep."

"Humph." She put her shoes on and stood up. She turned and remade the bed. "I got too much to do to be napping all day. We need to find out who killed April's husband before that trooper locks her up and ruins her career."

"If you're sure you feel up to it . . ."

"Of course I'm up to it. I been meaning to have a talk with that Marjorie Rivers anyway. Gotta find out where she's been all this time. I'm sure if I talk to her, then it'll all come back."

That was a good point. Hannah was back to herself. As long as she felt up to working, Michael thought it was good for her to keep going. She loved baking, and Baby Cakes allowed her to do what she enjoyed while surrounded by people who loved and cared for her.

I filled her in on the plans we'd made for today.

"I've got some of those apple turnovers downstairs, and I made a strawberry pie. We can take the pie. Nothing like a strawberry pie to loosen the tongue." She laughed. "Although I seem to remember Marjorie always loved lemons. I don't have time to make lemon pie, but . . . strawberry will have to do."

We went to the kitchen and grabbed the pie. Before we left, I wrapped up a couple of the apple turnovers too. If the pie loosened Marjorie's tongue, then I felt sure the turnovers would loosen Mayor Abernathy's.

It wasn't until we were in the car that I realized I didn't know where Marjorie was staying. I turned to Hannah and asked.

"I'm betting on Garrett Kelley's house." Hannah gave me directions.

The New Bison rumor mill had suggested that Marjorie Rivers had run off with Garrett Kelley's son. Garrett's son died years ago. If Garrett left his property to Marjorie, then the rumors must have been right.

I followed the directions Hannah gave and drove to a small farmhouse near Lake Michigan and the interstate. It was a small, eclectic neighborhood with small bungalows, farmhouses, and the occasional ranch thrown in to keep things interesting.

Any questions on where Marjorie was staying were answered when I pulled in front of the driveway and saw her on a swing on the front porch.

We got out and walked to the house.

"I don't know if you remember me. I'm—"

Marjorie hurried over and hugged Hannah. "Of course I remember you, Miss Hannah. How could I forget you? I certainly couldn't forget your sweet potato pie. Please tell me that's what you have under that foil."

Hannah chuckled. "This one's strawberry, but I'll have to make you a sweet potato pie and bring it by tomorrow." She turned to me. "This here's Maddy Montgomery, Octavia's great-niece."

Marjorie smiled and extended a hand. "I'm really sorry to hear about Miss Octavia's passing. I know Garrett was devastated. She was an amazing woman."

When I first arrived in New Bison, I wasn't sure how to respond to condolences about her death. I didn't know her. Surprisingly, since her death, I'd learned a lot about my great-aunt from her friends and the notes and messages that she'd left around the house. She was a smart, determined woman. She had a sound mind for business, and unlike me, she didn't have problems making decisions. Aunt Octavia knew exactly what she wanted and how to get it.

"Thank you."

Marjorie led us inside to the kitchen, which was small but clean. There was a small wood table with four chairs in a corner. "Coffee or tea?"

Hannah and I sat while Marjorie got cups and plates from the cabinets. She couldn't have been here more than a few days, but she knew exactly where everything was. Within minutes, we were all sitting at the table sipping coffee and eating pie.

"That pie was delicious." Marjorie leaned back in her seat. "Now, as much as I want to believe y'all came over here just to feed me, I'm guessing that's not why you're here."

I wasn't sure how to approach things since I didn't know Marjorie. Thankfully, Hannah came to the rescue. "I been meaning to come by ever since I heard you was back in town. How did you get mixed up with a slimeball like Clayton Davenport?"

Nothing like the direct approach. I wouldn't have been able to get away with being that direct, but older Black women could get away with saying things no one else could.

"After Garrett's death, that lawyer got in touch with me, Chris Russell. He told me Garrett had named me in his will."

She gazed out the window into the backyard. "Garrett had always been nice to me. He knew where I was all of these years, and he never told Paul." After a few moments, she snapped out of her trip down memory lane. "Not long after he reached out, I got a visit from Clayton Davenport." She scowled. "It was so close, that I thought Mr. Russell must have told him about me. At least, at first . . ."

We waited, but Marjorie blushed and took a sip of her coffee. She was holding something back.

"Clayton Davenport approached you about buying Garrett's bookstore, is that right?" I asked.

"Yes."

We sat in an awkward silence for several seconds while I tried to find the right words to ask what I really wanted to know. Fortunately, Hannah didn't share my indecisiveness.

"Honey, when you left that sleazy snake oil salesman, I just knew you had gotten free. How is it you didn't divorce the old goat?"

Unfortunately, I took that exact moment to take a sip of my coffee. When I heard Hannah's question, I spit my coffee out.

Marjorie hurried to the sink and came back with a roll of paper towels and helped me clean up the table.

I apologized over and over again.

When I was as clean as a Shout wipe could make me, we all settled back down.

"Now, where were we?" Marjorie asked, as if any of us had lost sight of the question.

"You were about to tell us why you never divorced Paul Rivers," Hannah said. For someone with dementia, she had a really good memory when it mattered.

Marjorie stared into her coffee. "I don't know. At first, I didn't want him to know where I was. If I filed for a divorce, then he'd find out. Later, when I heard he got remarried, I thought he must have gotten divorced in Mexico. I'd heard that you could do things like that."

"I saw that on an episode of *Perry Mason*. This man got a divorce in Mexico and then later, he married somebody else. Well, apparently his Mexican divorce wasn't recognized in the United States, or something like that. So, his ex-wife, who was a real piece of work, called the district attorney and filed charges claiming he was a bigamist." Hannah sipped her coffee and shook her head. "Perry Mason had his hands full with that one."

"What happened? How did Perry Mason get him out of it?"

"Someone killed her."

CHAPTER 17

Unlike me, Marjorie didn't spew coffee all over the table and down the front of her blouse. Instead, she nearly choked on it. She coughed and sputtered while tears ran down her cheeks.

I'm not good in emergency situations, especially medical situations. When I was a teen and living on base, I took a safety course that included training on the Heimlich maneuver and CPR, but my dummy died. My compressions were either too hard or too soft. My breaths were too shallow to fill its lungs, and every attempt to dislodge the object in my dummy's throat failed. My instructor suggested I keep my cell phone handy and call 9-1-1 if I ever found myself in a life-threatening situation. Considering my teenage plan was to marry a doctor, I didn't worry about failing safety training. Nevertheless, I pounded on Marjorie's back until she turned around and gave me a look that said *If you hit me one more time I'm going to punch you in your throat.*

After a couple of moments, she stopped coughing, and her face moved from maroon to puce to blush. I took that as a good sign and returned to my seat. My nerves were shot, and my hands were shaking. Watching someone nearly choke to death was exhausting.

"I'm fine," Marjorie said. "My coffee just went down the wrong pipe."

"Well, that was scary," Hannah said. "I'll bet you need something stronger than coffee." She reached into her purse and pulled out a small flask.

Marjorie's eyes widened. After a moment, she shook her head. "No, thank you. I think I'm just going to get a glass of water." She got up and went over to the sink, filled a glass from the faucet, and took a few sips.

Hannah shrugged and offered the flask to me.

It took everything in me not to grab that flask and take a long swig. Instead, I declined and took another sip of my coffee. I wondered if Michael was aware that his grandmother carried a flask in her purse. I also wondered what was in that flask.

Marjorie put her glass in the sink and turned to face us. "I'm a bit shaken, and I think I'd like to lie down. I hope you understand."

I understood. She wanted to get rid of us without answering the question, but there really wasn't much we could do.

Hannah and I stood. Hannah promised to return with a sweet potato pie. I stood and mumbled how I hoped she was okay and wouldn't have any ill effects. Then we hurried out to the car.

"Well, that was awkward." I glanced at the car's backup cameras and then turned and looked over my shoulder for good measure as I backed out of the driveway. It was a habit I hadn't broken. The Admiral taught me to drive in a military jeep that was likely manufactured during World War II. It had a manual transmission with no power steering, no power brakes, no rear or side assist cameras, and the numbers on the gear shift were probably last seen during the Korean War. In the large picture window of the house, the curtains moved, and I caught a glimpse of Marjorie watching us as we left.

"I'll come by tomorrow with a sweet potato or a lemon meringue pie," Hannah said. "I'll get the truth out of her." She said it with a lot more confidence than I felt.

"How?"

"Nothing loosens the tongue like a slice of my sweet potato pie."

I smiled. "I love your pies, but isn't that asking a lot from one pie?"

She waved her hand. "That's nothing. I've got a recipe for chicken that'll make a grown man drop to his knees and propose marriage." She gave me a glance from the corner of her eye. "I'll write down the recipe for you. After all, I'm not getting any younger."

I had to swerve to avoid hitting the curb.

CHAPTER 18

My next stop was the New Bison Police Station. In addition to housing the New Bison police force, the lighthouse-themed building was also where Jackson Abernathy moved his office after he took over as mayor.

I parked, and we got out and went into the building. I'd called earlier to make sure the mayor was available.

The mayor's office was an ode to 1980s décor. Mauve carpet and mauve flowered wallpaper. The most impressive part of the office was the view. A wall of floor-to-ceiling windows covered by plastic vertical blinds. Any one of the Golden Girls would have been quite comfortable.

We knocked and were admitted into the purple paradise.

Mayor Abernathy waved an arm toward two guest chairs with wooden arms and legs. "Please, take a seat."

Jackson Abernathy's office location may have changed from the first time I visited him in an old building downtown, but one thing remained the same. There were papers strewn all over the desk, folders piled on every flat surface, including the floor, and a wastebasket overflowing with paper.

I moved a pile of folders from one chair so Hannah could sit and placed them on the edge of the desk before repeating the steps for my own chair.

After we were seated, Abernathy leaned back in his chair and folded his hands across his stomach. "Now, how can I help you?"

"The workers have finished the renovations at Baby Cakes. I believe the underwriter completed his final walk-through, so—"

"Yes. Yes." He sat up, opened a drawer, and pulled out an envelope. "The final check from New Bison Casualty and Life. I'm glad Jacob is out of the hospital so I can focus on the insurance side of the business and don't have to help out with the underwriting." He passed the envelope across the desk. "Although, I still need to swing by and do a final walk-through. Take pictures. You know." He waved a hand.

"Thank you. I'm sure having the underwriter back has made things a lot easier."

"Yes. Now that I'm the mayor, I have a lot more responsibilities. I can barely keep up with my speaking engagements and committee meetings, and I'll be working on my reelection campaign in a few months, although I don't expect that it'll be much of a contest." He smiled. "I just don't have time to run my dad's insurance company and my own business of breeding and showing dogs." He shook his head. "There just aren't enough hours in the day."

Hannah grunted, turned her head to the side, and mumbled something that sounded like, "The big blowhard."

"What was that?" Mayor Abernathy asked.

Based on the flush that rose up his neck, I knew he'd heard her just fine.

"The breeding is the reason that I'm here," I said. "I wanted to ask—"

"Don't tell me you've finally decided to offload that mastiff.

I knew it was just a matter of time. That's a mighty big dog for a little lady. Mastiffs are powerful and stubborn and need a firm hand. Well, I've been thinking about downsizing the breeding business. I just don't have the time to show dogs like I used to, but I'd be happy to take him off your hands. A champion stud dog like that will make money without much effort." He paused but then quickly added, "Of course, he has to be handled properly. You can't treat a stud dog like a common pet. I knew it was just a matter of time before you saw that for yourself and came to your senses." He smiled and reached into his jacket and pulled out a checkbook. "I'm sure we can come to a reasonable agreement regarding the terms."

"I'm not here to sell Baby."

"What?" He stared with his pen poised over the check. "Your message said you wanted to discuss Baby."

"I do want to discuss Baby, but I don't want to sell him. I just want to ask you a few questions."

He stared for a few moments and then ripped the check from his checkbook and tore it into pieces. When he was done, he put the pieces into the trash and then leaned back in his chair and waited.

"He's been acting . . . different lately. I was wondering—"

"Different how?"

"He's not eating much and doesn't want to play. He just lays around and . . . well, he mopes."

"Mopes?" He rolled the word around on his lips. "Mopes? How does a dog mope?"

"He, well, he just doesn't seem interested in food or treats or playing. It's not like him."

"Did you take him to the vet?"

"Yes. Michael checked him out and he says there's nothing *medically* wrong with him. In fact, that's where he is today, having blood work done."

Abernathy squinted at me. "If there's nothing physically wrong with him, then I don't understand the problem."

"He's not himself. I was hoping—"

"Not himself? He's a dog, not a person. If he's not sick, and he's eating and drinking, then I don't see what the problem is."

"The problem is I think he may be sick . . . emotionally. I think he's lovesick." As soon as the words left my mouth, I knew I'd made a mistake in sharing.

There was a slight pause, and then Jackson Abernathy let out a roar of laughter. He laughed long and loud until tears fell from his eyes. Whenever he tried to stop, he would glance at me or Hannah and start up again.

The scowl on Hannah's face and the way she clutched her handbag told me that if Abernathy didn't gain control of himself, she was going to wallop him with that purse.

"Mayor Abernathy, please," I said. "This isn't a laughing matter."

He laughed a bit longer and then reached into his pocket and pulled out a handkerchief to wipe his eyes. "Oh my goodness. I can't tell you the last time that I've laughed like that."

Hannah mumbled something, but the only words I could make out were, "Crazed hyena."

"Mayor, I kept a record of Baby's eating for the past week." I put the folder that I'd brought in with me on top of his desk.

"Baloney." He pushed the folder aside and brushed against one of the many piles on his desk. The pile toppled like an avalanche in the Swiss Alps, burying my folder.

This isn't working. I heard the Admiral's voice in my head. *Counter-attack.* It was time to regroup and try a different tactic. I took a deep breath, plastered a big smile on my face, and twirled the ends of my hair with my finger. I leaned forward. "Mr. Abernathy . . . Jackson, I hate to admit it, but you're right." I giggled. "I don't know anything about dogs." I swallowed hard to avoid puking. "That's why I came to you. I know you're an expert when it comes to dogs and especially English mastiffs. I was just hoping that you could help me."

Gaah!

Hannah shot me a look out of the side of her eye that indicated she had questions about my sanity. I avoided returning her gaze. Frankly, I had the same questions. The only person who didn't think I'd suddenly lost what wits I had was Jackson Abernathy.

Abernathy's chest expanded. His shoulders went back, and his face lit up like he'd just learned that Santa Claus was indeed real. "I do have many years of experience with dogs. English mastiffs are smart but very stubborn dogs."

He launched into a long monologue on the history of the breed, their proper care and feeding, and an outdated view on dog training that made me cringe. It's hard to maintain a smile while you're mentally zoned out; however, I had honed my skills over many years dating sailors who thought naval artillery was the most fascinating topic on earth. Jackson Abernathy paused for a breath, and I was prepared to make my escape when there was a knock on the door.

Abernathy frowned. "Who can that be?" He pushed a button on his desk. "Holly, I'm in the middle of a conference and can't be disturbed."

The door swung open and Trooper Bob waltzed in, followed by a girl who looked about fifteen. She had long red hair and freckles.

"I'm sorry, Mr. Mayor," Holly said. "I tried to stop him, but he wouldn't even let me announce him."

Trooper Bob glared at me. "What're you doing here?"

"That's none of your business," Mayor Abernathy said, jumping from his seat. "You have no right to barge in here. I'm in conference."

Trooper Bob tapped his shield. "This gives me the right to barge wherever I need to. I'm investigating a homicide, and I want to talk to you about the argument you had with Clayton Davenport. Now, we can do this here, or I can take you over to my office. Your call."

Oh boy. Mayor Abernathy argued with Clayton Davenport? When did that happen? With any luck, Trooper Bob will forget that I'm here.

All of the blood drained from Jackson Abernathy's face.

Trooper Bob held the door open and swept his arm, indicating the path I was to take. "Miss Montgomery."

I should have known he wouldn't forget. Darn!

Hannah and I stood. I stared at the pile of papers and folders on the mayor's desk. I rummaged for a few moments until Trooper Bob yelled, "Stop stalling or I'll arrest you for interfering in a police investigation."

I grabbed the first folder I saw and tucked it under my arm. Then, I pivoted, clicked my heels, gave a perfect salute, and marched out of the office.

Hannah followed, and as soon as she cleared the door, I turned to give Trooper Bob a scathing response, but I should have saved my energy. He slammed the door in my face.

"Why, that low-down dirty male chauvinist son of a goatherder," Hannah said.

I turned to the mayor's young secretary to apologize but was surprised when she winked. "Which one?"

Hannah folded her arms across her chest. "Take your pick."

I stared at the door to the mayor's office. "I would pay a fortune to be a fly on the wall for that conversation."

"I've got a few friends coming over this weekend," Holly said, smiling. "How about one of those Chocolate Soul Cakes?"

I raised an eyebrow. "Ah . . . sure."

She put her hand up to her lips and shushed us. Then, she pressed a button on the intercom.

Trooper Bob said, "I have a witness who heard you and Clayton Davenport arguing. Do you want to tell me what that was about?"

"It was a personal matter."

"I'm investigating a murder. There are *no* personal matters when it comes to murder."

"You can't honestly believe that I killed him? I'm the mayor."

"That and three dollars will get you a bottle of water from that overpriced vending machine in your lobby. I want to know what you and Clayton Davenport were arguing about."

"That's none of your business."

"This is a murder investigation," Trooper Bob said, his voice booming. "Everything's my business."

"I don't have to answer. I'm the mayor. My conversations are . . . privileged. Someone in my position has a number of conversations that could be detrimental if the general public were to catch wind of them."

Abernathy was lying. I didn't need to see his face to know it. His voice was shaky, and he stammered so much that I was sure Trooper Bob, like a shark, could smell blood in the water.

"Mr. Mayor, you can tell me here, in the privacy of your office, in which case *if* I determine that your information isn't relevant to my investigation, then it stays here. Or I can haul you downtown in handcuffs and hold you in a cell for twenty-four hours for obstructing a police investigation, withholding information, and any other charges I can think of."

Abernathy gasped. "You wouldn't dare."

I could almost hear the soundtrack from *Jaws*. *Dada . . . dada.*

"Wouldn't I?" Trooper Bob asked.

There was a long pause. I imagined Trooper Bob circling the mayor as the beat increased. *Dada . . . dada . . . dada.*

"It was nothing. Just a . . . a . . . misunderstanding."

"Maybe you should let me be the judge of what's important and what isn't."

Dada. Dada. Dada.

Abernathy folded like a house of cards. "Clayton Davenport had papers that . . . well, if they were released, might be embarrassing. They were from years ago."

"What papers?" Trooper Bob asked.

The soundtrack reached its crescendo just as the shark leapt from the water, mouth wide, ready to take a huge bite out of his prey. *Dadadadadada.*

"He found out I was dismissed from the military, and he threatened to make it public. It might have ruined my political career. I pleaded with him, but he just laughed . . . laughed." Abernathy sniffed. "I didn't kill Davenport, but if you want to know who did, maybe you should question that baker over at Baby Cakes. He has a crush on Sheriff Johnson. Or it could be that Candy Rivers . . . Candy Hurston . . . whatever her name is. She was furious about losing her shop to Rivers's first wife . . . ah, current wife . . . whatever. Marjorie. Either of them could have killed Davenport."

"I'll get to them in due time."

"Well, there are lots of other people who had a real reason to want Clayton Davenport dead. Even that airhead, Maddy Montgomery. She was about to lose her bakery. Davenport goaded her into betting her bakery in the Spring Festival baking competition. Everyone in town knows she can't bake anything other than Octavia's Chocolate Soul Cake, and Davenport got the committee to agree that recipes that won in the past weren't eligible for resubmission. There's no way she could have won on her own, and Davenport knew it. How come you're not badgering her?"

"Why, that weasel," I whispered.

"Is he crying?" Hannah asked.

"Who said that?" Abernathy asked.

We heard footsteps but didn't have time to get out.

Holly turned off the intercom just as Trooper Bob opened the door.

"What are you two still doing here?" he asked.

I turned to Holly. "So, that was one chocolate cake and two dozen thumbprint cookies, right?"

Holly tapped her pen for a few seconds. "You better make it four dozen thumbprint cookies. You can never have enough of those."

I glanced up. "I'm just taking a catering order." I turned back to Holly. "It'll be ready. All I need is the address."

She handed me a scrap of paper where she'd written her address. Then, she turned to Trooper Bob and smiled. "Sorry, Dad. I'm afraid it's all my fault. I saw Miss Montgomery here, and I just couldn't resist getting one of her delicious Chocolate Soul Cakes for my party this weekend."

I glanced from Holly to Trooper Bob. "Dad?"

She nodded. "Work study. It was either here or the police station." She rolled her eyes. "This is definitely better than that."

Trooper Bob frowned. "Perhaps I need to see you two out to your car." Trooper Bob took me and Hannah by our arms and marched us outside. I barely had time to grab my folder from the desk before he propelled me out the door.

Once we were outside in the parking lot, he turned and leaned down so that he was only inches from my face. "Miss Montgomery, I take a very dim view of nosy busybodies who think they're some kind of Nancy Drew wannabe and interfere in an active police investigation. Especially when they may just be a prime suspect in a murder."

When I was young, I loved reading Nancy Drew. As an adult, I hated the association. "Trooper Bob, I am *not interfering*. And I resent—"

"Save it. Just stay out of my way, or you'll regret it." He

glared and then spun around and marched back toward the building.

I searched my mind for a scathing remark I could hurl back at him, but he was moving fast and was almost back at the building. "And by the way, Nancy Drew had a perfect record when it came to solving mysteries," I yelled at his retreating back.

"That'll have him shaking in his boots," Hannah said.

I unlocked the doors to the car, and we got inside. I tucked the paper with Holly's address on it into my folder and tossed it on the back seat.

Hannah's anger at being kicked out of the mayor's office and marched out to the parking lot had fueled her wrath, and she had muttered a few half-hearted threats at Trooper Bob as he practically dragged us to the car. Once she was inside and buckled in, her anger drained out like the air inside of a balloon. After a few moments, she turned to me. "That's one nasty policeman."

"Is that all you have to say? We've learned a lot of information and are well on our way to figuring out who killed Clayton Davenport."

"What was all that drivel you spewed at that idiot Abernathy?"

It took a few beats for me to figure out what she was talking about. When I did, I chuckled. "It was sickening, wasn't it? I used to be able to fawn and play dumb at the drop of a hat, but I'm out of practice."

"Hmm. I thought you were about to go into your Butterfly McQueen impersonation from *Gone With the Wind*. 'I don't know nothin' 'bout birthin' babies, Miss Scarlett.'" She said it in a high-pitched Southern drawl. "Ugh."

I laughed. "I can't believe he fell for it."

"Hmm. I can. That man's dumber than a box of rocks. He's a complete idiot."

"Maybe he is . . ." Twenty minutes ago, I would have agreed with her. But now, I wasn't so sure. In a short period of time, Jackson Abernathy had wiggled out of Trooper Bob's net and cast a line of suspicion at Leroy, me, and Candy in one fell swoop. He might not be as dumb as I'd first thought. No, Jackson Abernathy wasn't a *complete* idiot. But the question remained: Was he a murderer?

CHAPTER 19

Like a flower left in the sun too long, Hannah began to wilt. I made a detour and took her home to rest before driving over to the Carson Law Inn to meet April for lunch. The drive helped me sift through everything I'd learned, and it had the added benefit of helping me forget that I wouldn't be able to reenter Aunt Octavia's Chocolate Soul Cake in the Spring Festival Bake-Off.

Marjorie Rivers was hiding something. Why did Clayton Davenport go to all of the trouble to track down Mayor Rivers's ex-wife . . . first wife . . . whatever, and bring her back to New Bison? And why did Marjorie agree to the scheme?

I took a breath and immediately started coughing. "'Something is rotten in the state of Denmark.'" I quoted from *Hamlet*. I pushed the button to make sure that all of the windows were raised and then turned the air conditioning up to help eliminate the rotten stench that made me want to gag. "Denmark isn't the only place where something was rotten." Something's rotten right here in New Bison, Michigan. The first time I'd smelled the foul odor, I learned that steel plants in Northwest Indiana were embroiled in a battle with environmental protectionists and local surfers to prevent contamination of Lake Michigan.

I pulled up to the Carson Law Inn, parked, and entered the Georgian-style mansion.

The interior was elegantly decorated in period furnishings, including lots of ornately carved wood moldings and furniture. I learned from browsing a brochure in the lobby that the 26,000-square-foot mansion was built in the late 1800s and had over forty rooms. Seventeen of which were now guest rooms. I walked into the foyer and felt as though I'd stepped back in time. Wood-paneled walls and a coffered wood ceiling screamed wealth to all who entered. Heavy drapes and the Aubusson rugs softened the masculine feel and lightened the room.

I walked to the podium, and a stiff older man who looked as though he would have made a great butler double for *Downton Abbey* told me that April was waiting for me in the conservatory.

He picked up a menu and escorted me through a room that was probably the parlor at one time, through another room that was lined with books, and out to a small glass room.

April was seated at a bistro table near the window, and after the maître d' left, she leaned forward and whispered, "This is my favorite spot in this dark old mausoleum."

"I can understand why." I glanced around the light-filled space. Unlike the other parts of the house that I'd seen, the only wood in this room was in the small wooden tables and chairs. The floor was red brick set in a herringbone pattern. The bottom half of the walls were stone, and the top and ceilings were glass. There was a stone fireplace in the corner. The conservatory was built at the back of the house, with an incredible view of a beautiful, lush, and well-tended garden.

"Those flowers are amazing."

April reached over and turned a crank that opened the casement window and then took a deep breath. "Smell that."

I took a deep breath. "I have no idea what those flowers are, but they smell wonderful." I picked up my phone, snapped a few pictures, and posted them. **#LoveFlowers #TheCarson-LawConservatory #FoodFlowersFriends**

April smiled and pointed. "Those are hydrangeas, azaleas, tulips, peonies, and roses."

"I'm impressed. I didn't know you knew so much about plants."

"I love gardens. I used to dream of opening a flower shop when I was a kid. I wanted to be just like Eliza Doolittle from *My Fair Lady*. I thought Audrey Hepburn was beautiful." She smiled and then shrugged. "Who knows, maybe one day I'll be rich. I can retire and have a garden and grow beautiful flowers and drink tea and eat cookies all day." She smiled, but it didn't reach her eyes. "I guess I am retired. Who knew I'd be retiring at such a young age?" She sighed.

I reached over and squeezed her hand. "You aren't retiring. We're going to figure out who killed Clayton Davenport, and you're going to have that garden. No need to wait until . . . well, until later. You can plant whatever you want at home. That house is just as much yours as mine."

"For as long as I'm there. If I lose my job, I won't be able to pay rent."

I waved away her protest. "You don't have to pay rent. I can—"

"No. I won't stay there if I can't pay rent. When I moved in, we agreed this would be a business transaction, remember?"

The lightbulb went off in my head, and I squealed. "I just got the best idea. I love flowers, but I suck at all things horticulture-y. You love gardens. I could pay you to plant a few gardens. Maybe a flower garden and a few vegetables. I know Leroy would *love* fresh herbs. I would, of course, pay for the plants and any tools you would need. You'd just have to do all of the hard work." I frowned. "You'd have to take care of the plants too. I'd kill them."

She smiled. "Miss Octavia and I used to talk about plants. She said she had a brown thumb in more ways than one."

"I must have inherited that because I'm horrible with plants, but I do love them. What do you say? It would increase the property value, and we could have fresh flowers inside. I love fresh flowers, especially those big blue ones." I pointed.

"Hydrangeas."

"I thought you said those pink ones were hydrangeas?"

"They both are. The color of the flowers depends on the alkaline content of the soil."

"Well, I want all of those. What do you say?"

She smiled. "Okay, but we have to be fair. If I do it, then you subtract it from my rent."

"Deal." I extended my hand, and we shook. I had no intention of charging April rent while she was only working part-time, but I'd cross that hurdle when we came to it.

A waiter arrived to take our orders.

"I believe one of my friends said his mother works here," I said. "Maybe you know her. Mrs. Danielson?"

The waiter smiled. "Yes, I know Fiona. Would you like me to tell her you're here?"

We agreed, and he took off to place our orders and to notify Leroy's mom that we'd like to talk to her.

"I'm embarrassed to say I don't know anything about Leroy's mother. In fact, I didn't even know she worked here until he mentioned it. You've been here longer than me. Do you know her?"

She shook her head. "He never talks about his mother. At least not to me anyway."

"I wonder why."

Our drinks arrived. Not long afterward, a dark-haired woman wearing a housekeeping uniform came by our table.

"Are you Leroy's friends?"

It wasn't until she spoke that we realized Leroy's mother was British.

"Yes, I'm Madison Montgomery, and this is April Johnson."

"My name's Fiona." She smiled. "Leroy's told me a lot about both of you, but especially you." She nodded toward April, who blushed.

"Mrs. Danielson, I know you're working, but is there any chance you could join us? We're hoping you could help us."

She glanced at a clock. "I can take a short break."

Once she was seated, I asked if she would permit me to buy her lunch. She declined lunch but did accept a cup of tea.

At first glance, Fiona Danielson looked far too young to have a son in his midtwenties. However, a closer look showed the fine lines at her eyes and lips, and the gray around her temples indicated she was probably in her early to midforties. She had light gray eyes. Her hands were hard and calloused. She wore her hair in an asymmetrical bob. It wasn't until she turned her head at a certain angle that I noticed the scar that ran from her left temple down the side of her face to her chin.

"Leroy said you two wanted to ask me questions about the break-in." She sat very straight and folded her arms across her chest. "Well, I'll tell you the same thing I told the manager. I didn't take nothing, and if anyone says I did, they're a liar."

April reached out a hand and gave her arm a reassuring squeeze. "We weren't accusing you of taking anything."

Mrs. Danielson uncoiled like a spring. "Well, then what do you want to know?"

I glanced at April to take the lead in the questioning.

April smiled. "Mrs. Danielson, we—"

"Call me Fiona, dearie."

"Fiona, I heard that there was a break-in here at the hotel, but when my officer arrived, he was told the hotel didn't want to file a report. Now, I don't know if it's connected in any way to the man who was murdered, but he was staying here too. So,

I'd just like to make sure that the two events aren't linked in any way."

Fiona Danielson glanced around and then leaned forward. "It's funny you should say that because I think there was a connection."

"Why do you think the two were connected?" I asked.

"Because we never had no break-ins before. Not here at the Carson Law. It's a quiet neighborhood, and the guests are . . . well, you only get a certain type of clientele here. Not many folks can afford the rates." She sipped her tea. "I been working here twelve years. Never had no break-ins. No trouble of any kind. Then, we get a break-in and the room ransacked. Next thing you know that rich toff goes and gets himself killed. Well, if you ask me, that's mighty funny."

We stared at Mrs. Danielson as if she'd cast a spell. I was the first to break free.

"Are you saying the room that was broken into belonged to the same man who was murdered? Clayton Davenport?"

She nodded. "That's exactly what I'm saying."

CHAPTER 20

April was at a loss for words. "But that's . . . I mean, the hotel should have reported it. How?"

"Excuse me, Mrs. Danielson," I said. "I don't mean any disrespect, but how do you know all of this?"

"Because I was there. I was one of the first people on the scene after the break-in was discovered."

April and I exchanged a glance, then we waited for Fiona Danielson to continue.

"I usually work the day shift. There's only seventeen guest rooms, and typically, not all of them are occupied. Not much needed from housekeeping at night that the front desk can't handle. But with the Spring Festival starting, we're full up, and the manager, Mr. Appleton, asked for volunteers to help out." She sipped her tea. "I've been saving up my money for a trip home to visit me mum, so I could use the extra money. That's why I volunteered."

The waiter brought our food and verified that Fiona didn't want anything to eat before he left.

"No point in your food getting cold. Eat up." Fiona waved

for us to eat and then glanced around to make sure no one was within earshot. "The Studebaker and Upton Suites are in the east wing. They're the best rooms. Mr. Davenport was in the Upton Suite. It's a mite bigger than the Studebaker, with a private balcony that leads to the outside."

She topped up her tea and took a sip before continuing. "We had a late checkout in the Studebaker Suite, and I had just about got it finished when I came out into the hall and heard that Mr. Davenport swearing like a sailor. He came out, took one look at me, and then accused me of breaking into his room and trying to rob him. He claimed the Carson Law Inn was nothing but a fleabag shack and . . . well, he just ripped us apart." She shivered.

"How horrible," April said. "I'm so sorry he lashed out at you."

"That's the way of it. Someone misplaces a pair of expensive sunglasses, and they blame the maid. Drop their cell behind the nightstand, must be housekeeping." She shook her head. "Well, I told him in no uncertain terms that not only had I *not* taken one scrap of paper, but I was more than willing to go through a full search." Her eyes wide, she huffed. "That's when I pulled out my phone and called the police and then the manager. I *demanded* that someone come at once and search my cart, my pockets, and, if necessary, I was willing to strip down to me knickers so no one could say I took anything."

April's lips twitched, but she got them under control. "That was smart."

"Then I held up my keys. I have keys to get into any room in this building. Why would I need to break a window?"

"What did Mr. Davenport have to say to that?" I asked.

"Well, he backed down in a hurry. Mr. Appleton was too busy apologizing to Mr. Davenport to take notice of the likes of me. He just kept talking about *the reputation of the Carson Law Inn* and how *nothing like this had ever happened here be-*

fore. He's right about that. We never did have any trouble with thieves, but I suppose there's always a first time." She sipped her tea. "Anyway, by the time the police arrived, that Mr. Davenport had done a complete one-eighty. He didn't want a police report. He didn't want to file any complaints. He even apologized to me." She leaned forward. "He even tried to buy me off."

"How?" I asked.

"Smiled real big and said he didn't mean to accuse me of stealing. Claimed he was just . . . upset. Then, he pulled out his wallet and offered me money for my inconvenience." She pursed her lips as though she'd just sucked a lemon. "God knows I could have used the money, but there was no way I was letting him clear his conscience. Oh no, I took those bills and left them right there on his desk. Then I turned and marched right outta that room." She paused. "I have my dignity, and there's just some things that money can't buy."

"I'm so sorry," April said.

"What happened next?" I asked.

"I told Mr. Appleton, just as soon as I finished cleaning the Tippecanoe Suite, I wanted someone to go in and verify that nothing was missing and then I was leaving and wanted my last wage packet."

"Oh no," we said.

She chuckled. "That got his knickers in a twist. Anyway, he comes into the Studebaker suite and follows me around like a puppy, apologizing and begging me to stay." She shook her head. "I'd calmed down a lot by then. So, I told him I'd stay. I came out of the Studebaker and locked the door, and you'll never guess what I found in my cart."

"Money?" April asked.

She nodded. "You got it. That git must have slipped it in the cart while we were doing the other room. Well, that just got me het up all over again. So, I marched over there and knocked on the door, prepared to toss the money back in his face, but the latch must not have caught on the door. So, when I knocked, it just pushed open. That Mr. Davenport was on the phone with his back to the door, so he didn't hear or see me. But I heard him."

"What did he say?" April asked.

"Well, I'm not one to eavesdrop on conversations. The Carson Law is very strict about guest privacy."

"Of course, we know you'd never deliberately listen in on a conversation, but this is really important. And if you heard anything, it would be really helpful."

Fiona Danielson pondered for a moment.

"It could be really helpful to Leroy," I said.

That settled it. She glanced around and leaned forward. "I heard him say, *I know you took the photo and those papers, and I want them back, tonight.* Then he laughed." She shivered. "It wasn't what he said, but the way he said it, and then that laugh . . . I can tell you, that sent a chill right down my spine. Well, I just turned around and left. I put the money in an envelope, and I was going to give it back to him the very next day. But . . ." She shrugged.

"But he was killed," April said.

Fiona turned bright red and nodded. There was something more she wasn't saying. She kept her head down and didn't make eye contact with April, but I had an idea.

"Davenport, April's husband, was dead," I said. "And you were afraid that maybe the police might think Leroy was involved?"

She sighed and then nodded. "They had to know how he cared for her. And then if they found out that Mr. Davenport accused his mum of stealing and I was found with the money, well . . . I don't know, but it just seemed like I'd be mucking up dirt that might cause more trouble for my boy." She leaned toward me. "Leroy's a good boy. He wouldn't hurt a fly." She reached into her pocket and pulled out an envelope. She handed it to April. "I guess this belongs to you now."

April stared at the envelope as though it were a snake.

"Mrs. Danielson, it's obvious that Mr. Davenport wanted you to have this money," I said. "He gave it to you himself. I think you should keep it."

April slid the envelope back across the table. "Yes. I'm sure that would be best."

"Do you think I should report it?"

"I think if the police question you, then you should be honest and tell them the truth. However, I don't think there's any need to volunteer anything."

"That's what Leroy said. When I told him about it, he told me to tell you two and follow your instructions." Fiona slipped the envelope back into her pocket. She glanced at the time. "I better get to work."

"Mrs. Danielson, I don't suppose you know who Mr. Davenport was talking to, do you?"

She blushed. "No idea. To be completely honest, I wondered if he mightn't have been talking to you."

April frowned. "Me? What gave you that idea?"

"I heard him say, *Don't deny you took them. I know you too well. I'm sure the people of New Bison won't be happy if those papers became public, and they might just vote you out on your ear.*" She shrugged and walked away.

The color drained from April's face.

CHAPTER 21

It took several minutes before the color returned to April's cheeks enough to ease my fear that she wasn't about to pass out, despite her reassurances that she was okay.

She ran her fingers through her hair. "I'm just tired. I haven't slept, and I guess everything's just catching up with me."

It seemed logical. I was rather tired myself, but I still needed to figure out a recipe, and I had a date.

"Plus, I got a call from Clayton's personal assistant. He wants to discuss funeral arrangements."

"I don't want to sound rude, but isn't there someone else? I mean, you haven't seen him in eight years. Surely, he made other arrangements."

"I don't know. He didn't have any close family." She heaved a sigh and hoisted herself up. "He's dead. Helping to get him buried is the least I can do."

Outside, we made plans to meet and discuss everything the next day. Before we parted, April leaned close. "Did you know Leroy's mother was British?"

"No idea. I wonder if he is too."

"You think you know someone and then . . . you learn something new about them."

"I wonder if his father's British."

"I don't think he grew up with his dad around. At least he always talks about it being just him and his mom."

We said our goodbyes, and I elicited her promise to call if she needed anything.

For a few seconds, I wondered if I should follow her, just to make sure she made it home safely. *Was that too much? I trusted her. It's not like she'd been drinking.* By the time I made up my mind, April had pulled out of the parking lot and was halfway down the street.

One glance at my watch told me that I didn't have much time and better get back. I had a chocolate cake and four dozen thumbprint cookies to make for Trooper Bob's daughter's party.

I never baked before moving to New Bison, but since coming here and finding Aunt Octavia's recipes, I found it enjoyable. Mixing flour, sugar, eggs, and butter together and getting something yummy was somehow comforting. It was magical. Almost all of those ingredients tasted horrible if you ate them one by one. Even the dark baking chocolate and cocoa were bitter. However, mix them together and heat, and something truly amazing happened. Every time I pulled a cake from the oven, I was awed. I created that. Today was no different. The kitchen smelled chocolatey and sweet. If Baby were here, he'd be licking his lips, barely able to contain himself while saliva dripped from the corners of his mouth.

Thinking about Baby put a smile on my face. I had no idea how that dog stole my heart after only a few months. My smile was short-lived. My big boy was sick . . . lovesick. People didn't die from a broken heart in real life, but losing someone you cared about changed you. From everything I'd heard, my dad had once been a happy, carefree, extremely funny man when he met my mom. After she died, something inside him died too. I thought of the super serious career-military man who barely cracked a smile. Laughing was completely out of the question. *When was the last time I'd actually heard the Admiral laugh?* I racked my brain but couldn't remember ever hearing him just let loose with a good belly laugh. That settled things. *I can't let that happen to Baby.*

I put the cakes on a baking rack to cool, wiped my hands, and searched through my recent calls for the number for Daisy's owner. It didn't take long to get to a number I didn't recognize as a friend.

I pushed Call before I could think myself out of it.

"Hello."

"Hello, is this Mrs. Castleton? Sybil Castleton?"

"Speaking."

Her voice sounded cold, but I ignored it. After all, this was for Baby. "Mrs. Castleton, this is Madison Montgomery, Baby's owner."

"Yes. Madison, dear, how are you? And how's that great big hunk of a mastiff, Baby?"

Her voice suddenly oozed sugary sweet and phony. I rolled my eyes. *Don't call me dear.* "Baby's been rather sad. He really liked Daisy."

"I just knew those two would hit it off. The moment I saw him, I just knew he was the ideal candidate to sire Daisy's litter."

I took a deep breath and gritted my teeth. "I'm sure you're right. When did you say Daisy's next heat cycle was?"

"Oh . . . I don't really know. Let me see, sweetie."

Red flag number 412. I may not have been involved with

dogs and breeding long, but every breeder who had females knew exactly when they went into heat. "Do you remember when she was in heat last?" *And don't call me sweetie.*

"Umm . . . well, no. I don't really handle that."

Red flag number 413. How do you not handle that? Okay, maybe I am being too critical because I don't like her. Maybe she has someone who manages those things. "Okaaay, is there someone else I should talk to?"

"Umm . . . well, there was . . . but . . . he's not . . . I mean, I just don't know. Maybe I should call you back. Yeah, I think that would be best. I'll get in touch with . . . with my . . . hmm—"

"Breeder?"

"Yes. That's the word I was looking for. I'll get in touch with my breeder and call you back real soon, sweetie."

If she calls me sweetie one more time I'm going to . . . I unclenched my jaw. "Great. Do you need my phone number?" *Or my name, so you can use it rather than these stupid terms of endearment that mean absolutely nothing.*

"No, I have everything I need. Thanks for calling, dear."

I hung up and took several deep breaths to loosen the furl of my brow. *It's all for Baby. I'm doing this for Baby.* I rubbed my temples and tried to shake it off. The Sybil Castleton I spoke to was different than the one I'd talked to earlier. She sounded vague and confused. I certainly don't remember her using all of those "sweeties" and "dears" before.

I got a text from Michael. He was finishing up at the clinic, and he and Baby would be here shortly.

Yikes. Where had the time gone. I pulled off my apron and hurried upstairs to get ready.

I hopped in the shower and washed off the rest of the chocolate cake and frosting.

I went simple—in a form-fitting, pastel-striped jersey dress by Sergio Hudson, with gold sandals—so I could focus on my hair and makeup. By the time I was finished, I had a look that would work regardless of where we went in New Bison. In the three months that I'd been in New Bison and dating Michael Portman, I'd learned to be flexible in my attire. This outfit would be appropriate for walking on the beach, sitting at a burger joint, or eating coq au vin at La Petite Maison, the *only* French restaurant in New Bison. Michael appreciated good food, but he wasn't fussy. Regardless, he would appreciate the way the dress hugged my curves, and I would enjoy being with him.

I heard him and Baby in the kitchen and yelled, "Don't touch that cake. It's for a customer."

When I entered the kitchen, he was poised above the cake with a huge knife.

"Stop!"

He turned around and hid the knife behind his back. "I didn't touch it."

"I have to take that to a customer tomorrow. Please tell me you didn't cut it."

He ogled me. "You look amazing."

"Don't change the subject." I crossed my arms and waited. "Back away from the cake."

He stepped to the side and grinned.

I examined the cake and couldn't see any damage.

"I was just going to take a small sliver. You could stitch it together and your customer would never be the wiser."

"Dr. Portman, you may be able to stitch up a cat or dog after surgery, but you can't stitch a cake back together, no matter how small of a sliver you take out."

"Never mind the cake. I think I've found something else I'd like to nibble." He pulled me close and spent a few passionate moments heating up the kitchen. "Are you sure you want to go out tonight? Maybe we should stay in."

I chuckled and pulled away. "Oh no you don't. I'm starving."

Baby sniffed his food dish and then walked over to his dog bed and climbed in.

"How is he?" I asked. "Did you run the blood work?"

"Everything came out fine." He spoke about red and white blood cell counts, platelets, and a lot of other medical mumbo jumbo.

"I have no idea what any of that means," I said when he stopped to take a breath.

"It means he's perfectly healthy."

"Then what's wrong with him?"

"Nothing as far as I can tell. He's perfect. He's healthy. Of course, you're welcome to get a second opinion. I could recommend—"

I took his face in my hands and gazed into his eyes. "I don't need a second opinion. I trust you."

He nodded, and his shoulders relaxed. "I know you're just concerned about Baby, but he's fine . . . physically."

I took a deep breath and glanced at Baby. "Physically? What are you saying?"

"I'm saying there's nothing physically wrong with him. So, maybe his problem isn't physical. Maybe it's emotional. Maybe he's depressed." He glanced at Baby. "I researched his symptoms, and I even called my C.O. He said dogs can exhibit behavior consistent with depression in humans."

"You called your commanding officer? From the Army?"

"Yeah. I was an animal care specialist. My C.O. knew more about animals than anyone I've known either before or since."

"Did he have any recommendations?"

"Antidepressants."

I frowned. "I don't like the idea of pills. Surely, there's something else?"

"Diet. Exercise. The usual." He shrugged. "I'll keep looking. I promise. I care about Baby too."

"I know you do. Let's go eat, and we can talk about it."

I led Baby up to my bedroom. He climbed in bed, and I turned the television to his favorite show, a British sitcom, *Absolutely Fabulous*, or *Ab Fab*.

One of the things I found most surprising about this area in Southwest Michigan was the number of wineries. Neither Michael nor I were wine connoisseurs, but I was new to the area, and he was helping me get acquainted with it by showing me all of its attractions. The Spring Festival was taking advantage of the wineries by having a wine tasting and competition. The location rotated each year. This year, New Bison Vineyard was hosting the event. It was a working vineyard with a restaurant. Tonight, we headed to dinner at the restaurant. After dinner, we could explore the tents and sample the local wines.

New Bison Vineyard and Restaurant was a fully functioning winery surrounded by acres of grapevines tied in rows. Spring was too early for fruit, but the canes were pruned and tied to supports in preparation for the growing season. There was a massive tent and signs directing the Spring Festival attendees to a gravel lot down the road, where they could park and take a shuttle back to the vineyard. We had reservations at the restaurant and ignored the signs.

A barricade across the narrow dirt driveway stopped everyone who attempted to enter the winery. The young freckle-faced New Bison policeman who always reminded me of Opie from *The Andy Griffith Show* approached the car with a clipboard.

He smiled when he recognized me. "Hi there, Miss Montgomery. You folks eating dinner?"

Michael assured him we had reservations. He confirmed that our names were indeed on the list before removing the barricade and permitting us to pass through.

"Did you have to undergo a background check to get to park near the building?" I said.

He laughed. "Nope, but I know people."

"Really? What did you have to promise them?"

"Me? Nothing. But I might need a few dozen thumbprint cookies."

"Done." I smiled. "Who knew cookies could be used as currency in these parts?"

A large red farmhouse sat near the back of the property. We pulled into a parking space and inhaled the earthy scent. The view of the lush green fields, with row after row of vines, and the red farmhouse, was picturesque. I stopped, pulled out my phone, and snapped a photo before making our way inside. #NewBisonVineyard #WineFoodAndFun #OneLucky-Girl

The lobby featured a large bar arranged for wine tasting and purchases. We turned toward the right and gave the hostess our names. She crossed us off the list, grabbed two menus, and led us to a table near the window where we could look out onto the fields.

The dining room was small, with only enough space for twenty tables. All twenty were occupied. Several of the guests recognized Michael and waved. I must have frowned.

"Does it bother you?" Michael said. "Living in a small town?"

I shook my head. "I miss having access to more shops and restaurants, but I kind of like it here. It reminds me of being on a military base."

"How? There are thousands of people on a military base."

"True, but there's only one Admiral Montgomery. So, even

though I didn't know all of the sailors, they all knew me . . . or at least they knew my dad."

"I can't wait to meet Admiral Montgomery."

"Are you kidding? You're joking, right?"

"No. I want to meet the man who raised you. Don't you think he'd approve? What's not to like?"

I thought for a few minutes. "He'll like that you're a veteran, although he won't be impressed by the fact that you're Army instead of Navy. He'll like that you're stable and have a good job."

"Well, that's something. Will I need to salute when we meet?"

"Only if you want to earn brownie points. He likes that sort of thing."

"I was joking. Geez! I mean, did he like your ex . . . Elliott?"

"Not really. He thought Elliott had a weak handshake, soft hands, and he hated that he had highlights in his hair." I stared at him. "Does it matter what he thinks?"

"Yes. I want your father to like me."

"Why? As long as I like you, that's all that matters."

He leaned across the table and kissed me. "Then, I'm glad you like me."

The waiter came and brought bread and water. He gave us the daily specials and waited for our orders. I couldn't make up my mind between the braised short ribs and the rainbow trout. So, Michael ordered one, and I ordered the other. That was one of the things I loved about him. He didn't mind that I had trouble making decisions. He used it to his advantage.

Orders placed, I glanced around the room. "Is that Mayor Abernathy over there having dinner with Marjorie Rivers?"

He followed my gaze. "Looks like it. Seems odd for the previous mayor's ex-wife and the current mayor to be dining together, doesn't it?"

"Technically, she's not his *ex-wife*. She's his . . . widow?"

"Don't look now, but Chris Russell's here with Candy Hurston at nine o'clock."

I took a sip of water and glanced to my left. "This could get pretty ugly if they get into a fight here in the restaurant. Why do you suppose they're all here?"

"The wine tasting is a big event. Folks come from all over to see which wine is crowned Best of the Region. For people who are into wines, the judges are well-known. Besides, for a town this size, the Spring Festival's a big deal. Pretty much everyone will be here. There's not much else to do."

"Leroy even convinced April to come to the tasting. She needs to get out of the house."

"Like I said, everyone comes to the festival, even if they don't drink." He reached inside his jacket and pulled out one of the brochures that had been passed around the city like lollipops for weeks.

I hadn't paid much attention to anything other than the baking contest. I took the brochure he handed me and looked at the section on wines. The names were foreign to me, but I recognized the impressive-looking medals that the judges wore draped around their necks. Apparently, winning here at the Spring Festival would qualify you to advance to the next level of judging for a more prominent award and so on.

"I had no idea the festival and the wine competition were such big events. No wonder Mayor Abernathy was so concerned about the Spring Festival being successful." I told Michael about my day and all of the information I'd discovered.

"Let me get this straight. Clayton Davenport and the mayor had an argument. You think Davenport was blackmailing Mayor Abernathy? But why? Clayton Davenport was rich. He didn't need money, and Jackson Abernathy certainly doesn't have any. Well, not compared to Davenport."

"I don't think Davenport was blackmailing Abernathy for money. I think there was something else that he wanted."

"What?"

"I don't know, but when we figure out what it was, then we should be able to figure out who murdered Davenport."

CHAPTER 22

Our waiter brought our food, and all conversation about murder ceased. The food looked fantastic, and I managed to stop Michael from digging in long enough for me to snap a photo. **#GoodFood #GoodCompany #ItsWhatsForDinner #NewBisonWineryCooks**

Both entrées were delicious. The braised short ribs were tender and flavorful, but my favorite was the pan-seared rainbow trout. It was topped with crab, capers, and a lemon beurre blanc that was creamy, light, and refreshing. I didn't have room for dessert, but Michael ordered cheesecake and two forks. Another reason why I loved him.

"Did you talk to the mayor about Baby?"

"He wasn't at all helpful, but I decided to just swallow my objections and let Baby . . . service Daisy." I still hadn't come to terms with my dog's life as a stud dog, although his fees were quite substantial.

I shared the weird conversation I'd had with Daisy's owner. "Is that common? I mean, the other breeders that contract for

Baby's services are all very knowledgeable and at least know when their dog is going to be in heat."

"Maybe she's one of those wealthy dog owners who own the dogs and pay for everything, but they pay a professional handler to take care of the dog."

"Is that a thing?" I asked as I took my fork and sliced a generous portion of cheesecake.

"It is, but generally the handler is the one who makes arrangements for the stud services."

The cheesecake was light and melted on my tongue. I must have moaned. When I opened my eyes, Michael was smiling. "Do you need a moment alone with that?"

I licked my fork and put it down. When I glanced at the cheesecake, I saw that I'd eaten about two-thirds of it. "I'm sorry."

He smiled. "I don't need more than this. I've got that half-Ironman coming up."

"Don't you need to put on weight for that?"

"Not all calories are created equal. I need the right type of calories."

I listened while he talked about the competition and his training. Michael was in good physical condition but wanted to test his limits.

I sipped my coffee and my mind wandered.

"Earth to Maddy."

"I'm sorry. I really am. What were you—"

He waved away my protest. "When I went home to change, my grandmother was making sweet potato tarts for Marjorie Rivers. I just wondered if you'd figured out what you wanted to make for the Spring Festival."

"Not yet. I was leaning toward entering Aunt Octavia's Chocolate Soul Cake, but Clayton Davenport got the rules changed." I told him what I'd overheard while at the mayor's office.

"Well, Clayton Davenport's dead. That should take some of the pressure off. You don't have to enter the baking competition at all, if you don't want to."

I sighed. "I know, but . . . I want to. I mean, I want to prove that I can do it."

He reached across the table and squeezed my hand. "You don't have to prove anything to anyone, but if that's what you want to do, then let me know what I can do to help."

I don't think I've ever loved anyone more. The Admiral was great at making sure all of my material needs were met. However, never had I had anyone who cared so much about making sure that I was emotionally supported. I was on the verge of tears. "I'm going to cry. Excuse me." I got up and hurried toward the ladies' room.

The ladies' room was part of a newer addition to the farmhouse, which meant it was built in the twentieth century instead of the nineteenth century like the rest of the stone building. It was surprisingly large for a restaurant this size, with stalls that turned a corner and wrapped around the back of the room. I was further surprised to find the room empty. Sadly, the ventilation wasn't the greatest, and the staff usually propped a transom window open to help the airflow. The tissue dispenser hadn't been refreshed recently, and it wasn't until I turned the corner that I found tissue to clean away the raccoon rings left by my mascara. In the spirit of not letting the opportunity pass, I entered one of the back stalls to take care of business. The stalls were narrow, and women the size of an anorexic supermodel would have had to turn sideways to squeeze past the toilet-paper dispenser and a mammoth-size box that had been added for disposing of feminine products, while still navigating around the toilet. You had to be thin and extremely agile. Having spent most of my life on naval bases, I'd seen much worse. On the positive side, it was indoors. There were no snakes. And it didn't require the use of a Folger's Coffee tin. All positives. Plus, I am fairly agile, so I managed the acrobatic entry with ease. I was just finishing when I heard what sounded like a whispered argument coming from outside the open transom window next to my stall. I didn't think anything about it until "Clayton's dead" drifted through the window and over my door stall. I strained to hear more.

"Look, love. I was hired to do a job, and I've done it. Now, Clayton's dead. Job over."

I didn't need to see her face to recognize Sybil Castleton. Apparently, I wasn't the only person she called "love," "sweetie," and "dear." The other voice was softer and harder to recognize.

"No. No way, dearie. I want to get my money and get out of here. I'm done. I must have been a nut to agree to this craziness in the first place. If I hadn't needed the money so badly, you can bet your life that I never would have gotten myself messed up in this crazy scheme."

The other person said something else that I couldn't make out. Frustrated, I slipped the lock on the stall and gently eased the door open, careful not to let it swing too loudly. Unfortunately, the door hinges hadn't been oiled, and the door squeaked.

"What was that? Oh, Lawd, someone's here. I'm gone. I want my money. You can keep the horse and everything else. You got that, love? Either I get my money or I'm going to do what I should have done in the first place, go straight to the police."

The door opened, and two women entered the restroom. They were laughing and not paying any attention to me as I hurried around the corner and outside. There was a door a few feet from the ladies' room that led outside. I hurried through, but I was too late. Sybil Castleton and whoever she was talking to were gone. I rushed back inside and back to the main dining room and took a good look around. Sybil Castleton was nowhere to be seen.

Michael rushed over to where I was. "What's wrong? You look like you've seen a ghost."

"That's the problem. I didn't see a ghost or anyone else, but I might have just overheard a killer."

CHAPTER 23

I quickly filled Michael in on what I'd overheard. We ran outside and scanned the parking lot, but the sun had set. The winery had lights strung up outside and inside the tents, but it was still dim. As we'd been inside eating, the grounds had filled up with people. If Sybil Castleton was here, we couldn't find her.

Back inside, we returned to our table and took a closer look around at our fellow diners. The problem was there were a lot of familiar faces. People I knew as patrons of Baby Cakes Bakery or that Michael knew from his veterinary practice. Some were friends. A few were strangers, but no one acted overly suspicious.

Michael paid the bill, and we walked around the lobby and through the wine tasting room and gift shop. Again, we saw familiar faces, but Sybil Castleton wasn't one of them.

We went outside and walked around the tents. I couldn't focus on the tables set up for tasting, or the judges who were the center attraction at the event. My focus was in scanning the crowds for Sybil Castleton while trying to figure out whatever devious plot Clayton Davenport had hatched and Sybil's role in it.

"Are you sure you didn't recognize anything that will give you a clue about who she was talking to?"

I thought for several moments but eventually gave up. I shook my head. "Nothing. Whoever it was, they kept their voice low. I couldn't even be sure if it was a man or a woman."

"Maybe we should tell Trooper Bob and let him look into it."

"What are we going to say? I was in the bathroom and over-heard someone I thought was Sybil Castleton demanding money from someone?"

"Yes."

"He'd laugh me out of his office. Seriously, she said she was hired to do a job and now Clayton was dead. She wanted her money and was leaving. There's nothing illegal in anything she said." In explaining everything to Michael, I realized that I truly didn't have anything that connected Sybil to Clayton's murder. "It was more the feeling behind her words than the actual words themselves."

"I still think you should tell Trooper Bob."

"Have you met him?"

"I take care of his dog."

"Let me guess. He looks like a German shepherd man to me."

He chuckled. "Chihuahua, actually."

"Okay, I was stereotyping. I apologize. He just seems like a big dog kind of guy."

"You never can tell about people. I'm sure most folks would never look at you and say, *I'll bet she has a two-hundred-fifty-pound English mastiff.*"

"Touché."

Michael must have sensed that the mood had changed. We'd planned to enjoy the wine tasting, but that wasn't going to happen. Often after a romantic dinner, we drove to the lake and looked at the waves or walked on the beach, but tonight there wouldn't be a romantic interlude at Lake Michigan.

He pulled me into an embrace. "I know you've got a lot on your mind. Between Clayton Davenport's murder and Trooper Bob sniffing around you, April, and Leroy, it's got to be hard to focus on anything else right now. Plus, I know you're worried about the baking contest. Just tell me what I can do to help."

I snuggled close. "It's enough to know that you believe in me, but . . ."

"What?"

"I could use a good sous-chef."

"Actually, I have a lot of skills."

"Really? Like what?"

"It would be easier if I showed you." He kissed me, and for several moments the world stood still.

When we came up for air, I gazed into his eyes and realized that a romantic interlude wasn't completely out of the question. We locked hands and headed to his car. We were just about to his car when I noticed what appeared to be a bundle of clothes lying on the ground near the passenger door.

Michael stopped. "Stay here."

"Oh no you don't." I hurried to catch up to him. "We've had this discussion before. Classic slasher horror movie mistake. Never split up to investigate."

"Fine." He wasn't smiling, but he didn't try to stop me. "Stay behind me."

He didn't need to tell me twice. We approached the heap slowly, and I clung to his hand like plastic wrap.

Michael squatted down and turned the heap over.

What had once been Sybil Castleton lay on the ground. Her eyes bulged from her discolored face, which was permanently contorted into a grimace. A green scarf wrapped around her throat. Strangled.

A blood-curdling scream ripped through the air. It wasn't until Michael stood up and shook me that I realized I was the one screaming.

CHAPTER 24

People poured out of the tents in droves. Michael stood next to his car and held me close. I was shivering, and he slipped off his jacket and wrapped it around my shoulders.

April and Leroy were some of the first on the scene. April may have been suspended, but her training kicked in.

"You're hysterical," she said. "Do you need me to slap you?"

That sobered me up quickly. "No."

"Good." She gave me a quick hug and then went to work. She ordered everyone to step back away from the crime scene.

Opie arrived, and then moments later, the Pillsbury Doughboy trotted up. April immediately ordered them to work crowd control and protect the scene.

But she wasn't just firing off orders, she was multitasking. She whipped her cell phone out and immediately dialed for reinforcements and the county coroner. When she finished, she turned to Leroy and ordered him to take me inside and start pouring hot tea with sugar down my throat.

If she saw the scowl I threw her way, she didn't register it. Instead, she turned to talk to Michael.

Leroy may have worked for me, but he recognized the voice of authority when he heard it and shuffled me around the crowd and back inside the restaurant.

The bulk of the staff was standing around outside, but he found someone who wasn't curious who led us to a small employee lounge.

I was shaking and barely able to sip the disgustingly sweet tea, but Leroy didn't let that stop him. He had his orders. Whenever I faltered, he steadied my arm and helped me get the cup to my mouth.

After what felt like an hour, Trooper Bob marched in. He scowled at me as though I were the one who'd murdered Sybil Castleton.

He rocked on the balls of his feet and stared down at me. "I understand from Dr. Portman that you overheard a conversation he believes is pertinent to my investigation."

It was clear from his choice of words that he was only here because someone he respected, *Dr. Portman*, had told him to come.

There was a part of me that wanted to spew tea like a fountain, but I swallowed my pride along with a huge gulp of the disgusting brew. Trooper Bob had already threatened to arrest me once today for obstructing justice.

I opened my mouth, but before I could start to talk, there was a knock on the door.

Trooper Bob opened the door and in waltzed Chris Russell.

"I hope you aren't trying to interrogate my client without legal counsel," he said.

Trooper Bob growled but didn't say anything. He merely turned to me and waited.

I swallowed hard and took a deep breath. Then, I shared the conversation I'd overheard in the ladies' room.

When I finished, Trooper Bob frowned. He was silent for several seconds. "Is that it?"

I nodded. "That's it. Well . . . mostly."

He waited, and my habit of oversharing when I was nervous kicked in. That's when I shared the conversation I'd had earlier with Sybil Castleton about Baby. "Which was the main reason I'd gone to meet with Mayor Abernathy earlier today. I was worried about Baby because he hasn't been himself since he met Daisy, that's Mrs. Castleton's English mastiff . . . although, now I'm wondering if Daisy really is her dog. Michael thinks she might just be paying the bills, but she really isn't her dog—"

"Miss Montgomery, is there a point to this . . . babble? Because if not, I have a murder investigation to get to."

"Madison, I don't think you need to say anything more," Chris Russell said. He turned toward the state trooper. "Is there anything else?"

Trooper Bob grunted and marched out, muttering something that sounded like *Dumb as a bag of hammers*.

CHAPTER 25

Chris Russell spent five minutes lecturing me about not volunteering any information to the police. "Only answer questions that you're asked," he droned. And then he finished up with *never* talk to Trooper Bob, or any police, without legal counsel.

I assured him that I didn't plan to have any conversations with the police, with or without legal counsel.

However, a few minutes later, I was proven wrong when I went outside in search of Michael and found him in a confrontation with Trooper Bob.

"What do you mean I can't leave?" Michael folded his arms across his chest and stared down at Trooper Bob.

As a rule, Michael was even-tempered. Rarely had I seen him angry. In fact, this was a first. He'd been in the Army and deployed overseas. He'd seen unimaginable horrors, but he managed to stay positive and happy. Today, he was angry. His anger flashed in his eyes like a warning beacon, but Trooper Bob wasn't picking up on the signal.

"Your vehicle is part of my crime scene. It stays. As first on the scene, you're a witness, and you'll stay until we've finished our questions." He turned to me. "She's welcome to leave. I can have a patrol car take her home."

Michael swore. I'd heard plenty of soldiers swear, but again, this was another first in our relationship. He took a moment and explained exactly what Trooper Bob could do with his patrol car.

A vein on the side of Trooper Bob's head started to pound, and a purple wave moved up his neck and inflamed his ears. He reached inside his jacket and pulled out a tin of tobacco, took a pinch, and popped it in his mouth.

The men argued, and as much as I would have liked to have seen Trooper Bob knocked flat on his backside, I knew hitting a cop would *not* be a good career move.

Nose to nose and toe to toe, they argued.

"That's ridiculous. We found the body together. Why—" A lightbulb went on behind Michael's eyes. "Wait. You can't honestly believe Madison had anything to do with this murder?"

Trooper Bob squinted. "I didn't say she did, and I didn't say she didn't. But she argues with the first victim and then he's found with a knife in his back, and her fingerprints are on the weapon. She admits to talking to this victim earlier, and we only have her word for it that the conversation was amicable. Then she gives some cock-and-bull story about a conversation she overhears in the john, and then victim number two is found inches from your vehicle." He glared. "Frankly, I'm a fool for not locking her up right here and now. And I probably would have if it wasn't for that overzealous Clarence Darrow attorney."

The shock of hearing that Trooper Bob thought I had killed Clayton Davenport and Sybil Castleton had the opposite effect on me than it had on Michael. He was angry and clearly wanted nothing more than to put his fist through Trooper Bob's face, while hearing the accusations out loud simply tightened my resolve to find the killer. I needed to fire up my little gray cells. I put a hand on Michael's arm. I could feel the tension in his rock-solid bicep. "Stand down, soldier. It's okay."

"I'll make sure she gets home," Leroy said. "She can ride with me and April."

"I'm staying," April said. "There's work—"

Trooper Bob was shaking his head before the words were out of her mouth. "This is a crime scene—my crime scene. The only person with more of a reason to kill Clayton Davenport than she has"—he pointed to me—"was you."

April blanched. "What was my motive for killing Sybil Castleton?"

"Look, I don't have all of the threads tied up yet. Maybe you were helping out your friend. Or maybe you're a crazed serial killer. I don't rightly know, but I do know that you don't need to be anywhere near this active investigation as long as there's even the remotest chance that these two deaths are linked together."

April looked ready to spit bullets. One glance around and she swallowed whatever she was going to say. The crowds may have been held back by the yellow crime scene tape, but they were close enough to watch and hear the melodrama unfolding.

"Fine." She turned around and marched away.

"Was that really necessary?" I said.

"I'm investigating a murder," Trooper Bob said. "Two murders. And Sheriff Johnson may or may not have had anything to do with either one, but I have a job to do, and I mean to do it without any interference."

I turned to Michael. "You stay. I'm going home with Leroy. If it's not too late, swing by when they release your car."

He wasn't happy. He glared. He took deep breaths. Eventually, he must have seen the futility of the situation. He pulled me close and stared into my eyes. "Are you sure?"

"Yes. I'm sure." I hugged him. "Keep an eye on Trooper Bob and find out what he's up to."

"Is that it?"

"There is one more thing I need." I leaned closer and whispered in his ear. "Can you make sure Daisy is okay?"

"Make sure my girlfriend's dog's girlfriend is okay?" He grinned. "That's not exactly the sweet nothings I wanted to hear you whispering in my ear." He nibbled my earlobe. I could feel the warmth of his breath on my neck and a shiver went up my spine.

"What did you have in mind?"

He whispered something, and I didn't need a mirror to know that I was blushing.

Trooper Bob walked to the edge of the crime scene tape and spat. "All right. You two are steaming up my crime scene."

Nothing kills a romantic mood faster than the sound of a large wad of tobacco hitting the ground. We pulled apart, and I followed Leroy to his car.

April and Leroy must not have made reservations at the restaurant because he'd been forced to park quite a long distance away.

Leroy glanced down at my shoes. "Sorry, I could go get the car and pick you up, if you want to wait—"

I shook my head. "No way are you leaving me out here alone with a killer on the loose."

He glanced around anxiously. "I shouldn't have let April go off by herself. Do you think—"

"Not the same situation. April's the sheriff. She's probably packing heat, and she looked mad enough to shoot anyone who looked at her cross-eyed. Frankly, I pity the fool stupid enough to attack her."

We eventually made our way to Leroy's car and found April sitting on the hood.

"You okay?" I asked.

"I have never wanted to shoot anyone more than I wanted to shoot Trooper Bob." She hung her head down. "Mostly because he was right."

"Which part? The part about me killing Clayton Davenport? Or where I killed both Clayton and Sybil Castleton?"

"No. Of course I don't believe you had anything to do with either murder."

"Okay, what was he right about?"

"The part about it being his investigation. I mean, it is his case, not mine. I am too close to the murder victim, and shouldn't be anywhere near it." She took a deep breath and glanced through her lashes at me. "I heard today that the district attorney's office is reopening the investigation into Bradley Ellison's death."

Brad Ellison had been a real estate developer who had come to New Bison from Chicago with dreams of selling all of the lakefront property to some big-city developers. "Why on earth would they do that? And what could Bradley Ellison possibly have to do with Clayton Davenport?"

A couple passed by on their way to their car, cutting April's explanation short. "Let's go home."

We all got in the car, and while Leroy drove, April told us that Trooper Bob had found Brad Ellison's contact information in Clayton's phone.

"That makes sense if Clayton Davenport was one of the wealthy investors Brad was always bragging about," I said.

"It also explains how Clayton figured out where I was," April said.

We beat around a lot of ideas, but nothing rang a bell. By the time Leroy pulled into the driveway, my mind was spinning a hundred miles an hour.

I went to get Baby to let him out while April made tea and Leroy pulled thumbprint cookies out of the pantry.

We had just sat down at the table when there was a knock on the back door.

"Who could it be at this time of night?" I glanced at my

watch. Then I saw Baby standing at the back door with his tail wagging. "Whoever it is, Baby knows them and likes them."

I opened the door and found Alma Hurston.

"I'm sorry to bother you so late at night, but I saw the lights and took a chance that you were up."

Alma Hurston lived next door and was Candy's mother. Alma was petite with white downy hair and blue eyes. Tonight, those blue eyes, which were normally calm, were turbulent.

"Mrs. Hurston, what's wrong? Come in. Have a seat?" I pulled out a chair and urged her to sit.

"What's happened? I got a text from Candy that someone was murdered at the wine tasting." She paced back and forth. "I tried to text back, and I never got a response. I saw you posted from the winery. Were you there? Is she okay? Who was murdered?" Alma Hurston fired questions at the speed of sound.

"A woman named Sybil Castleton was murdered. As far as I know, Candy is fine. I saw her with Chris Russell."

Like a balloon that's been deflated, Alma Hurston flopped down onto the seat. Tears streamed down her face. "Thank God." She must have realized how that sounded, and she quickly corrected herself. "I don't mean thank God that poor woman was killed. I have just been so worried about Candy. I wasn't sure . . . I mean, I was afraid that someone . . . well, you know, after Paul and then this Clayton Davenport man . . . it was nerve-racking."

April handed her a tissue, and Leroy poured her a cup of tea.

I reached over and squeezed her arm. "It's all right. We understand. You were worried about your daughter's safety. That's natural."

"Thank you." She sniffed. "I guess I'm just overwrought between learning that Candy and Paul weren't really married and then Marjorie showing up after all these years with that slime-ball." She gasped and looked up at April. "I'm sorry."

April waved off her apology. "It's okay. I agree with your assessment."

"I intended to get with Candy to find out how things are going," I said. "I know Chris Russell got some type of legal order that allowed her to stay in her apartment."

Alma paused. "He did, which is good but . . . I just can't help thinking he's got ulterior motives."

I stole a glance in April's direction. "What do you mean?"

She gave a discreet cough. "I might just be an overprotective mother. That's what Candy says, but he's been wining and dining her. He sends her flowers and takes her for rides in his expensive sports car." She dabbed at her eyes and took a sip of tea. "That's bound to turn her head. Plus, she's still in mourning. It's only been three months since she lost her husband . . . well, Paul."

"It does seem a bit soon, but maybe it's not that serious. Maybe they're just good friends."

"You think so? I mean, I don't have anything against Chris Russell, except he's older than Candy and was good friends with Paul Rivers."

I didn't believe that for one minute, but I lied like a rug. "Sure, you know just because a man and woman hang out together doesn't mean there's . . . well, you know."

Leroy stood behind Mrs. Hurston and made a motion that indicated he thought I'd lost all of my marbles, and April made a motion that indicated my nose was going to start growing like Pinocchio any minute. Regardless of what my friends thought, Mrs. Hurston appreciated my lies. She finished her tea, gave Baby a scratch behind his ears that made his leg jiggle, and then got up and said she'd better get home.

When she was gone, April turned to me. "You are too smart to believe that Chris Russell and Candy Hurston are just *friends*." She used air quotes around *friends*. "Geez. The only reason he was able to get to Baby Cakes so quickly the night Clayton Davenport died was because he was next door with Candy."

"Did you honestly want me to tell her that the only reason Candy hadn't been arrested for killing Clayton Davenport was because she'd been . . . entertaining Chris Russell at the time of the murder and had an alibi?"

"I guess not."

My phone vibrated. I had a text from Michael.

Squid, Red Team, over.

I smiled and typed. **Go ahead, Red Team, over.**

Tango acquired, break.

I didn't have long to wait for the rest of his message.

Oscar Mike, over.

Wilco, over.

Roger, out.

April and Leroy waited for the translation.

"That was Michael. He has Daisy and is on his way."

A few moments later, Baby stood up and went to the back door. His tail wagged, and he gave a short, deep bark.

A few moments later, I opened the door, and Michael came in with an English mastiff that was so much smaller than Baby, I might have thought her a mere puppy.

For a few short moments, chaos ensued. Baby leapt in the air, and the two dogs greeted each other with barks, butt sniffs, and a rousing game of chase. We watched the happy reunion.

Baby bounced up and down and playfully nipped at Daisy's ears until she chased him through the kitchen, around the dining room, and back through the kitchen.

I picked up my phone and snapped a few pictures.

#EnglishMastiffsAtPlay #IHeartEnglishMastiffs #BabyFindsTrueLove

Eventually, the two dogs tired, and after downing a bowl of water, Daisy climbed on Baby's bed and made herself comfortable.

That broke the spell, and I leaned over and kissed Michael. "Thank you."

"My pleasure." He grinned. "Although, I think Trooper Bob was even more grateful than you."

I raised a brow. "Really?"

He chuckled. "Yeah. When I first suggested that I should go with him to Sybil Castleton's house, he pitched a fit." Michael puffed out his cheeks and mimicked Trooper Bob's accent and tone. "*No way a civilian is going to interfere with my investigation . . . blah, blah, blah.*"

He relaxed his cheeks and laughed. "After I mentioned that Sybil Castleton had an English mastiff that might not take kindly to strangers entering her house, he changed his mind."

I glanced over at Daisy, who was now curled up with Baby on the dog bed. "But she's so tiny. Surely, he wasn't afraid of a sweet girl like that?"

"I might have exaggerated a bit."

"Exaggerated how?" Leroy asked. "She may not be as big as Baby, but she's still a big dog."

"I know that. And you know that. But Trooper Bob had never seen her."

April sat on the ground in front of the dog bed and scratched Daisy's ears.

"But she's such a sweetie."

"She's sweet now, but I can tell you when Trooper Bob got to Sybil Castleton's house, she was not the pussycat you see before you."

I glanced at Daisy, meekly lying in the dog bed with Baby curled up beside her. An image of a different Baby came to mind. Instead of my gentle giant resting with his head on Daisy's backside, a vision of a fierce beast came to mind. Teeth bared. Drool drooping from the sides of his mouth like foam, and a look in his eyes that meant death. I'd only seen that side of Baby once while he leapt to my defense. I shivered. "What happened?"

"I went in first. Fortunately, I keep a towel in the trunk for drool remediation, and it had Baby's scent. I grabbed it and prayed she would remember me. She barked a bit, but as soon as she smelled the towel, her tail started wagging, and I was able to get a leash on her and get her in my car." He chuckled. "You should have seen the look on Trooper Bob's face. For a split second, I was afraid Trooper Bob was going to kiss me."

I reached up and kissed him again. "Thank you."

He reached for me, but I sidestepped. We had business to tend to.

"Now, soldier. Report."

He snapped to attention. Clicked his heels and saluted.

I gave him a playful swat and offered him a plate of thumbprint cookies, which he quickly grabbed. He shoveled about half a dozen in his mouth, quickly chewed, and washed them down with cup of tea that Leroy poured for him.

"Trooper Bob doesn't really think that April or I murdered Sybil Castleton, does he?" I asked.

He glanced sideways at April and took another sip of tea. He inclined his head toward me. "I don't think he believes you did it, although for some reason, he *really* wants it to be you."

I smiled.

"I assured him that apart from your trip to the ladies' room, you weren't out of my sight long enough to have murdered Sybil Castleton."

"Well, that's something," I said.

"So, he believes the two murders are connected?" April asked.

Michael nodded. "He does, but he doesn't know what the connection is yet. But New Bison is too small to have two suspicious murders within days of each other that aren't connected, unless there's a serial killer on the loose."

"He can't believe that. There's no indication that there's some crazed maniac roaming the streets of New Bison."

"I don't think he believes it. But he hasn't found the connection yet."

"What about the conversation Maddy overheard?" Leroy said. "Surely, that links the Castleton woman to Davenport."

"Look, he wasn't confiding his deepest thoughts to me. He knows I'm Team Maddy. I think he just wanted to get me alone to see if my story lined up with Maddy's before we had time to compare notes. Although, I did find out one thing."

"What?" I asked.

"I found out who Sybil Castleton was meeting at the wine tasting."

"Who?"

"Trooper Bob."

CHAPTER 26

There was a shocked pause that lasted for several beats. Then we all erupted like Mt. Vesuvius and fired questions.

He held up a white napkin and waved it like a flag of surrender. "Hold up."

April hopped up from the floor and paced the kitchen. "How is that possible? He should recuse himself. He can't investigate the murder of someone he was dating."

I folded my arms across my chest and frowned. "I thought he was married."

"When has that ever stopped a man from dating someone else?" April said.

"Whoa, Nellie," Michael said. "I didn't say he was dating her. I said she was there to meet him."

"What do you mean?"

"He said he got an anonymous call from a woman who claimed to have information about Clayton Davenport that might help find his killer. They agreed to meet at the wine tasting. He'd never seen her before. She told him she would wear a long green scarf."

The image of that scarf wrapped around Sybil Castleton's throat made me sick to my stomach. I closed my eyes and put my hand over my mouth. I felt myself being pulled down into a chair and my head pushed between my legs.

"Breathe, Squid. Slow. Deep breaths." Michael's voice was firm but soft.

I followed directions, and the nausea I felt just moments ago passed. When I was confident that I wouldn't puke, I sat up.

He looked me in my eyes. "You okay?"

"Fine. Thanks. And stop calling me Squid."

He grinned. "Now I know you're *really* okay."

Leroy handed me another cup of tea. I was sure I could float if I drank any more, but I didn't want to hurt his feelings. So, I smiled and took a sip.

"Did Trooper Bob mention why Sybil wanted to meet with him? He must have had some idea of what she was going to tell him?"

"If he did, he wasn't telling me."

"We need to figure this out."

Michael took a deep breath. "I think whatever we do, we're going to need to do it quickly."

"I agree, but why?"

"I overheard a conversation . . . well, an argument really, between him and the mayor. Trooper Bob wants to cancel the Spring Festival, he—"

"But he can't," April said. "It would destroy the town's economy."

"A lot of businesses have invested a lot of money in getting ready for this," Leroy said. "Plus, tourists come from miles away for it."

"He's right," April said. "Nearby towns have the Blossom-time Festival, the Harbor Shores Senior PGA Tournament, and the Winter Ice Sculptures. This is the only big event we have in New Bison."

Michael held up his hands. "I know. Mayor Abernathy pretty

much said the exact same things. Trooper Bob kept talking about public safety with a murderer on the loose. The problem is the mayor urged Trooper Bob to make an arrest."

"You mean he doesn't care if the wrong person is arrested?" I asked.

"Mayor Abernathy said an arrest will ease the public's mind, and it might lull the killer into a false sense of security, believing he or she had gotten away with two murders. Then, Trooper Bob could swoop in and nab the bad guy."

We stared at him.

"You're joking, right?" Leroy asked.

"That's so asinine, it had to come from that fool, Abernathy," April said.

I glanced at Michael. "Did the mayor have a recommendation for who this sacrificial lamb should be?"

April folded her arms and paced the kitchen. "Abernathy never did like me. He was always firmly in the *You're too pretty to be doing work like this* camp. I'd better go downstairs and grab my toothbrush. How long do I have?"

"Don't be daft," I said. "Trooper Bob hates me. He said as much at the winery. I'm the one who needs to grab a toothbrush."

Leroy stood up. "No way. There's no way I'm going to let him arrest either one of you. I'll confess."

We protested, but nothing shook Leroy's resolve. He simply dug his heels in and refused to budge. Eventually, he held up a hand to stop the conversation. "I didn't kill Clayton Davenport, although I would have loved to. And I didn't kill Sybil Castleton. You all know that. If we want this nightmare to end, then we need Maddy and April to figure out who really did kill them. You two are smart. You figured out who killed Paul Rivers, Garrett Kelley, and even Miss Octavia. You'll figure out who the killer is this time too. But you won't be able to do that if you're sitting in jail." He took a deep breath and gave a crooked grin. "Besides, it won't be my first time in jail."

CHAPTER 27

I don't know if I was more shocked by Leroy's courage or his revelation. *How did I not know he'd been in jail before? Did Aunt Octavia know?* Either way, I didn't have long to recover. Within minutes, there was a knock at the door.

Daisy and Baby woke up at the sound of the knocking, and Michael and I had our hands full containing the mastiffs. It took both of us to convince them to ignore the person knocking and to follow us into the bedroom. By the time we returned, I was sweating. Leroy and Trooper Bob were gone, and April was standing in the kitchen with tears running down her face.

April didn't want to talk. Instead, she said she just wanted to be alone and went downstairs.

"We've got to do something," I said.

"You will. We will." Michael stifled a yawn. "Give your little gray cells a rest tonight, and tomorrow we can figure out what to do."

One glance at the time showed me that it was after three in the morning. I didn't realize how exhausted I was until that point. My brain wasn't firing on all cylinders.

"You're right."

We said our goodnights, and Michael headed to the door.

"Umm, where do you think you're going?" I asked.

He turned. "I was going home, but if you want me to stay . . ." He winked.

I ignored the insinuation. "What about Daisy? I can't keep two English mastiffs. Baby is more than enough for me. Besides, Daisy doesn't know me. She knows you."

He walked back to the bedroom and opened the door. In the short time that we'd been gone, Daisy and Baby had curled up in my bed.

"Daisy, come."

Daisy lifted her head, stretched, and then hopped down. She trotted over to Michael and followed him out the door with barely a backward glance.

I thought Baby would object, but he merely sat up and stared after them. When they were gone, he yawned big and added vocals. It sounded like a wail.

"She'll be back tomorrow. I promise."

He gave another vocal response, this time without the yawn.

"I know, but it's just for a few hours. It's already three, and I'll take you to Michael's first thing and you can see your buddy."

He turned his sad brown eyes and stared at me.

"Besides, I don't know if I can handle two big dogs. Three months ago, I didn't think I could handle one English mastiff." I scratched his ear. "Now, here you are."

I climbed into bed and picked up the remote to turn off the television. I always turn on the television to keep him company when I leave. When I grabbed the remote, I dropped it, and the VCR started.

Three months ago, I didn't know what a VCR was. Another first. Aunt Octavia used to record messages on them. She'd recorded a message for me that her lawyer, Chris Russell, played when I first arrived in New Bison. Since then, I'd lo-

cated two more that she'd hidden around the house. Aunt Octavia believed someone in New Bison had been up to no good.
She believed someone had been out to get her. *A spy in the
camp.* That's what she called it. Turns out she was right. At
least, partially. Someone had been up to no good. Although, if
there was a *spy in her camp*, I never figured out who it was.

When Octavia's voice came from the VCR, Baby's head
snapped toward the television. He stared for several seconds
and then slid down like a sphinx and laid his head in my lap.

I stared at Baby, and tears ran down my face. "I'm sorry,
boy. All the women in your life keep leaving, don't they? First
Aunt Octavia. Now Daisy." I leaned down and hugged him.
"Well, I won't leave you. And I'm going to figure out a way to
bring Daisy here too."

I had no idea if he understood me or not, but together we
watched the last tape I'd found of Aunt Octavia. She was talking about a master criminal . . . a Moriarty who was manipulat-
ing things in New Bison. Elections. Land deals. Everything.
She didn't know who it was, but she felt it was someone in her
inner circle. *A spy in the camp.*

When she finished talking, Baby moaned. I picked up my
phone and sent Michael a text that I'd pick up Daisy tomorrow.

I knew it. LOL

#Liar

#Softie

We sent a few other messages, but nothing related to dogs.
When I heard Baby snoring, I put my phone down to charge
and tried to join him. As I drifted off to sleep, I made a mental
note of tasks that I needed to do.

First, I needed to post that Baby Cakes would be closed. I
didn't have time to think about baking, especially with Leroy
in jail.

Second, I needed to call Chris Russell and get him to repre-
sent Leroy. Maybe he could get him out on bail. Although, I

didn't know how that worked when you confessed to murder. I suspected bail wouldn't be an option, but Chris Russell would know.

Third, I needed to assemble the Baker Street Irregulars. We had to find out who killed Clayton Davenport and Sybil Castleton, in a hurry, and get Leroy out of jail.

Fourth, I needed to enter something in the Spring Festival Baking Contest.

Fifth, I needed to find out what Leroy had gone to jail for.

I tossed and turned and eventually grabbed my phone. I took care of items two and three with a couple of text messages. The last two couldn't be completed with a text or social media post. One post to social media and the first item would be taken care of too, but I waffled. *Do responsible business owners close their businesses when they have trouble? Or do they press through? If I close down too many times, will people decide they'd be better off with the Belgian chef that Clayton Davenport hired at his bakery? Speaking of which, I made a note to find out what happened to that bakery. Would it open? Would Marjorie know?*

I typed the social media post, and my finger hovered over the button that would post it on all of our social media sites. *Just because I am down one employee doesn't mean I need to close. What if Chris Russell can't get Leroy out quickly? We have plenty of baked goods. I could just sell what we have until we run out.* I deleted the message. *Word travels fast in a small town. People would hear about Leroy and flock here to find out whatever gossip they could. Would they think I was disrespectful NOT to close the bakery?*

I retyped the message. Before I pressed Send, I got another text from Michael.

Will drop off Daisy and Grandma Hannah in the morning.

I decided it was a sign from God. I deleted the message about closing and responded to Michael.

I lay in bed and let the thoughts of doubt and confusion drift around me. *What if my head baker is convicted of murder? What would happen to him? What would happen to Baby Cakes?* My last thought before I drifted to sleep was, *I wonder if Aunt Octavia knew about Leroy's past? Is there a possibility that he was the spy in the camp?*

CHAPTER 28

Dreams of Professor Moriarty flitted through my head, intermingled with 007. I woke up with no more answers than I'd had the night before. I wanted to close my eyes, pull the covers over my head, and forget this nightmare ever happened. However, an image of Leroy flashed through my mind, and I tossed the comforter aside and hopped out of bed. Well, it was more like a limp than a hop. Once I slid the leg Baby was using for a pillow from under his weight and shook the feeling back into it, then I hopped.

It didn't take me long to shower. I hadn't closed the bakery, so getting dressed was easy. A pair of leggings, an oxford shirt I borrowed from Michael, and my Sculpts. I refused to stress about my hair. I pulled it back into a ponytail and refused to think what my friends from L.A. would say if they saw it. Even my makeup routine was a lot simpler. Simple compared to my heavily applied *Real Housewives of Orange County* look, but still more makeup than any housewives of New Bison would ever wear. Some changes took more time than others. Just as I finished, the magical aroma of coffee drifted through the air.

166 / *Valerie Burns*

I inhaled the rich, nutty flavor and let it fill my lungs. "Let's go, big guy." Baby took a bit more coaxing, but eventually I convinced him that good things to eat would be in his future if he cooperated.

Downstairs, I found April and Candy sitting in the kitchen. There was a large mug of coffee sitting on the counter.

"Please tell me that's for me?" I asked.

April smiled and nodded.

I grabbed the cup and took a big whiff of the magical elixir. I could tell from one sniff that this wasn't your average, run-of-the-mill crushed coffee beans and water. No, this was something special. Similar to the experts who'd tasted and judged wines last night, I took a sip and allowed the liquid to roll around on my tongue. When the warm liquid went down my throat, I closed my eyes and let it infuse my soul. I might have groaned. When I opened my eyes, April was laughing.

"Is this a red eye?" I smacked my lips. "With a triple shot of espresso?"

Candy nodded. "That's amazing."

"Told you," April said.

"You were right. She really knows her coffee. I wasn't sure about the triple shot of espresso, but I figured you could use it since you were up so late last night."

April and I exchanged a glance.

"How'd you know I was up late?" I sipped my coffee.

A red flush rose up Candy's neck. She glanced down at her feet and then smiled. "I just happened to be with Chris Russell when you sent the text about Leroy getting arrested last night . . . well, this morning."

Both Candy and Chris Russell were consenting adults, so I didn't care what they did. "Is he going to be able to get him out?"

Candy shrugged, but she continued to avoid eye contact, so I knew there was more that she wasn't saying. I guessed she wouldn't be able to handle silence. I waited. She proved me right when she rushed to fill the silence.

"He said there's usually no bail on a murder charge, but he's going to go and meet with him."

I glanced at April. My normally stunningly beautiful pageant-ready friend looked haggard. She had dark circles under her eyes, and it was clear that she hadn't slept. I had a plan to keep her busy.

"I've got to get ready to open the bakery." I turned to April. "Can you do me a favor?"

"Sure."

"Can you drop this cake and four dozen cookies off at Trooper Bob's? His daughter ordered them yesterday, and I promised I'd deliver."

April seemed shocked, but she agreed.

"Michael's bringing Daisy when he drops off Miss Hannah. I trust Baby inside, but I don't know about Daisy. Could you keep them busy until we sell out?"

April frowned. "I don't need to be distracted."

"Me, distract? I wouldn't dream of it."

"Fine. What's the address?"

When I came home, I'd tossed the folder with the carefully researched data that I'd collected about Baby's eating and behavior habits on the counter. I picked up the folder and glanced through it. "This isn't my folder."

"What do you mean? Whose folder is it?"

"Jackson Abernathy's . . . at least, I think it is." I rummaged through the folder. It had Jackson Abernathy's name on the tab and included a picture of three young privates in the Army on the deck of a ship. I squinted. "It looks like a Navy ship, but they're dressed in Army uniforms, not Navy."

April glanced over my shoulder. "Hmm. That photo looks familiar. I think CJ had one just like it."

"The same photo?"

She frowned and then shook her head. "It looks like the same photo, but I can't be certain."

"Was Clayton Davenport in the Army?"

"He joined as soon as he turned seventeen."

"Interesting." A thought flashed through my mind.

"Why? Lots of people join the military. What's the significance?"

I searched my mind, but the momentary flash was gone. "No idea. My brain isn't working yet." I turned to Candy. "Is there more of this?"

"I don't think I've ever seen anyone drink two of those before. Especially with three shots of espresso." Her eyes were wide with awe and admiration. "Give me a few minutes." She went to the corner of the kitchen, and I saw that she had brought two carafes. One held the drip coffee and the other the dark, rich espresso. She measured the espressos and added them to the mug. After two she turned to me. "Three?"

"Yes, please."

She measured and added the third shot and handed me my mug.

Candy said she had to leave, and I thanked her profusely for making my day. I sat and savored the high-octane coffee.

Baby gave an excited bark, spun around twice, and then waited at the back door.

Hannah entered first, followed by Michael and Daisy. The mastiffs sniffed each other's butts, circled each other, and then took off in a rousing game of chase.

I turned to April. "See what I meant?"

"Maybe I should take them outside." She stood up. "Come on, guys, let's go outside."

Baby came running, followed by Daisy. Moments later, April and the mastiffs were outside, and a blanket of silence and peace descended.

Hannah laughed. "Whew! That's a lot of energy. I didn't know Baby had that much oomph left in him."

"I've asked Dr. Hanover to cover me for this afternoon," Michael said. "So, I should be back around one."

I folded my arms across my chest and stared. "You don't think I can handle two mastiffs?"

"You're so defensive. Actually, I thought I'd swing by the jail and check on Leroy. I'll check with April and find out what I can bring. I don't suppose you have time to bake a cake with a file? But I thought he might appreciate a razor, if they'll let him have one, and other toiletries, clean clothes. Grandma made treats and wanted him to have new underwear and socks."

I smiled. "I'm sure clean underwear and socks will make a big difference."

Michael helped Hannah and me carry the baked goods out to the garage. The cars were already starting to line up down the road.

Hannah and I were busy with no time to talk. We sold out in two hours, and I had five orders for cakes. It took longer than normal to get cleaned up without Leroy or Michael's help, but we managed. When we got back to the house, I was surprised to see April sitting at the kitchen table drinking tea with Fiona Danielson.

"Mrs. Danielson, what a pleasant surprise," I said.

"I hope you don't mind me coming by like this, and please call me Fiona." Her eyes were red. She'd been crying. She looked even more haggard than April.

"Of course not. I'm glad you're here. I just wish it were under better circumstances."

She sniffed. "My boy didn't kill that man."

April and I both placed comforting arms around her and muttered words of support and encouragement. We were both so engrossed in comforting his mom that we forgot about Hannah.

"Of course he didn't kill anyone," Hannah said. "Anyone with half a brain knows that, but sitting here crying ain't helping that boy one bit. Are you here for the meeting?"

I was shocked at Hannah's bluntness, but it was probably the best thing. It shocked Fiona into action.

Fiona Danielson sat up straight. Took a deep breath and wiped her eyes. "You're right. Here I am indulging in self-pity when I need to be working to get him free." She stared at Hannah with awe and hope. "You do think we'll be able to get him free, don't you?"

"Pshaw. We'll get him out, don't you worry. These are two of the smartest women I know. Octavia was brilliant, but Maddy's inherited a lot of good sense, and now that she's got more to do and think about than clothes and expensive shoes, she's using her brains. She'll get him out. Don't you worry. Now, I made a pound cake and put it aside for our meeting. Let's go get set up." She picked up her bag and helped lead Mrs. Danielson into the dining room.

When they were gone, April and I exchanged a glance. My eyes were wide and asked the question, *What just happened?*

April shook her head and shrugged. Her lips twitched, and she looked about to smile for the first time since the madness began, when her phone rang. She glanced down at it and frowned. After a few moments, she swiped and answered.

"Yes, this is April, although I go by Johnson, not Davenport. Who is this?" She paused, and the frown deepened. Eventually, she glanced at her watch. "Actually, it's not a good time. I'm really busy and—" She listened. "I suppose it would be okay if you came here." She glanced at me, and I nodded. "Sure. What time?" She waited. "I'll see you then." She listened a few moments and then said her goodbyes.

I waited for an explanation, although she certainly didn't owe me one. However, it was clear that the call had upset her.

"That was Clayton's attorney. He wants to talk to me about Clayton's will."

"His will? Are you inheriting something?"

She shook her head. "Honestly, I can't imagine CJ leaving

me a dime. He certainly wouldn't leave me anything that wouldn't explode rotten eggs or spray skunk oil all over me. Besides, I don't want his money. I really don't. You saw how he behaved. He was vengeful and mean."

"Do you want me to see if Michael can be here when he comes by?"

She shook her head. "That won't be necessary. I'm not afraid, and I can handle anything this attorney brings. Besides, I'm still the sheriff."

"Fine, but nothing comes inside that hasn't passed the Baby sniff test." I glanced over at Baby, who was curled up on his dog bed with Daisy. Sadly, he chose that moment to lift his leg and lick himself.

April and I looked at him and then at each other and burst out laughing.

There was a brief knock at the back door, and Baby stopped grooming himself long enough to go to the door. He didn't bark. He didn't growl. Instead, he stood, tail wagging, and waited. It was clearly a friend.

"Come in," I yelled.

Tyler Lawrence opened the door. Baby stood on his back legs, put his front paws on Tyler's shoulders, and licked him.

"Ugh," Tyler said.

"Baby, off," I said.

"What's up?"

"It wouldn't have been so bad if we hadn't just watched him lick himself," April said.

"Great." Tyler got a wet paper towel and washed off Baby's sloppy greeting.

Baby stood and watched Tyler and then turned on his heels and returned to his dog bed.

Tyler chuckled. "I think I hurt his feelings."

Hannah came in the kitchen. "Are y'all gonna stay in here and crack jokes all day or are we gonna meet?"

Properly chastised, we made our way into the dining room.

Fiona Danielson had undergone a transformation in the short time that she'd sat with Hannah. Fiona was no longer the sobbing wreck of a mother we'd seen earlier. Instead, she sat up straight, and her eyes sparkled. Her face was determined. Here wasn't a woman prepared to beg for her son's release. No. Here was a woman ready to march to the New Bison jail and demand his release.

April leaned over and whispered, "What's in that tea?"

I remembered the flask Hannah pulled out of her purse and wondered if she'd spiked Fiona's tea. However, I wasn't going to be the one to tell if she had.

"Now, Tyler, you take notes," Hannah ordered.

"Yes, ma'am." Tyler saluted and then quickly turned and winked. He hurriedly pulled his notebook out of his bag and hunted for a pen.

"Maddy, you give out the assignments," Hannah said.

I thought for a few moments. "Well, I know Michael plans to go to the . . . to visit Leroy this afternoon. Trooper Bob doesn't seem to dislike him as much as he dislikes April and me."

"That's not saying much," April said. "I thought Michael was going to punch his lights out last night."

Hannah waved away April's concerns with a flick of her hand. "Michael knows how to handle himself. He'll get whatever information you need outta that male chauvinist porcupine. You just tell him what you need. He'll do it." She leaned over to Fiona. "My grandson graduated at the top of his class."

"I'm counting on it," I said. "And what Michael doesn't find out, April can."

"Me?" April said. "He won't tell me the correct time of day."

"Maybe not, but I made two of those Chocolate Soul Cakes. One is for his daughter's party. The other one might just loosen the tongues of some of your patrolmen. I got the impression that they weren't big fans of Trooper Bob."

"They aren't. He yells and orders them around. Treats them

like children. I might be able to find out one or two things on the sly. And I apologize for thinking you were giving me busy work."

I grinned and turned to Tyler. "Are you still dating that woman who works at the bank?"

He rolled his eyes and groaned. "No . . . please don't ask me to talk to her. I just convinced her that we are over."

"I just thought—"

Before I could finish telling Tyler what I thought, Hannah smacked her hand down on the table. "Now, you listen here. This is no time to be thinking about yourself when Leroy's in jail."

"Yes, ma'am." He swallowed hard and turned to me. "What do you want to know?"

"Clayton Davenport invested a lot of money in this town. He bought the bookstore from Marjorie and paid for the licenses for the huge block party with Chloe. I was just wondering if she could see who else Clayton Davenport was paying. Specifically, Mayor Abernathy and . . ." I took a deep breath. "Candy."

"Candy? You can't think she had anything to do with it? She could never . . ." His face turned red. "I'm sure she wouldn't."

"Motive. Opportunity. Means. She was going to lose her coffee shop. She was right next door."

"And she's the one who found the tunnel that leads between the two buildings," April said. "So, she had the opportunity."

"The knife was right there in the bakery, so all she had to do was pick it up and use it," Hannah said. "I've known Candy her entire life. I don't think she's a cold-blooded killer, but if she were provoked, then . . . well, I guess it's worth checking into."

Tyler had a massive crush on Candy and didn't want to believe her capable of murder. "She had an alibi. She was with Chris Russell all night."

"I'm going to check with Chris Russell and confirm that she

was there all night," I said. "She could have slipped out while he was asleep."

Tyler wasn't happy, but he agreed to do it.

"Great," Hannah said. "Now, what about me?"

"And me," Fiona said. "I want to help too. I've let him down so many times in the past, I don't want to do that again." She wept.

April reached across and patted her hand. "Mrs. Danielson, I'm sure you were a great mother."

"No. I wasn't. Didn't he tell you? I'm the reason he went to jail the last time."

CHAPTER 29

I didn't realize I was staring with my mouth open until Hannah said, "Maddy, close your mouth or you'll catch flies."

I closed it and struggled to find the right words, but once again, Hannah came to the rescue.

She patted Fiona Danielson on the back. "Now, now. Maybe you'd feel better if you got it off your chest."

Fiona sniffed. "I've known Leroy's father my whole life. He was always a smooth talker. My mum used to say he could talk the cherries right off the tree." She shook her head. "Well, she was right. I was pregnant with Leroy before I graduated from secondary school. But his father wasn't interested in settling down, being a proper dad, and being saddled with a wife. Thankfully, I graduated before I was showing too much. I met James, Leroy's stepfather . . . stepfather doesn't express it well enough. He was more of a dad to Leroy than Edward ever was." She paused for a few moments and then continued. "Anyway, James was stationed at Lakenheath Air Force Base in Suffolk, England. He was so tall and handsome and kind." She smiled. "All the girls were jealous, but for some reason, he fell for me." She paused and then quickly hurried on. "We got married and moved to the States. He didn't even mind the idea of raising another man's child. Leroy came along, and I didn't think my life could get any better. Leroy was a chubby little thing, and James loved him so much . . . he loved both of us. He's named after his dad, you know. James Leroy Danielson."

I tried to imagine Leroy as a chubby baby, but I couldn't. I was going to need to see a picture. "Wait, Leroy's name is James?"

Fiona nodded. "His father said it would be confusing if both of them were James, and he hated Jimmy. So, we always called him Leroy."

"Amazing the things you learn talking to someone's mother," Tyler joked.

"Please go on," I said.

"Those first few years were amazing. But then James died. He was a pilot, and there was an accident." She turned to stare at Hannah. "That's why Leroy won't fly to this day."

I didn't know Leroy was afraid to fly.

"Suddenly, I felt lost. I was a widow in a strange country with a small child. James didn't have any family to speak of. And I didn't know how to do anything except be a wife and a mother. I never went to university . . . girls didn't much back then. Anyway, I felt overwhelmed. I tried to make a go of it for a few years, but it just got to be too much. That's when I packed up and went home. Leroy didn't want to go. He didn't want to leave his school and his friends . . . but I didn't know how else to make things work."

I didn't know Leroy grew up in the United Kingdom. I was really going to need to spend more time talking to him.

"Things in England were worse. My parents weren't used to an energetic youngster running around the house, and kids can be cruel. They made fun of his American accent." She stared at her plate. "He felt lonely and lost. So, I set out to find myself a husband and Leroy a father. I married the first man who asked me and looked able to support us. He was the town GP."

"What's a GP?" Hannah asked.

"General practitioner," Fiona said. "Horace Lee-Smythe was the town doctor."

I couldn't help but think of the similarities. *I used to want to marry a doctor too.*

"At first, I thought Horace would be the answer to all of my prayers. He was a doctor from a good family. But I'd just gone from one bad situation to another. Horace drank. He drank a lot. When he drank, he got violent. At first, he just yelled, but it didn't take long before it went from verbal abuse to physical abuse. He resented Leroy because he was another man's son, and despite his medical knowledge, he blamed me for not giving him a son. Leroy hated it. He hated his stepfather, and he hated me for marrying him and not being strong enough to leave."

April wiped away a tear and then reached over and squeezed Fiona's hand. "Leaving an abusive situation isn't easy. I know."

The two of them shared a look that spoke volumes.

"It wasn't long before I started drinking too. I drank to forget. I drank to give myself an excuse for all of the bad things that were happening."

"What do you mean?" I asked.

She paused for a few moments. "I was an alcoholic, so I deserved to be punished. It made the abuse my own fault." She shook her head. "It's taken five years of therapy for me to understand why I did what I did. Anyway, Leroy couldn't stand it. He hated the way Horace treated me. He spent as little time as possible at home."

"What about his biological father?" I asked.

"He had a gambling problem. He only remembered he had a son when he needed money." She paused. "I went from one addict to another. At the time, I didn't realize that gambling was going to be the lesser of the evils, but . . ." She shrugged. "Anyway, Horace and I used to argue all the time. When Leroy was about thirteen, he came home and interrupted one of our rows. Horace threw a bottle at me." She pulled back her hair and turned for us to see her scar. "That's when I got this. Well, Leroy flew into a rage. Honestly, I've never seen him so angry. He just lit into his stepfather like a tornado. I didn't think he would stop . . . I thought he would . . ." She choked back a sob.

We waited until she composed herself enough to continue.

She took a deep breath. "One of the neighbors called the police. It took five of them to pull Leroy away. I guess all the years of pent-up rage and frustration all came out at one time." She sniffed. "Horace was badly hurt, but he recovered. He put up charges against Leroy. He even tried to get him charged as an adult. He made false claims saying he was a juvenile delinquent and that he'd inherited his violent temper from his birth father. I was at my wit's end when some of James's friends from Lakenheath read about the incident in the papers. They paid for one of the best solicitors and involved the U.S. consulate because James was American and Leroy was born in America. I even put James's name on his birth certificate. At the time, I didn't think I'd ever see Edward again. In the end, the solicitors worked out a deal. I wouldn't prosecute Horace for beating me if he reduced the charges against Leroy. Leroy spent a month in a youth detention facility, but then served six months of probation with community service. When his probation was up, he told me he was going home to the United States one way or another." She shook her head. "One of James's friends said he'd help him. I pleaded with Leroy not to go, but he was determined."

"Who was the friend?" I asked. I would have bet money that I knew who she was going to name.

"Michael Portman."

I would have lost that bet. "Michael Portman? He never mentioned that he knew Leroy or Leroy's father, and Michael was in the Army, not the Air Force."

"Michael Portman, Senior," Fiona said. "Dr. Portman's father."

CHAPTER 30

"What about my father?" Michael asked.

We were so engrossed in Fiona Danielson's story, none of us noticed Michael's return.

"You never told me that your dad knew Leroy or Leroy's father," I said, trying not to sound accusatory.

"I didn't know he did." He glanced around. "Is it important?"

"I guess not. No . . . of course not. I just . . . no." I tried to figure out why that knowledge would matter, and for the life of me I couldn't come up with a good reason, other than it would be something that Leroy knew but hadn't shared with me. No big deal. He'd only known me for three months. No reason for him to spill his entire life story to a stranger.

Michael sat next to me and took my hand. "My dad was in the Air Force. He spent a lot of time overseas and going wherever the Air Force told him to go. I was in high school when he died." He paused for a few moments while he thought. "Yeah, it was my freshman year of high school. Now, can someone tell me what my dad has to do with Leroy?"

Hannah dabbed at her eyes with a handkerchief. "My Michael was a good boy."

I reached over and hugged him. "Nothing."

When he pulled away and looked at me it was clear that he didn't believe me, but he dropped it.

We quickly got him up to speed.

"So, my dad helped Leroy get to New Bison. I had no idea."

"There's no reason that you should."

It was clear from the way he looked at me that he didn't believe me, but that was okay. I would explain later. I looked at Fiona to continue.

"There's not much else. He came to the States. He got his GED, and I had hoped he would go on to college or maybe even join the Air Force like his dad, but . . . he still hates to fly, and I think a small part of him still blames the military for causing his dad's death. He got a job at the bakery, and Miss Octavia taught him to bake, which he loves." A smile broke across her face. "He always loved baking, even when he was just a wee little thing. I couldn't bake much when I first married James, so I remember going to the library and getting a cookbook for children." She chuckled. "I found a really simple peanut butter cookie recipe, and Leroy used to love to make those with his dad." She shook her head at the memory. "There were only four ingredients, and his dad used to sit him on the counter and let him pour each ingredient in the bowl." She clasped her hand over her mouth. "I'll bet that's one of the reasons he loves baking, because it reminds him of his dad."

Michael and Hannah exchanged a look, and then Michael smiled.

"You remember?" Hannah asked.

"Of course, I remember," he said. "You used to do the same thing with me. When I was little, my grandma used to let me bake with her. Only we made sugar cookies with sprinkles."

"Lawd, you used to love those sugar cookies. There'd be so

many sprinkles on top, you couldn't see the cookie." She joked. "He liked the chocolate sprinkles best."

For a few minutes, both April and Tyler shared their favorite childhood baking stories. They all seemed to have a memory of baking with their parents or grandparents and those recollections brought back warm memories. I listened quietly while they relived those baking moments. Sadly, I didn't have any memories of baking with the Admiral. If I wanted cookies, he bought them or ordered them from a bakery. Navy admirals didn't have time to bake with their daughters. Maybe if I'd spent more time with Aunt Octavia, I'd have baking memories too.

Michael must have noticed my silence because he took my hand and gave it a squeeze.

When the reminiscing died down, Fiona took a deep breath and continued. "Leroy leaving gave me the kick in the pants I needed to leave Horace. I went into rehab and got dried out. I haven't had a drop of alcohol in five years." She hung her head. "Although, I came close this morning when I heard he was in jail."

Hannah patted Fiona's arm. "We're not going to let you break that streak, so it's a good thing you came."

We all muttered words of encouragement, and I hoped that Hannah hadn't shared whatever she had in that flask she carried around in her purse.

"We need to get things moving so we can get Leroy out of that place." Hannah turned to me. "What do you want us to do?"

"I can't stop thinking about Marjorie. From what I've heard of the people who knew her, they all said she was a nice person."

"It's been years since I saw Marjorie, and she was a sweet girl. But people change. I don't know who that woman is that came into town with Clayton Davenport and caused all that trouble for Candy, but that's not the Marjorie Rivers I remember."

Hannah was one of the few people who remembered Marjorie Rivers, and now the dementia made her account less than reliable.

"We need to know what Clayton Davenport had on her that made her agree to come back to New Bison and sell Garrett Kelley's bookstore and help fleece Candy out of her share of Paul Rivers's estate," I said. "She's holding something back. I'm hoping a slice of your sweet potato pie will loosen her tongue."

Hannah looked at Fiona. "We'll get her to talk one way or another."

There was something about the way she said *one way or another* that worried me, but I looked at these two older women and immediately pushed it out of my mind.

"What are you going to do?" April asked.

"I'm going to talk to Chris Russell to get confirmation of Candy's alibi, and then I'm going to have another talk with Jackson Abernathy." I turned to Fiona Danielson. "Fiona, do you know what happened to Clayton Davenport's things? The items he left in his room?"

"I sure do. They're in the storage room at the inn. I packed them up myself."

I looked to April. "Does Clayton have any other family that you're aware of?"

She narrowed her gaze and shook her head. "No, but . . . you can't be thinking what I think you're thinking."

"I don't know what *you're* thinking, but I was only thinking that when you talk to Clayton's lawyer, maybe you could ask what he wants us to do with his things at the hotel. That's all." I said it as innocently as I could.

"Sure." She shot me a look that said *I know you're up to something, but I don't know what.*

I ignored the look. "Let's meet back here at five. I've got to meet Mayor Abernathy at the bakery to do a final walk-through from the renovations."

"That's unusual to have the insurance company also doing the underwriting, isn't it?" Fiona asked.

"He inherited the insurance company from his father and was just helping out the underwriters. In a small town, they sometimes share resources. One of the gazillion papers I had to sign at the time of the fire was my consent. So far, I guess it's been okay. Once everything's set, then I'll probably switch companies. I just want to wrap up everything with the fire first."

"That's smart," Hannah said. "It'll be good to be back in the bakery and not hauling food out to the road every day."

"It's nice that you have a commercial kitchen here in your home," Fiona said.

"Aunt Octavia started Baby Cakes right here," I said. I might not have been here from the beginning, but you wouldn't have known that from the pride in my voice.

"Lord, I remember when Octavia bought that building downtown and turned it into a bakery," Hannah said. "She worked her fingers to the bone baking, cleaning, and getting the word out." She laughed. "Lord, I think she musta gave away more cookies, muffins, and zucchini bread than she sold. Not like today, where you just snap a picture with your phone, and the next thing you know it's floating around out in the air and folks are lining up for a sale."

"Well, there's a lot more that goes into social media promoting," I said. "You really need to understand people."

"Well, Octavia always said, 'When you're good at what you do, you make it look easy.' She used to make baking look easy. Tyler makes knitting look easy, but when he tried to teach me, I had yarn everywhere." Hannah laughed. "I remember Marjorie used to love Octavia's lemon meringue pie. Octavia even tried to teach her to make it, but she just never could get the meringue right." She looked at me. "You have Octavia's recipe for lemon meringue pie. I'll bet if you whipped one up real quick, that would really loosen her lips."

"I don't know if there's time. Would you mind doing it?"

Hannah didn't respond.

"Miss Hannah?" I repeated.

She turned to stare at me. "Hello. Who are you?"

CHAPTER 31

Hannah wasn't going to be able to make a lemon meringue pie or anything else.

"I'd better take her home." Michael glanced at me. "I'm sorry."

"No apologies necessary. You take care of Miss Hannah. Then, swing by the jail and drop off the items you have for Leroy, including the sweet potato pie. I'm sure he's starving."

"He's always starving."

"Everyone have their assignments?"

Everyone nodded.

Fiona looked distressed. "I'd like to help Hannah. She's been so kind to me."

"Great. Go with Michael and then you can see Leroy."

"It won't take long for me to drop Grandma off at home, and then we'll go over to the jail," Michael said. "I'm sure Leroy will be glad to see you."

Fiona didn't look as sure as Michael was, but she helped escort Hannah to the car.

Before he left, Michael cornered me in the kitchen. "Are you sure?"

"Of course, with any luck, I'll be able to get a good video of the meringues this time." I pulled out the stand mixer. "Besides, the lemon meringue pie is super easy with Aunt Octavia's secret ingredient."

"Secret ingredient?"

"I'd tell you, but then I'd have to kill you." I reached up and kissed him. "Now, take care of your grandmother and let me know how Leroy's doing. I'll try to swing by tonight or tomorrow."

"Do you want me to take Daisy?"

I glanced over at the two mastiffs curled up in the dog bed together. I took my phone and got a quick picture.

#MastiffsInLove #BabyHasAGirlfriend #NotTheOnly-WomanInHisLife #BigDogsInLove

I don't know if it was the picture or the feeling of being watched, but Daisy lifted her head and thumped her tail. After a few seconds, she got up and stretched. She gave herself a shake and then trotted over to Michael. She stood on her back legs, placed both paws on his shoulders, and stared into his eyes.

"I was going to say you could leave them, but it looks like Daisy has other plans."

He smiled and petted her. "Don't you want to stay here and play with your buddy?"

Daisy's tail wagged so vigorously, I thought she was going to fall. I quickly snapped another photo.

#ShesAfterMyMan #ShouldIBeJealous #ShesLuckyShes-Cute #NoShameInHerGame

I folded my arms. "Is there something going on between the two of you?"

"Maybe." Michael grinned. "You're never this excited to see me."

I took my dishcloth and swatted him. "Fine, then you and Daisy can just go on. Baby and I have work to do."

Michael and Daisy left. Baby stared at the door for a few

moments after they left, but then he went back to his dog bowl and stared.

"Aww, ready for dinner, are you? Well, that means you're getting your appetite back." I went to the fridge and pulled out a bag of the special food Aunt Octavia used to supplement his regular dog food. I dumped the chicken and vegetable mixture into the bowl and stirred it up. Baby was a big dog, and it took quite a lot to keep him well nourished and energized.

He gobbled the food and then washed it down with about a gallon of water, sloshing a good deal of it on the floor. Normally, I would have reprimanded Baby for the spillage. However, it did my heart good to see him eating again. So, I happily wiped up the water.

Aunt Octavia's lemon meringue pie was truly simple to make, at least the lemon filling was simple. The meringue was a bit more challenging. The first time I tried, I didn't beat it enough and ended up with a thin, flat layer of foam. The second time I beat it too much and produced dry, stiff, crunchy mounds of Styrofoam. Leroy taught me how to tell when I hit the sweet spot, and the next time my meringue was towering white peaks of fluffiness that stood up to the heat of the oven and dissolved on your tongue.

I set up my ring light and recorded the process. This time, I remembered to lock the stand mixer in place and made sure the speed was set to low *before* I turned it on. A few short minutes later, I turned off the mixer, unlocked it, and lifted the head. The meringue was shiny, and the peaks stood at attention rather than curling over as they do when they are underbeaten or clumping together when overbeaten. I had enough for two pies, so I spooned the whites on top of the bright yellow lemony goodness and put them in the oven so the meringues could brown.

While I waited for the pies to set and the meringues to get golden brown, I thought about the baking memories my friends shared earlier. Simple cookie recipes had brought back memories that put smiles on their faces. I didn't have those memories, but maybe I could help parents create those memories with their kids. I hurried to the counter and found a notebook. I'd missed Mother's Day, but Father's Day was only a few weeks away. I could offer a Daddy and Me Baking Class. Maybe I could even pair it with a British tea. After the baking was over, they could have a formal British tea with sandwiches. *Hmm, I'm not sure most American kids would like watercress or cucumber sandwiches. But we could do peanut butter and jelly, and egg salad minus the crusts, of course. I'll bet Fiona could help make scones.* I pulled out my phone and looked up clotted cream. *Maybe I'll order it. I'm not sure I'm up to making that from scratch.* I loved this idea even more than the baking classes. I loved how it created an event that a kid could do with their dad and an opportunity to build a memory. That was something I never had with my dad. In that moment, I knew what I would enter for the baking festival.

"Hey, earth to Maddy." April waved her hand in front of my eyes and broke the spell I was in.

"Sorry, I just had a great idea for a new class to add to the schedule, and I was just working through how to make it work. Plus, I think I know what I'm going to make for the Spring Festival Baking Competition."

"Really? That's great."

"What's up?"

"I just got a message from Clayton's attorney. He should be here any minute. I can take him downstairs—"

"Don't be silly. You can meet in the living room. I'll head out and leave you alone so you can talk in private." The timer went off, and I took the lemon meringue pies from the oven. They looked delicious. They weren't as beautiful as the amazing pies by pie artist Stephanie, at Pie Lady Books, but they were quite lovely. I snapped a few pictures and uploaded them.

#LemonMeringuePie #NotAsPrettyAs@PieLadyBooks #Not-APieArtistStillYummy

"You don't have to leave. In fact . . . I was hoping you'd stay," April said. "You know, for moral support."

"Of course. I'll be happy to stay, but why do you think you'll need support?"

"CJ was vindictive. I can't believe he'd leave me anything short of a rattlesnake. Or maybe a pile of horse poop."

Baby's ears perked up. He gave a quick bark and barreled to the front door seconds before the doorbell rang.

April and I rushed to the living room. I grabbed Baby's collar while she opened the door.

I don't know what I expected, but the Greek god standing on the porch wasn't it. Tall, slender, tanned, with black hair and dark eyes and a smile that was dazzlingly bright.

"Hello, which one of you lovely ladies is April Davenport?" he asked.

"It's April Johnson." April extended her hand. "This is my friend Madison Montgomery."

He extended a hand to shake, but I needed both hands and a leg to pin Baby against the wall.

"Sorry, I'm not sure why he's being such a goofball," I said. "He's normally very sweet."

"Ah, no worries. What's this beautiful boy's name?"

"This is Baby."

"Baby, how amazing." He held out a hand for Baby to sniff.

That took courage considering Baby was acting like he'd like nothing more than to rip this stranger's arm off and bury it in the backyard.

Baby sniffed.

I tightened my grip on his collar and braced my legs in case he made a lunge for the stranger's jugular. But his muscles relaxed. The tension released, and his tail started to wag.

That's when the Greek god put his hands on both sides of Baby's head and scratched.

The drool poured out of both sides of Baby's mouth like a fountain, and he leapt up and gave the stranger a facial wash that left no spot unexplored.

When the shock wore off, I ordered Baby down.

"I'm so sorry." I didn't know whether to use my drool towel to remove the strands of drool hanging from Baby's face or offer it to the stranger. I chose Baby. After all, Greek god or no Greek god, he had worked for Clayton Davenport.

April opened the door wider and stepped back. "Please come inside, Mr. . . . . I'm sorry, I've forgotten your name."

"Nico Vassos. The stranger pulled a silk handkerchief from a pocket, wiped his face, and came inside. "I used to have a mastiff when I was a boy. That's a fine specimen."

Would the surprises ever cease? Prior to moving to New Bison, I'd never seen an English mastiff, let alone met anyone who'd had one. Now, I not only owned a mastiff, I knew people who knew what they were, and was seriously considering adding a second one to my pack.

We moved into the living room, and Baby's love affair with Nico Vassos wasn't over. In fact, once the lawyer was seated, Baby climbed up and sat in his lap.

Nico laughed. "Oh, big boy, you wanna hang out on my lap?"

April and I exchanged a look. Aunt Octavia always said that I should trust Baby's judgment, and so far he hadn't proven me wrong. April's shoulders relaxed, and she loosened her grip on the arms of the chair.

"Mr. Vassos," I said, "you've been so kind, but—"

"Nico, please."

"Nico. And you can call me Maddy." I walked over and pulled Baby off and escorted him down the hall to the master bedroom. I left him on the bed, closed the door, and hurried back to the living room.

April and Nico were making small talk. When I returned, Nico opened a briefcase that he'd brought in and pulled out an envelope. He rifled through the documents until he found the one he was looking for. He took a few moments to make sure it was the proper document and then cleared his throat.

"Mrs. Davenport . . . I mean Johnson. I—"

"April."

He flashed April another dazzling smile. "April, I know you and Mr. Davenport were estranged. His will is very . . . well, he says some things that are not very nice."

April waved her hand. "I expected that."

"Well, according to the terms of his will, you are to receive one dollar and this letter." He passed an envelope to April.

She took the envelope and rose. "Great. If that's all, I—"

"I'm afraid there's more."

April sat back down.

"You see, I'm new to the firm, and I didn't handle Mr. Davenport's business affairs. However, it looks that while Mr. Davenport removed you as his beneficiary and made sure that the terms of his will were clear, he failed to ensure that all of his business documents reflected his wishes." He cleared his throat. "It appears that in exchange for certain tax considerations, Mr. Davenport placed some of his business and real estate holdings in your name."

"My name?"

The lawyer nodded.

April shook her head. "That sounds like Clayton. I suppose now that he's dead, I'll be strapped with paying the taxes even though I don't own them?"

Nico waved his hands to calm April. "No. No. It's . . . well, it's a bit more complicated than that."

"How could it possibly be more complicated?" I asked.

"You see, Mr. Davenport was a hardy man. He intended to live for many years. Based on what I can figure out, he always transferred deeds into your name. He reaped the tax benefits and then transferred them back."

April released a long breath. "Oh good. Then, that all worked out. I get my dollar and all's well, right?"

"Mostly, but there are some properties that Mr. Davenport did not get transferred back to himself." He flipped through the papers. "There is a hardware store and a bookstore here in New Bison."

"Oh God." April closed her eyes and put her head in her hands. "Are you trying to tell me that I own those properties? How is that possible? I mean, his will states that I get nothing but a dollar."

"True, but technically you cannot give, or in this case fail to give, something you don't own. Mr. Davenport doesn't own those properties. So, he can't keep them from you. They belong to you."

"But I don't want them," April said. "Can't you just put them with the rest of his estate?"

Nico shook his head. "I'm sorry, but that would not be legal. As the owner, you are free to dispose of them however you'd like."

"Great. Then that's what I'll do. I'll dispose of them." She stood. "Is that it?"

"Here are the deeds for your properties." Nico pulled two folders from his briefcase. "There's just one more thing. Do you know anything about the Rucker-Merkel Diamond Mine?"

A smile broke out on April's face. She sat down. "I haven't heard that name in years." She paused and took a few deep breaths. "When we first met, Clayton used to say I was his diamond and one day he'd give me more diamonds than there were stars in the sky." She wiped away a tear. "On our wedding day, he gave me a deed to a diamond mine in Alberta, Canada, as a wedding present. It was worthless, but it was one of those nice gestures. There weren't diamonds in the mine. In fact, I think it flooded not long after he bought it." She chuckled. "We used to go outside and look up at the sky and laugh our heads off when we talked about that mine."

"I'm afraid the Rucker-Merkel mine isn't exactly a laughing matter," Nico said.

"What do you mean? Don't tell me someone actually found a diamond?"

Nico shook his head. "No . . . no diamonds have been found." He handed April an envelope. "Turns out the mine is full of ammolite."

I gasped.

"What in the world is ammolite?" April said. "Is it valuable?"

"Ammolite is only one of the rarest gemstones on the planet," I said.

April flopped back against her chair. She looked so pale, I rushed to the kitchen to get her a glass of water. "Don't you dare pass out on me. You know I'm not good in emergencies."

April took several deep breaths and then drank most of her water. "But I've never heard of ammolite. What is it?"

"Mollusks." I pulled out my cell and searched until I found an article that would explain it. "Ammonites, with an N, were marine mollusks that have been extinct for about sixty-five *million* years. The fossilized shell material is either ammonite, not valuable, or an extremely rare gem quality material called ammolite."

April stared at me and then Nico. "And that diamond . . . ah, mine has ammolite?"

Nico nodded. "My understanding is that the quality of stone in your mine is rare and extremely valuable."

April shook her head like Baby. "This can't be. Clayton would never have deliberately left me anything of value. You must be mistaken."

"Well, my understanding is that the mine belongs to you. The ammolite has only recently been discovered, and there have been efforts to locate you, but . . ."

Nico left April with the letter from Clayton Davenport, three folders, and one dollar.

When I returned from seeing him to the door, April hadn't moved. She looked stunned and pale.

"Are you okay?"

She lifted her head. "I can't believe how wrong I was about Clayton."

I swallowed the negative responses that leapt into my mind. Clayton Davenport hadn't changed. He was still the low-down, dirty-dealing slime bag. However, he was dead, and reminding her of that didn't seem wise. Obviously, she was feeling sentimental about him. So, I merely sat down, gritted my teeth, and tried to be a sympathetic friend. "If that mine has ammolite, then he definitely left you a very wealthy woman."

She shook her head. "That's not what I mean."

"How were you wrong about him?"

She paused so long I didn't think she was going to answer. Eventually, she sighed. "I thought the worst thing he could do to me was to leave me a rattlesnake or a pile of poop. By leaving me real estate and an ammolite mine, he's left me with the one thing I didn't have before—a good motive for murder."

CHAPTER 32

April was still dazed, so rather than have her perform her initial list of tasks, I agreed to talk to Marjorie and deliver the cake to Trooper Bob. April needed a few moments to recover.

The entire drive to Marjorie's home, I thought about what April had said. I couldn't believe she was a suspect, but sooner or later Trooper Bob was going to figure out that Leroy was lying. When he did, he was bound to go back to April as his number one suspect. I intended to find the real killer and get Leroy out of jail. I needed Leroy. Not just because he was my master baker. Leroy was my friend. No. That's not right either. Leroy was my family. He was more like a brother. Family was a strange concept for me. Prior to moving to New Bison, I hadn't given it much thought. My mom was dead, so it was just the Admiral and me. Since moving here, my blood relations hadn't changed, but the people I loved, the ones who I would give a kidney to, or fight to the bitter end to protect, had grown significantly larger. That list included both Leroy and April. That meant I needed to solve this murder quickly.

I pulled in front of Garrett Kelley's house. The front of the house had an abandoned air that I didn't remember from the last time I was here. I sat and stared at the house, trying to put my finger on what was different. The only thing I noticed was that the windows and doors were closed. Today was bright and sunny. Most of the houses had their curtains open, if not their windows and doors. Even the ones with central air-conditioning boxes on the sides of their houses and didn't need a fresh breeze from Lake Michigan opened their curtains.

Maybe Marjorie doesn't like sunlight. I carried the lemon meringue pie up the porch steps and rang the bell.

I waited and was just about to ring again when I heard a loud thump inside. I tapped on the window. "Marjorie? Are you okay?"

A few moments later, the door opened. Garrett Kelley's house wasn't the only thing that wasn't open and welcoming. Marjorie's face was anything but inviting. "Yes?"

I felt my left brow rise. I forced it down and the corners of my lips up. "Hi, Marjorie. I'm Maddy Montgomery. I was here yesterday with—"

"I know who you are."

"Great . . . well, when I was here before with Miss Hannah, she mentioned bringing you a sweet potato pie. She—"

"Is that what that is?"

"Ah . . . no, she wasn't feeling well and wasn't able to—"

"What is that?"

Maybe if you'd let me finish a sentence, I could tell you. "She felt bad about not getting here and remembered that you really liked lemon meringue pie, so I—"

"Ugh. I hate lemon meringue pie." She backed up and started to close the door, but I'd had enough of her bad manners. I stuck my foot in the door and scooched my body in so she couldn't shut me out. *Geez, if someone takes the trouble to*

bake you a pie, the least you can do is say thank you and take it.
You'd think I was trying to give her a fire-breathing, poisonous
reptile. Her behavior wasn't just rude . . . it was bizarre.

"How odd. Mrs. Portman remembered you as being exceptionally fond of lemon meringue pie."

"Doesn't she have dementia? She must be mistaking me for someone else. I'm really busy, so if you'll excuse me, I—"

"Mrs. Portman does have dementia, but when it comes to food, her memory is as sharp as a meat cleaver." I paused to watch her reaction. She was jittery, and her gaze darted around the street as though she were afraid to be seen talking to me. "Perhaps we should take this conversation inside. The neighbors can be exceptionally nosy in a small town." I didn't wait for a response. I used my knee to widen the opening and pushed my way inside.

Once I was inside, I stopped and waited.

She closed the door and glared. "Why are you here?"

Why am I here? I'm here to get information. Marjorie's behavior was extreme. Ideas tumbled around in my brain like a clothes dryer. Eventually, a thought came to mind, and I blurted it out before I had time to think. "I'm here to find out who you really are."

Marjorie's brave facade slid to the ground, and I found myself staring into the eyes of a terrified stranger.

"Oh God. I knew this would never work. I knew it wouldn't work. I knew it." She glanced around the room as though she were looking for someplace to hide.

"Why don't we sit down and talk. Maybe I can help."

"Help?" She laughed. "No one can help me."

"Do you want me to call the police?"

She went white as a sheet, and her knees buckled.

I placed the pie on a console near the door and caught her before she collapsed. I put my arm around her back and guided her to the kitchen. Once there, I put her in a chair and pushed her head down between her knees. At first, I wasn't sure what to do for someone who looked about to pass out, but then I remembered what April had done to Candy and Michael had done to me. It couldn't hurt.

I waited a few seconds, and she didn't seem worse, so I got a glass from the cabinet and filled it with water. I wasn't sure if I should splash it in her face, but I decided to just see if she would drink it. "Here, drink this."

She took the water, but her hands were shaking so badly, she couldn't lift the glass to her mouth. I held the glass and helped her drink like I would have done for a small child. After a few moments, she pulled away.

She sat at the table, shaking like a leaf.

I pulled out the chair where I'd sat during my last visit. "Okay, do you want to tell me who you really are and what you're doing here?"

She wrung her hands. "My name's Carla . . . Carla Lattimore."

"Okay, Carla. I guess it's safe to say you were never married to Paul Rivers."

"Never even saw the man."

"How'd you get mixed up in this?"

"I was a grifter in Chicago. A friend of mine, Brad Ellison, said he knew a way I could make a lot of money—"

"Wait, Brad Ellison, the Realtor?"

"Yeah, that's the one. Anyway, Brad had seen a picture of Marjorie, and he thought I looked enough like her that I could pass myself off as her and help them get some property. Brad said Paul Rivers's current wife was dumb as a box of rocks. She'd either roll over and accept that Rivers hadn't divorced his first wife, or they could give her a few thousand dollars and she'd just take it and blow out of town. Anyway,

Brad introduced me to Clayton Davenport. And Clayton told me all I had to do was stay here in this house and keep my mouth shut."

My mind raced. Brad Ellison planned this entire farce before he died. How was this even possible? "And you did it?"

"Of course I did it. He was going to pay me fifty thousand dollars. I would have done anything for that kind of money."

"Fifty thousand dollars is a lot of money. All you had to do was come to town and pretend to be Marjorie Rivers? So, what happened? Did Clayton want you to do more so you killed him?"

She stood up. "Oh no you don't. You're not going to pin that murder on me."

"If you didn't kill him, then who did?"

Marjorie . . . I mean Carla, shrugged. "I have no idea. Davenport told me to come to this house and stay here. I wasn't to talk to anyone unless he was here." She paced. "When he was murdered, I started to run, but I thought that might make me look guilty and then the cops would arrest me for the murder. I've got a record, and I lied about who I was, so they wouldn't believe anything else I said. But then I got a note telling me to stay put. Lay low. And I'd still get my money."

It took me a few moments to grasp what she was saying. "You got a note? From who?"

"No idea."

"Do you still have it?"

She reached in her pocket and pulled out a folded piece of paper with a few typewritten comments.

Lay Low. Stay Put and you'll still collect your 50k.

"Where's the envelope? Did it come in the mail?"

She shook her head. "No envelope. Someone shoved it under my door. I found it when I woke up."

"You must have some idea who sent it. It had to be someone who knew you weren't really Marjorie. It had to be someone who knew about this plan. Someone who was in on the scheme. Did Clayton or Brad talk about someone else?"

"No."

I didn't want to scare her, but it was time for a little tough love. "Brad Ellison and Clayton Davenport were in this scheme together, but both of them are dead. Someone else has to be involved. Someone else knows that you're not Marjorie Rivers. Someone knows enough about this entire plot to have killed Sybil Castleton and to slip that note under your door. Now, you need to think."

Carla's eyes widened. She paced in the small kitchen. "I don't know. I don't know. They didn't talk about stuff to me. I wasn't part of their inner circle."

She sounded sincere. The Admiral would say it was time to regroup. I thought for a few moments. "What was Sybil Castleton's role in this whole thing?"

Carla stopped pacing. "Clayton wanted her to get back at you."

"Me? Why me? He didn't even know me. Did he?"

She shrugged and continued pacing. "I don't know."

"You're lying. Look, either you level with me and tell me the truth, or I pick up my phone and call Trooper Bob."

Her eyes darted, and she looked like a frightened rabbit ready to run. I could almost see the wheels spinning as she weighed the likelihood of getting away. She must have realized she'd never get away fast enough. I was pretty speedy with a cell phone and slipped it out of my pocket and held it so she could see the screen showed 9-1-1. All I needed to do was press Send. "You won't make it to the end of the driveway before the police arrive."

She flopped down in her chair, and her shoulders lowered about a half inch. "Fine."

"Why did Clayton want to get back at me? And how did he plan to do it?"

"Look"—she turned toward me—"like I said, I wasn't part of his inner circle, but I know he blamed you and someone named Octavia for filling April's head with feminist nonsense. Octavia was dead, so that just left you."

"How was he going to get me?"

"He watched your social media feeds and thought the best way to get to you was through your dog."

My heart skipped a beat, and I gasped. "Baby? How?"

"He bought an English mastiff that has some kind of genetic heart problem. Once your dog bred with her, then the defect would pass to the puppies. Then, he could claim that your dog caused the birth defect that the puppies would inherit. He paid a vet who was going to swear that your dog was the problem."

"Sounds farfetched."

"He wanted to destroy everything you cared about. He was going to ruin your bakery and paid a fortune for the Belgian pastry chef to come to town. Then he was going to take your house and everything you owned. He knew about your great-aunt's will and if you left town before one year was up, then you'd lose everything. So he just needed to get you out of town."

Clayton Davenport was definitely thorough. If he wasn't already dead, I might have killed him. That man was evil. It was bad enough that he wanted to hurt me, but he was using innocent animals like pawns in a chess game without thinking about the poor puppies who would be born with a heart condition simply to get back at Aunt Octavia and me. Attacking me was one thing. Attacking my dog brought out feelings of rage on an entirely different level. Whoever killed Clayton Davenport did the world a favor. I wouldn't lose a minute of sleep if his killer was never brought to justice, were it not for the fact that my friends' freedom was in jeopardy.

I growled. "Tell me everything you know from the beginning."

CHAPTER 33

I didn't learn anything more to help figure out who murdered Clayton Davenport during the second, third, or fourth retelling of Carla's story. By the end, I was confused and Carla was exhausted. I made her promise not to skip town, took my pie, and left. There was a lot to process, and I had very little brainpower left to work it out.

I drove to the address that Holly Roberts, Trooper Bob's daughter, gave me. I don't know what I expected a state trooper's house to look like, but Trooper Bob's house didn't disappoint. It was a brick ranch on a large piece of land, set back from the road. There was a long driveway, and I imagined it provided a great line of sight from the house to any arrivals. There was a large garage off to the side, which I imagined was where he kept his arsenal stashed. When the zombie invasion happened, Trooper Bob would be leading the resistance. This is where the rebel forces would gather.

I pulled up in front, grabbed the chocolate cake, thumbprint cookies, and the lemon meringue pie too. No sense in letting a perfectly good pie go to waste. Aunt Octavia wasn't into marketing, but in addition to the new aprons, I'd ordered white boxes with the new Baby Cakes logos. Branding was important. Plus, the boxes made it a lot easier to carry baked goods.

At the door, I juggled the boxes to free my hand to ring the bell, but I needn't have bothered. There were security cameras directed at me, and I couldn't help smiling and making sure my hair was still in place. Before I could press the doorbell, the door swung open, and I found myself staring into Trooper Bob's steely gaze. He glared and looked ready to spit nails. "Thank God you're here. What took you so long?"

I don't know what words I expected to come out of the state trooper's mouth, but that wasn't it. "I'm sorry. I was—"

"Never mind. Just get in here." He stepped back and opened the door wide for me to enter.

I stepped over the threshold and was immediately attacked by five pounds of pure attitude in the form of a Chihuahua. "He's so cute. He looks just like the—"

"Yeah. Yeah. He looks like the dog on the Taco Bell commercials. Save it. I've heard it a thousand times." Under his breath he mumbled, "Today." He scooped up the scrappy little dog that had gotten the string from my Sculpt shoes between his teeth and was intent on taking me down to the ground, shoe first. "Follow me." Trooper Bob took off down a hall.

I scrambled to keep up, remembering the way drill sergeants would make the sailors march double time. As we marched through the house, I got glimpses of colorful quilts, sturdy wooden furniture, and walls overflowing with pictures. The kitchen was a montage to the 1970s with a harvest-gold single wall-oven, fridge, and dishwasher, oak cabinets, and red laminate countertops. Despite the outdated décor, the addition of rooster-themed accessories gave the room a comfy, lived-in vibe.

The kitchen was at the back of the house, and a large sliding-glass door led out to a backyard oasis. Large, lush green trees followed the perimeter of the house and hid the six-foot privacy fence, which was dotted with security cameras. Old-fashioned flowers burst into bloom, including many of the same ones April had identified for me at the Carson Law Inn—roses, peonies, hydrangeas, and wildflowers. In the center of the yard was a concrete patio and large in-ground pool. Outside was a small platoon of teens enjoying a water volleyball game, while the bass from Chloe's latest hit boomed so loudly the glasses on a nearby table vibrated. He slid the glass door open, dropped the Chihuahua on the ground, and closed it before the dog could sneak back inside.

I was impressed by his speed in closing out the dog. "That was fast."

"Not my first rodeo."

Trooper Bob turned and glared at me. He dabbed at his ears. "Are my ears bleeding?"

I chuckled. "Looks like Holly has a great party going."

"She wanted a few of her closest friends. I'm pretty sure I've seen some of those kids on Wanted posters, but I've been strictly forbidden against running any fingerprints."

"I'm sure they're good kids."

He worked to hide a smile. "Most of them. Anyway, I'm glad you're here. Holly accused me of being mean to you when I escorted you from the mayor's office. She's been screaming, crying, and having fits all day, afraid I'd scared you or made you so mad that she wasn't going to get her Soul Cake and thumbprint cookies. So, I guess I should thank you for saving my sanity." He rubbed his hand over his head. "I told her you didn't scare easily."

"I was raised by a Navy admiral who could make grown men cry. No offense, but it's going to take a lot more than a grumpy state trooper to frighten me. Not only did I bring the cake and cookies, but I threw in a lemon meringue pie for good measure." I handed over the goodies. "I gave her my word. I couldn't go back on that. No matter what."

He took the treats and gave them a critical eye, and then he held the boxes up to his ear. "You sure it's not a bomb?"

I crossed my heart and held up three fingers. "Scout's honor."

"I'll be right back." He stacked the boxes by size, with the thumbprint cookies on top, opened the patio door, and slipped outside. He placed the boxes on a table under a bright pink patio umbrella.

Holly glanced over, saw the boxes, and screamed. "Soul Cake!"

The teens clambered out of the water as if they'd just spotted a great white shark and descended on the table like vultures picking flesh off a carcass in the Sahara.

I snapped a photo quickly, careful not to include any faces, just arms and legs, as the teens descended on the baked goods. #JustWhenYouThinkItsSafe #SoulCakeEmptiesThePool #SunFunAndChocolateCake #BabyCakesCatering

Trooper Bob hurried out of the way and back inside. He watched out the door as the teens feasted. "I probably should have cut a slice before I took it out there."

"I should have brought two. I had no idea how many—"

He waved away my words with a swipe of his hand. "I had no idea how many she invited either, so there was no way for you to know." He reached in his back pocket and pulled out a wallet. "How much do I—"

This time I shook my head and waved a hand to wipe away his words. "No charge. It's my pleasure."

Trooper Bob frowned. "I prefer to pay my debts. I can't accept favors. Someone might misinterpret your well-meaning gesture."

I shook my head. "No gesture. Holly and I had a deal, and I'm paying up."

He tilted his head to the side and waited, but I didn't elaborate.

I certainly couldn't tell him that his daughter had let me listen in on his interrogation of Mayor Abernathy in exchange for baked goods.

After a few moments, he returned his wallet. "Thank you."

We stood in an awkward silence for a few moments until I blurted out, "You don't honestly believe Leroy killed Clayton Davenport and Sybil Castleton, do you?"

He scowled, but there was a glimmer in his eyes that told me he wasn't serious. Maybe it was being home or perhaps it was the fact that he wasn't wearing his uniform. Whatever it was, Trooper Bob let down his mask, and for a few moments, I saw the real man, not the state policeman. In that moment, I saw my dad, the Navy admiral who barked orders faster than an M16 assault rifle with the power to send terror up the spine of burly, hardened sailors. Yet, in the hands of his daughter, he was putty.

"You don't believe it." I smiled. "You're much too smart to fall for that."

"He confessed." He worked to control his lips, but they twitched. He eventually lost the battle and smiled.

"I knew it."

"Look, I shouldn't be talking to you. You're a suspect yourself."

It was too late. He'd lost his tactical advantage. Now, I was in control. "You know good and well that I didn't kill Clayton Davenport or Sybil Castleton. If you thought I had, I'd be the one in that cell, not Leroy." I flashed him my biggest smile. "You're setting a trap for the real killer, aren't you? You arrested Leroy so the killer would think he or she was safe, but then you're going to do a rear maneuver and circle around behind and pounce."

"I have no idea what you're talking about." He turned away to keep me from seeing his smile, but it was too late. I had him pegged.

"Come on. If you tell me your full plan, maybe I can share what I know."

That got his attention.

"I hope you're not implying that you've been withholding information from the police."

"Would I withhold information?" I gave him my most innocent look. "Now, you tell me something, and I'll tell you something."

"Okay. You first."

I was shaking my head before the words left his mouth. "Nope. You first. How about you tell me what time the medical examiner thinks Clayton Davenport was murdered."

He narrowed his gaze and hesitated. "Okay, Nancy Drew. The coroner estimates Davenport died between two and four a.m. based on the stomach contents and the last time he was known to have been alive."

I gave him an easy one to see if he was going to play along.

"Now, your turn, Nancy Drew. What information have you uncovered?"

I hated the Nancy Drew reference. It grated on my nerves and caused me to want to wipe that smug smile off his face. "Well, I know that the woman who's been claiming to be Marjorie Rivers is really a grifter named Carla Lattimore who Davenport and the late Brad Ellison hired to cheat Candy Rivers out of her inheritance."

"What?" He pounded the table with his fist and leaned close. "How do you know that?"

"I just talked to her." I knew I'd lost my advantage, and in my nervousness, I overshared. I told him not only about my conversation with Carla Lattimore, but about the visit from Davenport's lawyer, the ammolite mines, and Sybil Castleton's plan to taint Baby's lineage.

When I ran out of steam, he sat staring at me as though I'd suddenly grown another head. After what felt like an eternity, he rubbed his hand over his head, pushed himself up from the table, and paced around the small kitchen.

I'd seen this behavior before. Whenever the Admiral was so

angry with me he couldn't speak, he paced. Several times, Trooper Bob stopped. He walked to within inches of me, held up a finger, but then swallowed hard and paced a bit more.

"Would it help if I said I'm sorry?" I asked.

He growled, turned, and pounded both hands on the counter. "You . . . you could have . . . *grrr.*" His face was red. "Where is she? Carla Lattimore."

"She was still at Garrett Kelley's house when I came here."

He pulled out his cell phone, pushed a few buttons, and then ordered a patrol car to the home of Garrett Kelley to pick up Carla Lattimore. He gave a brief description. "At the moment, she's a material witness in a murder investigation." He hung up, but before he could put his phone away, it rang. "Fled the scene?" He turned to glare at me. "Pick her up. She's wanted for questioning in connection with two homicides." He jabbed his finger to disconnect and slammed the phone down on the counter. He turned and scowled. "Now, start from the beginning and tell me everything you know, or so help me, you'll be sitting in a cell right next to your tenant and your head baker."

CHAPTER 34

By the time I finished repeating my conversation with Carla Lattimore for what felt like the hundredth time, I was exhausted. Trooper Bob's phone didn't ring, which meant that Carla hadn't been picked up, yet. For a brief moment, I was afraid he meant to make good on his threat about locking me up. However, the teens started making their way inside, and I took that opportunity to sneak out while he was distracted.

I sent Michael a text that I would meet him at Baby Cakes, and then I headed for my appointment with Jackson Abernathy.

I parked in my usual spot, in front of the sign Aunt Octavia had that read OWNER, DON'T EVEN THINK ABOUT PARKING HERE! That sign always brought a smile to my face. I was the owner. I snapped a picture and quickly uploaded it. #StillLoveOwningABusiness #StillLivingMyBestLife #GrandReopeningComingSoon

At least, I hoped I would be reopening and not sitting in jail.

I noticed Abernathy's truck parked in front, but I didn't see the mayor anywhere in sight. *He's probably shaking hands, kissing babies, and campaigning for votes.* I also noticed Chris Russell's Spider parked down the street. That McClaren Spider was hard to miss, especially in a town the size of New Bison.

I unlocked the back door and entered the bakery. The construction was done at last. The new bakery looked **#Amazing**. I walked through the entire building, snapping pictures. **#NewDecorSameGreatTaste #GrandReopeningAllWelcome #BabyCakesBackInBusiness**

I couldn't help running my hands across nearly every surface. The glass display cases were empty, but I couldn't wait until they were filled with cakes, cookies, and all kinds of delicious treats. The demonstration area was open and bright and just waiting for Leroy to work his magic. It was very different from the bakery I'd inherited from Aunt Octavia, but deep down inside, I knew she'd approve.

The construction crew had the building professionally cleaned, but I wanted to do something. I wanted to polish or sweep or bake. Since no groceries had been delivered yet, baking was out of the question. Besides, while my repertoire of items that I knew how to bake had increased, I wasn't ready to get my new bakery dirty by actually baking something. So, I opened a closet and hunted for a broom and a dustpan. Just as I found the elusive dustpan at the back of the closet, I heard voices. For a few seconds, I stood up and strained to hear where they were coming from. That's when I remembered the passage that connected Baby Cakes to the building next door.

I had never used the passage and didn't plan to use it this time. Whoever Candy was entertaining, she didn't need me dropping in on her. Broom and dustpan in hand, I was just about to close the door when I heard my name and stopped in my tracks.

Why would anyone be talking about me?

I strained against the back of the closet, but I could only hear every fifth or sixth word.

I should walk away. So what if they are talking about me? Maybe they want to buy cookies. It probably doesn't mean anything.

I pushed the door to the passage open a crack. *This is stupid. What am I thinking? Dumb woman enters a dark passage . . . ALONE had to be the dumbest classic horror mistake, EVER.* Still, I took a deep breath, clutched my broom like a baseball bat, opened the door wider, and walked through.

This is stupid. I should absolutely NOT be walking down this passage.

I ignored my sage advice and followed the rumble of voices. I prayed that I wouldn't see or hear anything scurrying around. When I estimated that I was mere feet from the coffee shop door, I stopped and listened.

The voices were clearer, but still I struggled to understand every word. I made out three different voices. One was Mayor Abernathy. One voice belonged to Chris Russell. The third voice was familiar, but still, I couldn't quite make it out. In fact, I couldn't tell if it was male or female.

I had a jolt and a moment of déjà vu as I remembered overhearing a conversation between Brad Ellison, Jackson Abernathy, and someone whose voice I couldn't make out. In that moment, I had a strong desire to run. I didn't care what they were saying about me. It didn't matter. The blood rushed to my head. I was dizzy. My heart raced, and my hand shook.

I need to get out of here. I turned to leave and ran into a solid wall.

Suddenly, a pair of arms wrapped around me like a vise.

I took a deep breath and filled my lungs, prepared to scream, when a hand covered my mouth.

I wiggled but could barely move. My brain froze, and the blood pounded in my ears. I struggled to recall the self-defense classes I'd taken from the Navy. *What was the acronym I was supposed to remember? SING, SIGN? Shin. Instep. Nose. Groin.*

Or was it Shin, Instep, Groin, Nose? Did the order really matter? I stopped struggling. *The Admiral always said to Stop and Assess my situation.* I decided that the instep was going to be my only option. I wished I was wearing my Louboutins rather than my Pyer Moss Sculpt sneakers, but I intended to put my entire body into the task.

I pushed back and heard a thud as my attacker's back hit the wall of the tunnel. Just as I was about to deliver a crippling stomp, I leaned back and got a whiff of cologne. I recognized that scent.

Then, I felt two large paws on my shoulders as Baby stood up on his hind legs and licked my face.

I moved my head to avoid a sloppy mastiff kiss.

The hand on my mouth loosened. "Baby, off."

"Shhh, what are you doing?" Michael whispered in my ear.

My knees buckled from relief. Before I hit the ground, Michael scooped me in his arms and carried me back through the passage, through the closet, and back to the Baby Cakes kitchen. He took me to one of the chairs in the demonstration area, got down on his knees, and checked my pupils and pulse.

"I'm fine."

"People who are fine don't collapse."

I swatted away his hand. "They do when someone scares the crap out of them."

"I'm sorry. I didn't mean to scare you." His eyes reflected the concern I heard in his voice.

I reached across and kissed him. "I know you didn't mean to scare me."

He returned my kiss, and we lost track of time for a few moments. When we came up for air, he turned serious again. He gazed into my eyes. "Are you sure you're okay?"

I grinned. "I'm a bit hot and bothered at the moment, but other than that I'm fine."

"Well, I might be able to fix that." He reached for me again.

There was a noise at the back door. Someone was entering the building.

Michael and Baby both went into protection mode. Both stopped, stood still, and listened. Baby gave a short bark and trotted to the back door. His tail was up, and he didn't show any indications of fear. Whoever was coming into the bakery was a friend.

A few seconds later, I heard Tyler Lawrence's voice. "Hey there, Baby. How are you, boy?"

I gasped. In that moment, I recognized the voice I'd heard earlier coming from Candy's shop. Why was Tyler Lawrence talking with Jackson Abernathy and Chris Russell? Could Tyler's voice have been the sinister voice I'd heard a few months earlier? The voice that promised, *If she gets in my way again, I won't miss next time.*

After recognizing Tyler's voice, Michael's shoulders relaxed, but after hearing me gasp, he turned. His eyes asked for an explanation, but I merely shook my head.

"There you are." Tyler came into the demonstration area. "What's going on?"

"Nothing. What brings you here?"

Michael's tone was sharp, and Tyler stopped. "Hey, if I'm interrupting something, just tell me."

I stood up and forced a smile. "You're not interrupting anything important. We were just admiring the finished results. I can't wait until all those display cases are filled."

Tyler glanced around. "It looks great. You've done a fantastic job."

"Thank you. I hope Aunt Octavia would approve."

"Absolutely. She would love it."

Michael was still in protection mode and not yet his normal friendly self. Tense and on high alert, he looked ready to pounce at any moment. I could feel the tension between the two men. I plastered on a big smile. "What brings you down?"

"I just came from talking to my friend at the bank," Tyler said.

First lie.

"Really? Were you able to find out anything helpful?"

"Just twenty-four hours before Clayton Davenport was murdered, Jackson Abernathy withdrew nine thousand, nine hundred dollars from his savings account in cash."

"That's curious," I said. "Why such an odd amount?"

"Just under the limit for federal reporting?" Michael said.

Tyler nodded. "Exactly."

I glanced from Tyler to Michael. "I don't understand."

"Financial institutions are required to report withdrawals of sums over ten thousand dollars to the federal government," Michael said.

Tyler pulled a notebook from his pocket and read. "It's called structuring. It's supposed to help against money laundering. Apparently, it's part of the Bank Secrecy Act from 1970."

Michael's shoulders relaxed, but I could tell by the way he flexed his hands, he was still not fully at ease. "The act was modified in 2002 by the Patriot Act to try to stop the funding of terrorist organizations after 9/11."

"That's what my friend told me too," Tyler said, flipping through his notes. "Although the Patriot Act included a lot of other things and expired in 2020."

"Okay, so Abernathy withdrew just under ten thousand dollars," I said. "What's the big deal? Maybe he wanted to go shopping?"

Based on the way Tyler and Michael stared at me, I had obviously put my foot in my mouth.

"What?"

"Most people don't withdraw ten grand to go shopping," Michael said.

"Whatever. Well, that's great. Nice job, Tyler."

"Wait, it gets better. The same day that Abernathy withdrew nine thousand, nine hundred dollars, Clayton Davenport deposited nine thousand, nine hundred dollars *cash* into one of his numerous bank accounts."

"That's a big coincidence," I said.

"If you believe in coincidences, which I don't, then it's a big coincidence," Michael said.

I was still flustered, but I wanted . . . needed to know what Tyler was doing with Abernathy and Russell. "Did you just leave the bank?"

"Yeah. It's going to cost me a dinner, but that's it." His cell phone rang. He glanced at the screen, and a flush rose up his neck. "I need to take this. I'll talk to you guys later." He hurried out the back with his phone cupped to his ear.

When he was gone, Michael turned to face me. "Okay, what was that about?"

Briefly, I told him about hearing Tyler's voice from Candy's shop while I was in the tunnel.

Michael listened patiently. "Could you make out what he said?"

I shook my head. "No. I only recognized his voice, but I couldn't make out what they were talking about."

"Are you sure he wasn't the voice you heard a few months ago in Abernathy's office?"

I thought. "No. I recognized Brad Ellison and Jackson Abernathy the last time. I didn't recognize the third voice."

"So, it might not have been Tyler."

I flopped down in the chair. "I really hope it wasn't Tyler, but if he wasn't mixed up in this mess, then why was he meeting with Abernathy and Chris Russell? And why did he lie about it? If it was just an innocent meeting, then why not just say, *Hey, Maddy. Guess what. Mayor Abernathy just commissioned an alpaca sweater for Christmas?*"

"Jackson Abernathy doesn't strike me as an alpaca sweater kind of guy."

"No wardrobe is complete without an alpaca sweater." I waved away the joke. "No, there's something going on between them. Something Tyler didn't want to talk about. Remember, Aunt Octavia said she thought she had a 'spy in her camp.' What if Tyler was the spy? And who was that call from? Did you see the way he turned red? And he didn't just say, *Oh, this is my friend Lisa calling, I need to take this.* He didn't want us to know who it was."

Michael frowned. "Who's Lisa?"

"I don't know. I made it up. I was just making a point."

"Maybe I should have a talk with Tyler."

"No, you'll just scare him."

"Me? Why would Tyler be scared of me?"

I tilted my head to the side, folded my hands across my chest, and glared. "Seriously, Dr. G.I. Joe? You military types can be very menacing to normal civilians when you get all . . . special ops, flexing muscles, like *I can kill you with a paper clip.*"

He laughed. "I have never said I could kill someone with a paper clip."

I raised a brow and gave him *the look.* "But can you?"

He paused a beat. "That's not the point."

"What is the point?"

Before he could answer, my phone vibrated. I had a text. I responded and glanced up. "That was Jackson Abernathy. He said he's going to be late."

"Why?"

Before I could respond, my phone rang. When "Anchors Aweigh" played, I didn't need to look at the picture to know who was calling. For a moment, I thought about sending it to voicemail, but at the last minute I changed my mind. "Hi, Dad."

Conversations with the Admiral didn't often require a great deal of input from me, especially when he was in a mood, which he almost always was. Today was no different. The theme for today's rant centered around the dangers of New Bison. I put the phone on speaker, sat down, and waited: "Two murders in a town with less than two thousand people is a dangerous place to be. And how are you mixed up in this? If you took the time to think instead of making impulsive decisions, you would have figured out a way to offload the bakery and move to a town where you'd be safe. This is why you need a husband. You need someone responsible to help you make decisions."

Baby had a psychic sixth sense that honed in on when I needed extra attention. He came and put his head on my lap and looked up at me with his big, soulful eyes. His eyes radiated the love and affection he had for me and helped bolster my self-esteem.

I gazed into Baby's eyes and zoned out on my dad's well-meaning but completely soul-shattering rant. I'd had a couple of decades to perfect the art of tuning out the Admiral. I completely forgot that Michael was still there. That is until he reached over and took the phone.

"Sir, you don't know me, but my name is Michael Portman. I'm a veterinarian, a veteran of the Army, and your daughter's boyfriend. I heard what you've said. I've only known your daughter for three months, but you obviously don't know her at all. Madison is smart, funny, intelligent, clever, and caring. She's a successful business owner with an amazing skill for marketing. If you can't recognize that, then I'm sorry, but I'm not going to stand around and allow anyone to speak that way to the woman I love." His voice was soft but full of iron. He pressed End and handed the phone back.

I stared at him.

He took several deep breaths. "I'm sorry. I know I shouldn't have gotten involved, but I couldn't take the way he was talking about you."

I stood up and flung myself in his arms and kissed him hard.

When he came up for air, he stared in my eyes. "You realize I've just destroyed any chance that your father will like me. He'll probably disown you and may send a submarine to attack New Bison."

I gazed into his eyes. "He won't disown me. I'm the only family he has, but if he does, so what?" I shrugged. "I don't need his money. I'm an independent businesswoman with a successful bakery. And I have the support of a wonderful man who isn't afraid to stand up for me. What more could a girl ask for?"

He kissed me, and I lost all sense of time until Baby had enough of being ignored and got up on his back legs and forced his way in between us.

Michael smiled and scratched Baby's ears. "Obviously, I'm going to need to have a conversation with your dog next."

Baby's ears perked up. He gave a short, quick bark and then trotted out of the room.

Michael stopped and stood perfectly still.

"Hey, Baby," Candy Rivers cooed. "Have you been a good boy?"

Michael's shoulders relaxed for the second or third time since he'd arrived.

Candy and Baby came around the corner. She saw Michael and stopped. "Sorry. I didn't mean to interrupt."

We stepped apart.

"You're not interrupting," I said.

She entered the demonstration room. "This place looks amazing. When is the grand reopening?"

"I hope tomorrow. I was waiting for Jackson Abernathy to sign off on the final paperwork for the insurance. He was supposed to come today, but—"

"Oh, he just left. He looked awful."

"Really? Is he sick?"

She shook her head. "Worried. He looked like he hadn't slept in days. He kept mumbling about something falling apart." She leaned close and whispered, "I think he's in some kind of trouble. I guess that's why he needed to talk to Chris. He must've needed to talk to a lawyer pretty badly."

"Really? I don't suppose he mentioned why?"

"No idea. Chris asked if I'd mind giving them a little privacy. You know, client privilege or something like that. I decided to do a little shopping." She turned away so I couldn't see her eyes, but I did notice a flush go up her neck.

"Was it just the two of them?" I asked.

"What?" Candy snapped out of a daydream. "I guess so, yeah. I didn't see anyone else."

Michael and I exchanged a glance.

Candy wasn't artfully deceptive enough to be a good liar. Tyler could have come and gone while she was out, so she never saw him. Or maybe I was wrong. Maybe I hadn't really heard his voice. I was almost certain I had. But, then again . . . I shook myself like Baby in an attempt to clear my head. Now wasn't the time for waffling. I had heard Tyler's voice. I needed to stick to the facts.

"Candy, do you mind if I ask you a personal question?"

She smiled. "Of course not. I'm an open book."

Before I could ask, Michael stepped forward. "I think that's my cue to leave."

"Coward," I said. "You're willing to take a Navy admiral on full steam, but you run away from a conversation between two women?"

"I know my limitations." He kissed me and left.

When he was gone, I turned to Candy and gave her the sly *let's have some serious girl talk* look. "I'm just curious about you and Chris Russell. Are you two serious? I mean, when Clayton Davenport was killed, I couldn't help but notice his fancy sports car parked out back, and he made it down here in record time." I winked.

"That just happened. I mean, he came up to go over some

documents with me about the building and Paul's will, and then we decided to have a drink . . . or two or three. We had a lot of drinks." She giggled. "The next thing I knew, I woke up butt naked, and he was right there, snoring."

My brain was going one hundred miles an hour. "So . . . you don't remember anything?"

She shook her head and leaned closer. "I'm afraid to tell him I don't remember it. Men can be so sensitive. Plus, he's been super nice and attentive. He sends me flowers every day, which is sooo cool."

"And neither of you . . . left?"

"For what?"

"You know . . ." I gave her a knowing look, even though I had no clue what I was implying or hinting about.

"Oh . . . no. I'm covered." She shook her head. "Good thing too."

I needed to try a different tactic. "I'm sorry if I woke you when I called."

"You didn't wake me. I didn't even hear the phone. Chris told me what happened when I woke up. Frankly, I'm surprised he woke up. Both of us are really sound sleepers. I got up once to go potty, and he didn't budge. I could have tap danced on the kitchen table and he wouldn't have woke up."

Isn't that interesting. I'd pretty much discounted Candy as a suspect in Clayton Davenport's murder because she was having a romantic interlude with Chris Russell all night. But Candy could have snuck downstairs and stabbed Clayton Davenport, and Chris Russell would have slept through it. Ugh . . . I didn't want my mind to go there. I liked Candy, and I didn't want to believe that she killed Clayton Davenport.

"So many men have a crush on you. You have your pick of suitors. Why Chris Russell?"

She scrunched her nose and tilted her head to the side. "I don't know. I mean, he's a lawyer, and he's super smart."

"And . . ." I egged her on to share more.

"And I'm really flattered that he asked me out . . ."

"Why do I sense a *but* coming?"

"But I don't know. I mean, it just feels wrong."

"Oh, Candy, I'm sorry. I'm sure it must feel wrong to be dating again, so soon after your husband's death. It has only been three months." I reached over and squeezed her hand.

She shook her head. "It's not that. Paul and I were over long before he was murdered. We were separated, and I know now that I wasn't really in *love* with him." She used air quotes around *love*. "I think I was flattered. He was the mayor, and he talked about a lot of nice things." She paused and then shrugged again. "I think I feel much the same about Chris. He's so, so smart. I feel flattered that he wants to go out with me. He went to college and then law school, and I barely finished high school. I know I'm not very smart, and most men just want . . . well, you know, but when I tell people I'm dating a lawyer, then they look at me differently. They treat me differently."

In that moment, I felt closer to Candy Rivers than ever before. We were both insecure. While my insecurity came from my dad's criticism of my decision-making ability, Candy was young and beautiful, but she was also insecure because she didn't feel smart enough.

"Candy, you are smart. You're opening your own business."

"Maybe, I mean, I wasn't smart enough to verify that Paul was divorced before I married him. That was pretty dumb."

"Actually, I don't think you were dumb at all." I thought for a few minutes. I felt confident that Trooper Bob wouldn't want me spreading rumors or sharing what I found out from Carla Lattimore. But, he didn't tell me I couldn't talk about what I knew. Of course, I'm sure he didn't think that I'd run into Candy Rivers right after I left his house. Besides, it would all come out soon anyway.

I shared. I told Candy that Marjorie was really Carla Lattimore and that it was all a big scam.

Candy stared at me open-mouthed. "But where is the real Marjorie?"

"No idea. But maybe your lawyer friend could look into it and find her."

She squealed and hugged me. "You are amazing. That's the best news I've heard in days. I can't wait to go tell Chris." She hopped up from her seat. She reached down and threw her arms around Baby's neck. "You big, wonderful boy. You are such a good boy. Aunt Candy is going to find you a nice big bone." She stood up and turned to me. "And you get free redeye coffees for life!" She hugged me again and then hurried out of the back door.

I stood in the same spot and stared at the door. "I wonder if the local penitentiary has a coffee shop. Because you just might be making those red eyes behind bars."

CHAPTER 35

Baby and I stood where we were for several minutes after she left while I tried to put the pieces of the puzzle into place. What did I know?

I paced.

"Chris Russell couldn't be a witness for Candy because he was a heavy sleeper. Candy could have left the apartment, come downstairs, and stabbed Clayton Davenport. Then, hurried back upstairs and gotten back in bed without waking him up."

Baby sat up straight and watched me pace.

"But I don't think she did it. Do you?"

Baby yawned.

"I didn't think so. Let's see. Candy had the means. The killer got the knife from the kitchen. Easy-peasy. She had the opportunity. She was right upstairs. She knew about the passage, and she could have used it to sneak over, stab Clayton, and then sneak back upstairs." I looked at Baby.

He turned his head away and refused to make eye contact.

"I know you like Candy. I like her too, but that doesn't change the facts. She had means, opportunity, and she had a motive. Clayton Davenport was threatening to take away her independence, her coffee shop, and any insurance money she had left."

He slid down so he looked like a sphinx.

"I'm not saying she did it. I'm just saying, she could have done it. Who else had a motive?"

Baby lifted his leg and began to lick himself.

"Ugh. You're not helping. Okay, besides Candy, who else do we have?" I paced. "Carla Lattimore. She had the opportunity and the means, but why would she murder Clayton Davenport? Or Sybil Castleton? They were all in the scheme together. As far as we know, she didn't have a motive."

Baby rolled over on his back and wiggled from side to side with his paws in the air.

"Mayor Abernathy was being blackmailed by Davenport. So, he had a motive. He was at the winery, so he had the means and opportunity to kill Sybil Castleton. I don't know if he had the opportunity and means to kill Davenport. I suppose anyone could have gotten in here, but why on earth would they?" I froze and stared at Baby. A chill went up my spine. "Whoever killed Davenport must have lured him here. They wanted him found here at Baby Cakes. They wanted me or someone close to me to be accused of the murder."

Baby barked his approval.

"Sometimes it takes me a while, but I catch up eventually, boy." I scratched Baby's ear until his leg jiggled.

"I can't focus on that for now or I'll freak myself out. I need to think about this objectively, like Sherlock Holmes."

Baby nudged my hand until I continued scratching him.

"Abernathy . . . blackmail is a really good motive for murder. I wonder what Davenport had on him? Whatever it is, it must have had something to do with his time in the military."

As if on cue at the mention of the military, my phone vibrated, and the Admiral's face appeared. I debated answering, but I knew resistance was futile.

"Hi, Dad."

The Admiral was apologetic. He didn't mean to make me feel bad. He loved me. Blah. Blah. Blah. I truly believed that my dad cared about me. He just wasn't equipped to express himself. Maybe if my mom had lived, he wouldn't have buried his feelings. Maybe he would have learned to talk things through. To show his feelings in ways that didn't involve money. Regardless, being away these past few months, running Baby Cakes, learning to bake and take care of Baby, had taught me that I was capable of making good decisions, and even if I was impulsive from time to time, that was okay too. I would simply have to live with those decisions. Unlike my dad, if I made a bad decision, no lives would be lost.

Thinking of lost lives led me to thoughts of Clayton Davenport.

"Hey, Dad. I need a favor."

He immediately went to money by asking how much I needed.

"No, I don't need money. Baby Cakes Bakery is doing well. The renovations are done from the fire, and we are ready for the grand reopening. I was thinking about the man who was murdered. His name was Clayton Davenport. Apparently, he was a very wealthy investor." I took a few minutes and filled him in on the little I knew about Davenport's business dealings. "I think he might have been in the military."

The Admiral's estimation of people always went up when he found out they served their country. His opinion dropped a few notches when I told him Davenport was in the Army instead of the Navy.

My next move was tricky. "Dad, I had no idea the Army had ships."

The Admiral spent the next couple of minutes telling me about the history of ships in the various branches of the military and then finished with a bit of trash talking about why the Navy was superior when it came to sailing. That was good. I had him right where I wanted him.

"That guy who was murdered in the bakery, Clayton Davenport, was stationed on one of those Army ships. I saw a picture, and I think it was of the mayor, Jackson Abernathy, with two other men."

The Admiral spent a minute talking about the importance of military service and how the discipline you learned there prepared you for life.

"Right, so I think there may have been some type of . . . oh, I don't know, negative stuff that happened. I don't suppose you could find out what happened. I mean, that was the Army, and you're *just* in the Navy, so if you can't find out, that's fine. Maybe I should talk to Michael. He was in the Army, and he may have more connections—"

Bingo! My dad was not about to concede that anyone, especially anyone in the Army, was capable of doing something that he couldn't. The fact that he was still testy over the tongue-lashing he'd gotten from Michael, a lowly Army vet, was still in his mind. There's no way my dad was going to accept that there was anything he, and consequently the Navy, couldn't do faster and better. If I knew my dad, he was already tapping away on his computer. He'd have an answer soon.

I remembered April's comments that Clayton Davenport had been in the military too. "Hey, Dad. Can you run a couple of other names while you're at it? I'm just curious." I gave him the names of all of the men I knew that had any connection to Mayor Abernathy regardless of age, including Paul Rivers, Bradley Elliott, Tyler Lawrence, Chris Russell, Clayton Davenport, and Michigan State Trooper Robert Roberts. That should keep him busy.

"Sure. I understand you need to go. I'll talk to you soon." I glanced at Baby and held up my hand. "High five."

He raised his paw and touched my hand, just one of the many tricks Aunt Octavia had taught him.

My phone rang again. This time it was April.

"I talked to Al Norris—"

"Who's Al Norris?" I asked.

"You call him the Pillsbury Doughboy."

"Oh, yeah."

"Two things. First, I suggested he get Clayton Davenport's suitcases from the Carson Law Inn and search them. As his next of kin, I authorized the search. Anyway, guess what? He found a flash drive in his suitcase."

"Really? Were they able to open it?"

April sounded giddy with excitement. "It was password protected, but you'll never guess what the passcode turned out to be."

"Hmmm, your birthday?"

"Close. Our anniversary." I could hear the smile in her voice. She cleared her throat and continued. "Anyway, Clayton had been investigating someone in New Bison. I think it was *him*."

It took me a few moments to connect the dots. "Him? You mean the guy who wanted Clayton to trade you in a business deal?"

"Yes. I'm almost certain. CJ didn't name him. He just re-ferred to him as Nemesis. Just like that Miss Marple movie we watched a few weeks ago. You remember?"

I absolutely remembered, and a chill ran up my spine. "I don't understand."

"Me either, but it looks like CJ figured out who he was, and whoever it is, he tracked him to New Bison."

I ignored the fact that April no longer seemed repulsed by her late husband and focused on what she was saying. "Plus, there's some shady real estate things going on. It's weird, and I don't understand everything. Trooper Bob has it. He's going to send it to Lansing for tests and deciphering."

"That's a lot to process. Good job."

"I'll let you know what I find out. You be careful. Whoever this Nemesis is, he's dangerous."

I hung up and looked at Baby. "That's a scary twist. What's the likelihood that Clayton Davenport's nemesis could be in New Bison, Michigan?"

Baby shook his head.

I mulled over everything April said. The shady real estate dealings sounded similar to things Aunt Octavia had mentioned in one of the videos she'd left. She'd ordered special reports about the land, but if she'd received them, I hadn't found them, yet.

I paced and tried to make sense of everything.

I wasn't surprised when my dad called back less than ten minutes later.

"Hey, Dad."

He had the scoop. I expected him to be pleased with himself and maybe the slightest bit cocky that the Navy got an answer before the Army. Yet, I hadn't expected the anger.

"Wait, hold up. Are you sure it's the same Jackson Abernathy?" *Geez, how many of them could there be? It has to be the same one.*

"Dishonorably discharged?"

According to the Admiral, not only was Jackson Abernathy on the ship, but so were Clayton Davenport and Chris Russell. The Admiral was thorough if nothing else.

"Wow. That's . . . wow." I had no words. Of course, my dad had plenty of words. Most of them were only four letters long, which was a definite indication of his frustration. No matter how angry he was, my dad rarely swore in front of me. I needed to stop the flood of expletives and think. "Hey, Dad. Thanks for the information, but I have to go, someone's coming in the bakery. I'll—"

The Admiral wasn't about to disconnect without a warning for me to be safe.

"I promise. I will be careful. Now, I have to—"

Just when I thought my dad could no longer surprise me, turns out I was wrong.

"Wait. You're coming where? Here? To New Bison?" *Holy macaroons.* "Of course, I want to see you. I just thought you'd be busy. I mean—yes. I have a pencil." I fumbled through my purse to find a pencil and something to write on. Eventually, I gave up and put his flight information into my phone. "Great. Yes, I have it. I'm looking forward to seeing you too."

Boy, was this going to be a disaster. Admiral Jefferson Augustus Montgomery was about to invade New Bison, Michigan.

CHAPTER 36

I paced to keep my head from exploding. "Baby, this is *not* good. According to my dad, Jackson Abernathy, the mayor, was dishonorably discharged from the Army."

If I'd been paying attention, I would have noticed the change in Baby's demeanor. He stood up. His ears went up. His body was tense. He growled and then charged around the corner.

"Baby, come," I screamed.

But he wasn't listening. Baby stood in attack mode. Every muscle in his body was flexed and ready to pounce. He bared his teeth and drool dripped from the sides of his mouth.

In the kitchen, Jackson Abernathy was backed up to the counter with a knife in his hand. "Call off your attack dog. If he so much as scratches me, I'll have him put down."

"That won't be necessary." I grabbed Baby's collar. "Baby, stop." I said it with more confidence than I felt.

Like the well-behaved dog that he was, Baby stopped barking. However, he was tense. I could feel the tension. His hair stood up, and he stared at the mayor as though one false move and he'd take a bite out of him. Every fiber of his being longed to lunge.

Abernathy pointed his knife in Baby's direction. "Take him out. I don't trust him."

"Fine." I took Baby outside and put him in the Range Rover. I made sure the windows were down for ventilation but not enough to allow him to escape. *You'd think someone who raises English mastiffs would know how to handle them.* I reentered the building.

In the kitchen, Jackson Abernathy stood with his back to me. "Baby won't bother you. He's locked up."

Jackson Abernathy turned around slowly. He still had the knife in his hand, but this time, it was pointed at me. "Good. We wouldn't want that mutt getting in the way, now would we?"

CHAPTER 37

Crap. What have I done? I tried to look Jackson Abernathy in the eyes, but I struggled to look away from the knife. "Mayor Abernathy, what are you doing?"

"I'm making sure that you don't ruin everything I've built up. Now, who were you talking to? Who told you that I'd been dishonorably discharged?"

"I don't know what—"

"Don't lie to me! I heard you."

"I wasn't talking about you. I was just talking to my dad. He's in the Navy. He was telling me about someone I knew. That's all."

He hesitated and squinted. "Who?"

"You wouldn't know him. Just a sailor I used to date. Lieutenant Commander Riker."

"Riker? That's not a real person. You got that from *Star Wars*."

Actually, I got it from Star Trek: The Next Generation, *but now is not the time to quibble.* "Lieutenant Commander Andrew Riker. We dated for almost a year before I met Elliott." I had dated a sailor named Andrew, so I was able to talk with confidence that I didn't feel. And I needed to keep talking. "Drew and I were pretty serious at one time. That's why my dad was telling me about him. Apparently, he was dismissed from the Navy, which is the same as a dishonorable discharge for an enlisted man, but since he was a commissioned officer, he was merely dismissed."

"What did your boyfriend do?"

"Murder. He killed someone." I racked my brain to remember any cases of someone being dismissed and lit on one. "He got married a couple of months after we broke up. I'm sure they were dating while we were together, but given what happened, well, I'm glad he wasn't faithful. Anyway, he caught his wife with another man and shot him. My dad said—"

"I don't care what your dad said."

"Sorry, I thought you wanted to know what happened."

"I don't believe you. I think you asked your father to investigate me. That's what I think. I think your dad found out that I was dishonorably discharged from the Army for leaking secrets to a Russian spy."

I shook my head. "I had no idea." I worked to make my voice sound as sincere as I could. "My dad didn't mention anything about Russian spies. How interesting. I've never met a spy before. Was it like in the movies? I mean, was it all cloak and dagger? James Bond? Did they pay you a lot of money? Or did you do it for ideological reasons? Honestly, I—"

"Shut up."

"Sorry, I talk a lot when I'm nervous. Looking at that knife makes me very nervous. Perhaps you'd consider putting it away. I mean, I'm sure we could come to an agreement. After all, I don't think Trooper Bob has a clue that you killed Clayton Davenport and Sybil Castleton. He thinks it was Carla Lattimore. He's—"

"He knows about Carla?"

Oops. I've been oversharing again. "Well, I went by earlier and told him about the conversation I had with her before she skipped town and—"

"Whatdya mean, skipped town?"

"Well, when he sent a patrol car to pick her up, she was gone, so I guessed she skipped town. I suppose she could have just gone to the store."

He rubbed his forehead. "I need to think."

"Maybe you could just slip out of town too—"

"I'm the mayor! I can't just slip out of town."

"Why not? No one knows anything about the treason with Anna Chapman. You could—"

"I thought you didn't know anything about it?"

"I don't."

"Then how'd you know Anna Chapman was the name of the spy?"

Crap. "Lucky guess. I mean she was famous. So, when you said you gave secrets to the Russians, I just assumed it would be someone like Anna Chapman. She's legendary, but my dad never mentioned names. I just guessed. I—"

"Shut up. You're a horrible liar."

"They don't know you murdered Clayton Davenport and Sybil Castleton. So, if you were to leave town, the police would have no reason to keep looking for you."

"I don't care about the police. The police are the least of my worries."

"Well, you could just go and—"

"Shut up."

I shut up.

Outside, I could hear Baby barking along with a pounding noise that sounded like he was hammering against the car in an attempt to get out. I cringed at the thought of the damage. I took another look at the knife that Abernathy was wielding, and I didn't care if Baby ripped that car apart like a can opener tearing into a can of peas.

"I can't think with all that noise. You need to shut that mutt up. He's going to have the whole neighborhood here."

"Sure thing." I turned and headed for the door, but Abernathy wasn't having it.

"No, you don't." He moved in between me and the door, my only means of escape. "You stay right there."

My eyes darted around the renovated and empty kitchen. Nothing. A box on the floor that we'd packed up held a skillet and some pots, but the knives were on the other side of the room, and there was no way I could get to them without Abernathy tackling me first.

"I should have drowned that mutt when he was born instead of just tossing him in Lake Michigan."

CHAPTER 38

My neck snapped around. "What? You were the person who left Baby to die when he was just a puppy?"

"Yeah." He grinned. "He was the runt of the litter. Scrawny cuss. Didn't think he stood a chance. I took the humane route—"

"Don't you dare talk about drowning a defenseless puppy as *humane*. You're a monster. Aunt Octavia was right." Arguing with someone who'd already killed at least twice and was threatening a third kill wasn't my smartest move. However, learning that Jackson Abernathy had tried to kill Baby was more than I could handle. Something snapped. In that instant, I could have ripped Abernathy apart with my bare hands.

"Don't lecture me. I know more about dogs than you and that crazy aunt of yours ever will. She never said anything, but she knew I was the breeder. How could she not know? I was the only person within fifty miles breeding mastiffs. She never said anything, but I could tell by the way she looked at me that she knew. And she wanted me to know that she knew."

He spat on my newly installed and recently cleaned floor. Inside. He spat as if he were outside in a barnyard.

Between the revelations, the spitting, and the taunts, my brain refused to focus. There must have been a part of me that recognized that Jackson Abernathy was a desperate man. He'd already killed twice and was threatening to kill me and my dog. But whatever the rational part of the brain is that processes things like these, mine wasn't working.

Abernathy was still talking, but the blood pounded in my ears, and I couldn't hear. Words came in between the pulsing.

"Murder . . . pawn . . . duped . . . fall guy."

"What are you talking about?"

"I'm not taking the fall. I'm not a murderer, and I'm not going down for murders I didn't commit."

Baby barked. The car horn blared.

From the corner of my eye, I saw the door to the broom closet open slowly.

"Stop that noise. God, I'm going to take a lot of pleasure in killing that beast this time around." Abernathy moved toward the door.

That was the last straw. I reached down and grabbed the cast-iron skillet from the box and swung it like Hank Aaron.

There was a loud thump as it connected with the side of Abernathy's skull. His eyes crossed in confusion before they rolled back in his head. The knife dropped from his hand. His knees buckled. He spun around and his legs wobbled.

Glass shattered outside.

A loud shot rang out.

The bullet hit Abernathy and knocked him backward, and he finished his descent to the floor. Dead.

CHAPTER 39

Baby crashed through the back door, splintering the wood. He bounded into the kitchen. Blood dripped from his paws and small pieces of wood, foam, and metal clung to his skin.

I dropped to my knees and threw my arms around his neck. "Oh my God. Are you okay?"

I turned and stared into the barrel of a gun and the eyes of Chris Russell. For a moment, I glimpsed into a pair of cold, dark eyes. A shiver went up my spine.

Baby growled.

I held him tighter. If we died, we would die together.

Will this nightmare never end?

CHAPTER 40

Sirens blared.

Chris Russell took a step in my direction, but Baby wasn't allowing anyone else to get in between the two of us. He growled, and I felt the power as he prepared to lunge.

Footsteps raced through the door.

"Drop the weapon."

Chris Russell placed the gun on the counter and held up his hands.

Trooper Bob glanced around. "You okay?"

I tried to drag my eyes away from the gun lying on the counter, but they wouldn't move.

Trooper Bob took a step in my direction. "Maddy?"

Baby growled, barked once.

I could feel that he was ready to spring. From the corner of my eye, I saw the two patrolmen, their weapons drawn and pointed at Baby. That brought me back to earth.

"Baby, stop," I ordered.

Michael pushed through the patrolmen and rushed to my side. "Maddy. Oh God. Are you hurt?"

I threw my arms around his neck and collapsed.

When I woke up, Michael was holding me, shining a light in my eyes.

He dropped the light and kissed me long and hard.

Trooper Bob cleared his throat loudly. "Doctor, I don't want to interfere in the treatment of your patient, but I need to get a statement."

"Are you up to answering questions?" Michael asked.

I nodded. "Wait." I glanced around. "What about Baby?"

Michael gave a bashful glance. "I checked him out first. He's got some scratches from busting out of your car and breaking through the back door, but he'll be fine. I gave him a tranquilizer and—"

I threw my arms around his neck and kissed him. "I love you."

"Good Lord, let's not start that again," Trooper Bob mumbled.

Michael must have carried me to the demonstration area. I sat up and tried to ignore the stretcher that was wheeling out a body.

"Now, what the hell happened?" Trooper Bob asked.

I shared what I'd learned from my dad and how Abernathy surprised me.

Trooper Bob asked a few clarifying questions, but didn't press me too much. "So, Mayor Abernathy killed Clayton Davenport and Sybil Castleton to hide the fact that he was a traitor." He turned to the corner where Chris Russell sat. "And where do you come in?"

"I was next door. I came to see Candy . . . ah, Mrs. Rivers. I'd been there earlier having a conversation with the mayor and Mr. Lawrence—"

"Why?" I asked.

"Why what?"

"Why were you two meeting with Tyler?"

"We hoped to convince him to join the town council. We

need younger blood. Tyler's a smart young man, and Candy thinks very highly of him."

"He never mentioned it." I exchanged a glance with Michael.

"We asked him not to say anything until we had a chance to discuss it with the other council members. If he turned us down, we didn't want the next person we asked to think . . . well, that they were second fiddle."

Trooper Bob tapped his pen on his notepad. "Great. Now, back to the shooting."

"Like I said, I was upstairs visiting with Candy when Baby started barking." He shook his head. "I've never seen him act like that before. Candy said something had to be wrong. She called the police and I came over through the secret passage."

"What secret passage?" Trooper Bob asked.

"Candy discovered a tunnel or passage that led between the two buildings. She discovered it during the renovations. I made her stay upstairs where it was safe. Then, I snuck down. I was just about to come through the door when I heard Jackson talking." He shook his head. "I realized immediately that Maddy was in danger."

Trooper Bob held up the weapon. "Do you have a license for this gun?"

"I most certainly do." He reached in his pocket, but Trooper Bob waved it away.

I tried to think of the reasons why a respectable lawyer and member of the town council needed to carry a concealed weapon, but I don't suppose he needed a reason.

Trooper Bob smiled. "It's a good thing you had it. Miss Montgomery might have been a goner if you hadn't been around to rescue her."

"I didn't need rescuing. Baby and I had things under control. In fact, Jackson Abernathy denied killing Clayton Davenport and Sybil Castleton. There might have been someone else involved. Now, we'll never know." I glanced around and couldn't help noticing the *You poor pitiful deluded fool* glance Trooper Bob exchanged with Chris Russell.

"They always deny it," Trooper Bob said. "The prisons are full of killers who are still proclaiming their innocence."

"I'm afraid that's true." Chris Russell shook his head. "Just like Brad Ellison. He denied pushing your Aunt Octavia down those stairs, but . . ." He held his hand up and shrugged.

"It's over. Now, you've been through a lot and you've got adrenaline rushing through your body from all of the excitement, but trust me. It's over," Trooper Bob said.

I wanted to argue. I wanted to wipe those smug looks off both Chris Russell and Trooper Bob's faces, but Mayor Abernathy was a traitor and a liar. Plus, only a monster would try to kill a poor, defenseless puppy. He tried to kill Baby. He would have killed him today if he could. Jackson Abernathy was a monster. Maybe they were right. Maybe, I was hyped up on adrenaline and two or three red eyes. Suddenly, I felt exhausted.

April rushed in. "Maddy, are you okay?" She flung her arms around my neck.

"I'm fine."

She glanced around. "Baby?"

"We're both fine. Michael said it's just lacerations, but nothing serious."

She released a heavy breath. I didn't know if it was for me or Baby. Either way, it was nice to have my friends nearby.

"I'd better go and check on him," Michael said. "He was snoring like a sailor when I put him in the back of my truck." He kissed my head and gave my hand a squeeze. "I'll call you as soon as I have him patched up."

He left, and April took his place next to me.

"I was so worried when I heard on the police radio that there was a shooting at Baby Cakes Bakery." She shivered. "I kept thinking *not again*. Then, I got here and saw your car." She turned to face me. "Good Lord, what happened to your car?"

"Baby."

"Oh . . . I'm so sorry, but I don't think you'll be able to fix that."

"It doesn't matter. The important thing is that Baby and I are safe."

"The streets of New Bison are safe now that a murderer is off the street," Chris Russell said.

"Does this mean April gets her job back?" I said eagerly. "Full-time?"

"I can't wait to get out of this crazy town," Trooper Bob mumbled.

April gave a big smile. "I guess this means you can let Leroy out of jail."

Trooper Bob rubbed the back of his neck. "Just as soon as I get back to the precinct."

Chris Russell stood. "Great. I'll go with you and help expedite the paperwork."

CHAPTER 41

Tyler and Leroy worked late into the night to get a new door on Baby Cakes Bakery. I snapped photos of the progress and uploaded them so people would know that we would be ready for business and our grand reopening, as originally planned. #GrandReopening #NoMastiffsWereHurtInThisRenovation #BabyCakesANewBisonOriginal

It didn't take long for news of Mayor Abernathy's death to make its rounds. News travels fast, especially in a small town. New Bison is too small to have a daily newspaper. Most residents who want daily news subscribed to the *Daily Herald*, a newspaper from a town about thirty minutes from New Bison with a population of fifteen thousand. The *New Bison Times* comes out once per week unless there's a special occasion. Exposing the town mayor as a two-time killer constituted a special edition. The paper hailed Chris Russell as a hero. There was even talk of a medal of commendation.

"I'll bet he started that talk himself," Hannah said. She sat at the counter and grumbled as she read. "If anyone deserves a medal, it's you and Baby. Y'all are the ones that took down that slimy weasel."

I reached over and gave Hannah a hug. "Thank you. If it wasn't for that skillet, I might not be here today."

She grinned. "I told you. No better weapon in the world than a good cast-iron skillet."

After Leroy finished with the door, he insisted on going to a twenty-four-hour grocery and stocking up on baking supplies. Then he went to work.

"You should get some rest," I told him.

"I've done nothing but rest for the past couple of days. I need to bake." He grinned. "Besides, we've got to fill those display cases."

Hannah brought pies, two caramel cakes, two Chocolate Soul Cakes, and dozens of cookies. Those cases were filling up quickly.

I baked lemon squares, thumbprint cookies, lemon meringue pies, and peanut butter cookies. Baking was a great distraction. It kept my mind off Clayton Davenport and Sybil Castleton's murders and my near murder. More importantly, it kept my mind off the fact that the Admiral would be in town later today. I wasn't sure Baby, me, or New Bison were ready for a full-on naval invasion, but we had little choice in the matter. Once he'd made up his mind, he wouldn't change. The Admiral was coming.

Candy started the morning by bringing a carafe of complimentary coffee and what she assured me was only the first of many red eyes. "I owe you big-time. Mr. Russell confirmed that since Carla Lattimore wasn't Marjorie Rivers, she didn't have any legal claim to Paul's property."

"Mr. Russell?" I sipped my red eye and felt the caffeine flowing through my veins. "You're being rather formal with someone you're . . . dating, aren't you?"

Candy's checks flushed with color. "We aren't dating anymore."

"Oh?"

"It's still pretty early after Paul's . . . you know . . . murder. I need some time."

"Good idea." I wondered if this was Chris Russell's idea or Candy's. Either way, Tyler would be happy.

"Hey, you know how much I love Baby, right?"

"Sure." I wasn't sure where this was heading, but I hoped she wasn't going to ask what I thought she was.

"Well, my mom worries about me a lot since I moved out. Then, with the murders and everything, well, I was thinking maybe I should get a dog, like Baby. So, I was wondering if you were planning on keeping Daisy?"

"I don't know. I hadn't really—"

"She's just the sweetest dog."

"Clayton Davenport bought her. So, I guess technically she belongs to April. You should ask her."

"I did. She said she was okay with it as long as you were. I promise I would take great care of her, and she'd just be next door, so you and Baby could spend as much time with her as you wanted and—"

"Yes."

Candy stopped with her mouth hanging open, prepared to beg longer. "Really?"

"Yes. I think you'd give Daisy a great home."

She clapped like a small kid, threw her arms around my neck, and squealed. "I'm so excited. This is just the best day ever. You can have all the free red eyes you want."

I laughed. "You may not want to promise that. I'd hate to bankrupt you."

She literally bounced in her seat with joy. "I can't wait to go shopping. I saw the cutest pink collar at the pet store, and I'm going to paint her nails and put big pink ribbons in her ears. Daisy is going to be the most stylish mastiff in all of New Bison . . . no, in all of Michigan."

"I'm sure she will." I was happy to hear that Daisy was going to get a new home. "Did Michael tell you about her heart condition?"

Candy's eyes teared up, and she fanned to stop from crying. "He did. That poor thing. I'm sorry she won't get to make babies with Baby, but he said he will make sure she has a good long life. And I intend to make sure that however long she has, that it'll be happy."

Now, it was my turn to get teary-eyed. Big dogs like mastiffs didn't live as long as smaller ones, and with a heart condition, Daisy's time could be even shorter. I was glad to know that she was going to have a full life with someone who cared about her as much as Candy did. Plus, Baby would be happy to have his friend nearby.

Michael brought Baby home last night. After a good night's sleep, Baby was back to his normal, goofy self. None of his abrasions required stitches, and apart from antibiotic ointment that needed to be applied twice every day for five days, he was as good as gold.

I ordered a second dog bed for the bakery, and Baby curled up and slept while Hannah, Leroy, and I tended to the crowds. And it was crowded. I was glad to see that many of the same people who patronized Baby Cakes also stopped by Higher Grounds Coffee and Tea. New Bison might be a small town, but every town needs a good coffee shop.

Fear of a second bakery in New Bison faded when April learned that one of the real estate properties that Clayton Davenport had hurriedly put in her name to avoid tax implications, was Garrett Kelley's old bookstore. She wasn't sure what to do with the building yet, but the one thing it would not be was another bakery. The Belgian pastry chef was already on his way back to Belgium. I hoped one day April would turn the building into a flower shop. For now, she was still the sheriff.

Both April and Trooper Bob were still looking for Carla. So

far, she'd managed to elude the law, but I had a feeling this wouldn't be the last we'd see of her.

The Spring Festival kicked off with a bang. I didn't know if the crowds were due to curiosity about the renovations or the desire to see a real-life crime scene. Whatever the reason, the public's curiosity was piqued. At various points, the line for Baby Cakes Bakery was down the block. When the Spring Festival Committee stopped by to get the Baby Cakes entry into the baking competition, I turned in my new creation. I called it Peanut Butter Dream Cake. It was a combination of Aunt Octavia's Chocolate Soul Cake and Leroy's peanut butter cookies.

I didn't expect to win, so when the committee brought the blue ribbon, I was genuinely shocked. I ugly-cried like a baby. Michael held me close while I blubbered. Baby stood on his hind legs and licked my face until I was covered in mastiff drool and tears, but I didn't care. I snapped a picture of the ribbon. #CarryingOnTheTradition #PeanutButterDream #Living-MyBestLife #NewBisonSpringFestival #LetEmEatCake

Recipes from Baby Cakes Bakery

Great-Aunt Octavia's Chocolate Soul Cake

Ingredients
2 cups granulated sugar
1³/₄ cups all-purpose flour
³/₄ cups unsweetened cocoa powder
1 teaspoon baking powder
2 teaspoons baking soda
¹/₂ teaspoon salt
2 large eggs
1 cup coffee (if you're feeling brave, try espresso)
1 cup buttermilk
¹/₂ cup vegetable oil
1¹/₂ teaspoons pure vanilla extract

For the frosting
6 ounces coarsely chopped semisweet chocolate
1 cup butter
2 cups confectioner sugar
1¹/₂ teaspoons pure vanilla extract
¹/₂ cup sour cream

Directions
1. FOR THE CAKE: Preheat oven to 350 degrees F and place oven rack in the center of the oven. Butter, or spray with a nonstick vegetable spray, two 9-inch cake pans. Then line the bottoms of the pans with parchment paper.
2. Whisk together the sugar, flour, cocoa powder, baking powder, baking soda, and salt in a large bowl.
3. Whisk together the eggs, coffee, milk, oil, and vanilla extract in a separate bowl. Add the wet ingredients to the dry ingredients and stir until combined. (The batter will be runny.)

4. Pour the batter into the prepared cake pans and bake for about 27–32 minutes or until a toothpick inserted into the center of the cake comes out clean.
5. Remove from oven and let cool for about 10 minutes. Then remove the cakes from their pans and cool completely on a greased wire rack before frosting.
6. FOR THE FROSTING: Melt the chocolate in a heatproof bowl placed over a saucepan of simmering water. Remove from heat and let cool to room temperature.
7. Beat the butter until smooth and creamy (about 1 minute). Add the sugar and beat until it is light and fluffy (about 2 minutes). Beat in the vanilla extract. Add the chocolate and beat on low speed until incorporated. Increase the speed to medium-high and beat until frosting is smooth and glossy (about 2–3 minutes). Add the sour cream and mix until smooth and combined.

Maddy's Peanut Butter Dream

Start with Great-Aunt Octavia's Chocolate Soul Cake, but instead of chocolate frosting, make peanut butter frosting and chocolate ganache.

Ingredients
For the peanut butter frosting
2 sticks unsalted butter, room temperature
1$^1/_4$ cups creamy peanut butter
2 teaspoons vanilla extract
$^1/_2$ teaspoon salt
2 cups powdered sugar
2 tablespoons milk

For the chocolate drip
$^1/_2$ cup heavy cream
1 cup semisweet chocolate

Directions
1. FOR THE FROSTING: Cream butter and peanut butter in a stand mixer. Add vanilla and salt. Gradually add powdered sugar, one-half cup at a time, beating well on medium speed. Scrape the sides and bottom of the bowl as needed.
2. Add milk, one teaspoon at a time, and beat at medium speed until light and fluffy.
3. Assemble the cake layers with a thick layer of frosting in between each layer.
4. Apply a thin layer of crumb coat icing to the entire surface of the cake, scraping away any excess with an offset spatula or bench scraper to create a spackle-like coating. Refrigerate until hard, about 15–20 minutes.
5. Spread the remaining frosting in an even layer all over

the cake. Refrigerate while you make the chocolate drip.

6. FOR THE DRIP: Place the chopped chocolate in a heat-proof bowl. Bring the heavy cream to a simmer then immediately remove from heat and pour over chocolate. Cover for a few minutes then stir until smooth.

7. Allow to cool until it has thickened but is still pourable, about 10 minutes. Test the consistency of the drip by pouring down the side of a glass. If it's too thick, microwave for 5–10 seconds. If it's too thin, allow to continue to cool.

8. Spread over the top of the cake and allow it to drip down the sides.

Optional

9. Decorate the top with chocolate sprinkles, crumbled peanut butter cookies (see Leroy's Easy Peanut Butter Cookie recipe) or mini peanut butter cups. If you want to be really adventurous, use them all!

Leroy's Easy Peanut Butter Cookies

Ingredients
1 cup granulated sugar
1 cup peanut butter
1 large egg
1 teaspoon vanilla extract

Directions
1. Preheat the oven to 350 degrees F. Line a baking sheet with parchment paper.
2. Beat together sugar, peanut butter, egg, and vanilla extract until thoroughly combined.
3. Using a tablespoon, scoop out dough and roll it into balls.
4. Place the balls of dough on the prepared baking sheet 2 inches apart. Use a fork to press a crisscross pattern in the dough.
5. Bake for 10–12 minutes.
6. Cool on a baking sheet for 5–10 minutes.

Michael's Easy Sugar Cookies

Ingredients
1 cup unsalted butter, room temperature
$^2/_3$ cup + 3 tablespoons granulated sugar
2 cups + 1 tablespoon all-purpose flour
1 teaspoon pure vanilla extract
Rainbow sprinkles (optional)

Directions
1. Preheat oven to 325 degrees F. Line a baking sheet with parchment paper.
2. Beat together butter and 2/3 cup sugar until combined.
3. Add in flour and blend well. Then blend in the vanilla.
4. Roll the dough into 1-inch balls.
5. Press down on the balls of dough with the bottom of a glass to flatten, and place them 2 inches apart on the baking sheet.
6. Bake for 14–16 minutes or until just slightly golden around the edges and on the bottom.
7. Sprinkle with the remaining 3 tablespoons of sugar and add the sprinkles (if using).
8. Cool on the baking sheet for at least 10–15 minutes.

Quick and Easy Lemon Meringue Pie

Ingredients
8-inch graham cracker piecrust
$1/2$ cup lemon juice
1 can Eagle Brand condensed milk
1 teaspoon grated lemon rind
3 eggs, separated
$1/3$ cup sugar
$1/4$ teaspoon cream of tartar
$1/2$ teaspoon vanilla

Directions
1. Preheat oven to 350 degrees F.
2. Combine condensed milk, lemon juice, lemon rind, and egg yolks in a large mixing bowl and stir until mixture thickens.
3. Pour into piecrust and place in the oven to warm while you make the meringue.
4. Add cream of tartar and vanilla to egg whites and beat until almost stiff enough to hold a peak.
5. Add sugar gradually, beating until stiff and glossy but not dry.
6. Remove pie from oven and pile the meringue onto the pie filling.
7. Bake at 350 degrees F until meringue is lightly browned (approximately 15 minutes).

Visit our website at
KensingtonBooks.com
to sign up for our newsletters, read
more from your favorite authors, see
books by series, view reading group
guides, and more!

BOOK **CLUB**

BETWEEN THE CHAPTERS

Become a Part of Our
Between the Chapters Book Club
Community and Join the Conversation

Betweenthechapters.net